**Praise for the novelette, "The Last Battle" in Tree House Tales**

"The Last Battle is a powerful tale that harkens back to the halcyon days of classic fantasy. Thompson's deft skill with description and emotion immersed me in Anna's world and left me yearning for more."
- Michael Dunne, author of The Fire of Iblis and The New Kingdoms

**Praise for Narenta Tumults #1: Seabird**

"Narenta is a tangible world--mysterious, inviting, frightening. Cara completes a visible character arc, (as she becomes) a champion. A must-read for CS Lewis fans."
- Asgard, BlogCritics Magazine, April 16 2008.

**Praise for Narenta Tumults #2: Earthbow**

[Earthbow is] noticeably darker [than Seabird] and the characters the reader meets face difficult choices and situations, as well as their own uncertainty and inner struggles.

One new character, Coris, is quite interesting, and Harone is back. And while it is gloomy in the beginning (Coris just can't seem to do anything right at first), Khiva soon appears to provide some (not out-of-place) entertaining relief.

Over all, I think I may have enjoyed reading "Earthbow" more than I did with "Seabird." It reads smoothly and quickly, and the three intertwined storylines were all enjoyable, so I didn't mind when they changed from one to another. And, while it is grittier than "Seabird," it still has a quality that reminds me of J. R. R. Tolkien, Charles Williams and C. S. Lewis, the better-known members of the Inklings.
    - Andrew Beussink, Amazon reviewer.

Other works by Sherry Thompson

Narenta # 1    Seabird
               First edition published January 2008. Out of print.
               Revised edition, forthcoming Spring 2015

Narenta # 2    Earthbow
               First edition published 2010.
               Revised edition, forthcoming Spring 2015

Narenta # 3    The Gryphon & the Basilisk;  Working title of a
               novel that thinks it's a trilogy
               Forthcoming Summer 2017, if it behaves.

Narenta # 1.5  Marooned.
               Forthcoming Spring 2015

Narenta # 0.5  Da Boid, da Tree-Rat 'n' da Loser; working title
               Forthcoming Spring 2016


Short Stories

"Shadow Harper" first appeared in UnCONventional: Twenty-Two
Tales of Paranormal Gatherings Under the Guise of Conventions.
Spencer Hill Press: January 2012.


"Baffled by the Green Door" first appeared in the Written Remains
Writers Guild anthology' "Stories from the Inkslingers":
Gryphonwood Press: 2008.

# TREE HOUSE TALES

BY

## SHERRY THOMPSON

*Scroll Chamber Press*
**2014**

# Scroll Chamber Press

All entries within the sections titled "Fantasy, Mostly" and "Extracts From Five Narenta Novels" are works of fiction. Names, characters, places, and incidents are products of the author's imagination or are used fictitiously. Any resemblance to actual events, locales, or persons living or dead, is entirely coincidental.

Contact Scroll Chamber Press via The Scroll Chamber Blog, for permission to reproduce limited extracts from "Tree House Tales".
Please leave a comment and email address on the following page,
http://scrollchamber.blogspot.com/2014/10/tree-house-tales-collection-due-out.html

First Edition: December 2014.
978-0692348444
0692348441

Thompson, Sherry (author)
Tree House Tales; a collection of short works and art. (title)

The author acknowledges the copyrighted or tradesmarked status and the copyright and trademark owners of the following wordmarks mentioned in these works of fiction:
Mountain Dew; Girl Scouts; Tupperware; Rolex; Google; Hippety Hopper (Warner Bros); Frisbee, "The President's Analyst" [theatrical film] ; "Life With Father" by Clarence Day [book]; Babylon 5 [television series]; "The Babylon 5 Cygnets" email group for use of the expression,"Under the Couch"; "Darkover"; "DarkoverCon"; Nevil Shute's "On the Beach" [book]; Walter Farley's "Island Stallion" and "The Black Stallion" [book]; Wikipedia for an extract from their "Hurricane Hazel" entry; "The Story of Kup-Ah-Weese", as collected in "Legends of the Delaware Indians and Picture Writing", by Richard C. Adams.

My story, "Shadow Harper" first appeared in UnCONventional: Twenty-Two Tales of Paranormal Gatherings Under the Guise of Conventions. Spencer Hill Press: January 2012. Used with permission.

My account, "Baffled by the Green Door" first appeared in Written Remains' "Stories from the Inkslingers": 2008.

The author also acknowledges the copyright status of "Wooden Whistle", "Jug O' Punch", "Teddybear's Picnic"; "Waltzing Matilda", "Handel's Messiah"; and the copyright status of the lyrics to "Green Door".

"I Need a Horse" was inspired by Anton Baklashov's photograph, as posted on Tumblr woodendreams.

"The Smashed Fairy Song Cycle" was inspired by "Lady Cottington's Pressed Fairy Book" (1994), by Terry Jones (Author), Brian Froud (Illustrator).

With gratitude to Demaris Hollembeak, my longtime coworker,
fellow fantasy reader & gamer, and my almost-sister
—for her unfailing & unassuming support over the decades.

With thanks to the Lost Genre Guild authors, publishers and art designers—past
and present—who have been my companions, tutors, role models, and sounding
boards for daft ideas and sometimes even author-related stuph.  I stopped being
a lonely author in a garret when Frank invited me to join LGG in 2008.
(p.s. I think he stole the garret.)

Thanks, Mike Dunne, long-distance geographical friend and longtime fellow
author and editor. Foremost a dear friend, a fellow believer, and a most patient
reader of wingeing emails so long that many of them require subject headings
for paragraphs and even footnotes. Maranatha!

Thank you to Grace Bridges owner and editor of Splashdown for her patient and
neverending assistance to this novice publisher. Grace spent hours shepherding
me through the intricacies of preparing my manuscript for submission. And
when all else failed—including my brain—(semi)voluntarily took on the task of
upgrading my graphics file for Tree House Tales' book cover. Grace also
offered advice with regard to choosing Amazon "categories" and writing a
"Book Description" which might possibly make sense.
Without her, the finished version of this work might never have existed.

A special thank you to God, without whom nothing would exist. Thank you for
loving us so much you chose to create us and--through the willing sacrifice of
Your Son--even provided a way for us to be reconciled to You.
I'm sorry about the messes we've made of our lives and souls, our relationships
with You and with others, and the mess we're making of what was once a
perfectly good planet.

# Table of Contents

## FANTASY, MOSTLY 9

*"Imagination is the one weapon in the war against reality." -- Jules de Gaultier*

## REALITY, WHATEVER THAT IS 151

*Reality is that which, when you stop believing in it, doesn't go away.*
 *--Philip K Dick*

## END OF REALITY...

(That's a relief!)

# Extracts from Five Narenta novels

## How I Write

## The End

## Pages with Artwork

The original artwork from which these thumbnails were derived will be posted at my "Daily Scroll" blog shortly.

# FANTASY, MOSTLY

"Imagination is the one weapon in the war against reality."
-- Jules de Gaultier

*Illustration for, "I Need a Horse!"*

**Inspired by Anton Baklashov's photograph, posted on Tumblr
woodendreams.
Thanks, Anton!**

# *I Need a Horse!*

*I can't just look at a photograph or a painting.*
*I start wondering what happened earlier*
*or what's going to happen next.*

I need a horse.

Don't know why—maybe I have an important message to deliver—or swarms of four-legged rainbow trout are after me. Maybe I'm just lazy.

Loosening the noose dangling conveniently from my neck, I sneak up on my wannabe steed. Who doesn't want to be.

I tumble over the edge of the slope, through the trees, and land face down in an oozy puddle. Trust me, there's a puddle down there behind the fir. No, not that fir. The other one on the right.

Drip. Glop. Ouch! Now I really need a ride. And a bath.

As for the ride, the Aardvark messengers' road is less than an hour away and I've got enough coin left from my last job to bribe a hostler.

~~~~~

Too late! The fastest trout in the flock find me!

Their leader spits in my face. Those who arrive with her do the same. My attackers whisk off to the mountain stream for more ammo but the slower ranks are catching up!

Eyes half-closed against the slithery attack, I grope my way toward the messenger road. The queen trout & her entourage are back! Fresh stream water runs down my face & soaks into my shirt.

Such fortune! Every trace of ooze should be gone by the time I reach the road.

## A Sailor's Tale

Time period: Just before the Revolutionary War.
Location: Maryland Colony, somewhere along the coast of the Chesapeake Bay.
Characters:
Jacob:        keeper of the lighthouse (perhaps at Hooper Strait)
Anne:        Jacob's daughter
Michel:      Jacob's helper at the light.
Narrator:    a nameless sailor.

Look on the southwest side of the Bay Light, and you'll still see the sign. You may have to look hard and long but it's there amidst the overgrown grasses—a cast-iron plaque to mark the place where they say Anne fell. The plaque was her father's idea. The framing edge of seagulls, mine. Make what you can of the plaque, if you'll not believe an old sailor's memories or the court testimony records.

Anne was only 16 the October her father found out she was in love. To say he was furious would be to speak faint of the man's cold rage. To find her in love would have been nothing. But the galling fact was she loved a common sailor from the British courier ship, 'Albatross'. And that could not be borne.

The lighthouse keeper was not a staunch Royalist. Some even whispered that Jacob sided with those who thought of insurrection. The same murmuring voices said it made his teeth grind to keep the lighthouse signal fire burning when the king's own ships were due in harbor. Jacob was never my friend but I'll say this for him. He was a principled man. No matter the provocation, he would never have let the Bay Light go out when any ship was due in port.

It was midafternoon before the night that the 'Albatross' was expected. 'Vengeance' had seen and hailed her with a rocket, only hours before the fog began closing in. She reported the 'Albatross' due to touch dock after midnight, bearing messages from the royal governor at the great port north of the town. But in those few hours the fog was thickening and billowing. And tempting Jacob.

Michel was Jacob's help at the light. Michel and I--and Jacob of course--knew Anne to be strange. Jacob couldn't help but know this. He'd married Anne's mother despite the rumors, not because he had never heard the gossiping tongues.

You needn't spy his daughter Anne up on the rocks with her arms aloft, her loosened hair like a great sail streaming at her back to wonder about her. You could see it in Anne's black eyes, just as you could have seen it once in her mother's—a reflection of the sea but not as the sailors see it on their wooden steeds, nor even as the townsfolk see it from their quays. It was a giddy thing to look into Anne's eyes. Those who encountered her in the town played it safe and scarce even looked into her face. She held her head the higher in answer.

Jacob knew all this. He might even have suspected in one part of his soul the strange truth hidden in rumor. But he'd loved Anne's mother once. And he'd shut out that part of his whispering soul, the more comfortably to keep loving her.

And her daughter, his beloved Anne? Well, hadn't he done what he could with the priest's holy water? Yes, he'd done all he could. But the townsfolk talked, and his soul whispered. And Anne's eyes kept on reflecting the sea.

Michel's testimony is still stored at the old courthouse if you've a mind to read it. You see, Michel loved her too. And he thought he knew the truth about Anne. But that night, oh those many years ago in October, Michel knew something else even stronger and more urgent. The man Anne loved was on the "Albatross" and was due in port in just a few hours. And, for all the grinding of Jacob's teeth, Jacob would do naught about it.

So Michel set to work. The ale in this mug tastes fine, but the dew in Michel's flask was stronger. And Jacob was of a mind to partake, though both men knew that spirits weren't permitted aboard the light.

Evening wore into night, with the mess fire burning brightly, and the bottle passing back and forth between them over the tiny mess table. Anne peeked into the room of occasion, her face a battle of lover's anticipation and anxiety.

Michel, facing the door, watched her face change as the night grew darker and his plans went on apace. He told himself, as he added more whiskey to both men's cups, she didn't realize what he was about, she'd be asleep by the time he'd doused the light. She'd understand some day and turn to him. His thoughts warned otherwise through the whiskey haze—but like Jacob did about the whispering in his mind—he refused to listen.

Last Michel saw of Anne, it was near midnight. Jacob was nodding in his chair, and mumbling about the light. Michel heard Anne struggling to lift the locked hatch to the signal fire deck, then the patter of her feet down the steps. Her pale form flitted past the mess door and was gone.

Michel wondered to where she was bound, but he had little time. He bounded up the narrow, bent steps to the next level, and then up the last tiny flight. In his haste, his head nearly cracked against the trapdoor frame as he wormed his way through. The fire buckets were full and he used them to best effect. When the last of the signal fire was nothing but hissing embers and steamy fog, Michel plunged back down through the trapdoor hatch, and went looking for Anne.

The window of her tiny room was open. The fog was chill and thick right to the room's door. But Anne wasn't there. Michel tried the other rooms, his ears attuned the while for the ding of a ship's bell in the distance. As he burst through the outside door and into the yard, he could still hear it. Close, but not so close yet. Time still to find her...

Some say he found Anne's discarded gown in the yard, just at the hour she found me.

I make no claims. All I know is that it was a gleaming white seagull which came to me at forward look-out, and warned me of the rocks. A seagull with Anne's eyes.

## Sisyphus

Evil pressed its inexorable hand on Leslie, forcing her down against the mattress. Her despairing whimper caught and died in her throat.

It was happening again. She knew what she had to do—what she had done in each relentless repetition of this nightmare. The lurking malice in the unlit bedroom grew stronger the longer she tried to ignore it. She had to try to stand or the malice would smother her. It didn't matter if she succeeded in moving or if she failed. Either way, it would do no good.

Leslie tried to move. Something—perhaps the silent voice of the haunting presence—reminded her she never succeeded in shifting so much as a finger or toe. It warned that the more she struggled, the more the feeling of terror and evil would grow.

It lied.

There. Her right index finger twitched. That accomplished, she had to continue straining muscle and bone against smothering immobility. She worked and fought and strained until her right hand lifted away from the mattress.

This had happened before. Awakening. Her finger. Her hand. How many times now had she battled, striving to reach an ever-receding goal? Older memories, of sun and music and familiar voices, faded before the countless echoes of her struggles. She knew one thing beyond any doubt or hope—each tiny triumph of movement only made the path to the final horror worse.

The heavy weight pressing on her poured away over the edge of the bed. She took her first unlabored breath. What should she do next? Move a foot? Her head?

It was watching in the dark, ready to mock and gloat. Already insinuating that her choice didn't matter.

The skin-tight prison wrapped about her had only pretended to flee. It hid in nothingness. It gathered its strength. It crept back to teach its favorite message--it will do no good.

She refused to let the dark hold her in place. The bedside lamp was so close. Maybe she would be better off not trying but she had to try to reach its switch. The darkness was ominous but suppose it was hiding something worse? Better to know. Better to see.

Leslie put all her will into moving her hand toward the lamp. Eternity passed. And eternity again.

Her fingers hung in mid-air, heavy and limp, as she tried to push them a little bit further toward the switch. Then, at last, the cool metal touched her fingertip. She drew a breath and strained, twitching desperately with a reluctant muscle.

Light sprang into warm existence around her but it brought no comfort. She was in the bedroom. Her enemy hid beyond, just outside the door.

Leslie turned to one side and managed to get her right elbow under her. She kept her rebellious muscles pushing until she was sitting on the edge of the bed.

Amid a tangle of sweat-darkened light brown hair, her pale face gazed at her from the vanity mirror. A cold shiver passed through her soul, unreflected by movement within her body. Something horrifying awaited her. If, perhaps, she could get into the next room—into Paul's study—perhaps someone would be in there. Paul would be in there.

The presence answered her thoughts. How many times now had she chosen to do this, only to find horror where help should be?

Too late now. She had given into the need to move and she couldn't stop what she had started.

Leslie looked down at her bedroom slippers on the old braided rug. Her toes twitched but she couldn't make her cold feet slide into their beckoning warmth. A shard of memory confirmed the reason. She hadn't put the bedroom slippers on before so she couldn't put them on now.

She pressed her feet against the cool of the rug and willed herself to stand. The gravity of an ocean bottom dragged at her. She pressed the knuckles of either hand into the bedclothes under her, until she felt she must be boring great holes into the mattress. At last, her body lifted between her straining arms, and she was on her feet.

A tiny revelation shimmered on another splinter of memory. From here on it was physically easier but more terrifying. Why hadn't she stayed hidden in the dark? Had it really been so bad?

Too late. Leslie slipped quietly toward the half-open bedroom door. Silence overwhelmed the throb of her heart. Walking into the dim hall required little effort but every pace away from the bedroom lamp's light added to her foreboding. Was the feeling of malice growing around her or was she drawing closer to its source?

She pattered down the cold hardwood of the hall until she stood in front of a closed door. A dim band of light shown on the floor, casting fugitive reflections on her toenails. Good. The lamp was on in Paul's study. Her body moved freely now but her will was barely strong enough to force her hand toward the dim gleam of the brass doorknob. Her fingers shrank from the first touch of its cold surface. She tried again. Opening the door and looking inside were the last things and then it would be over.

She reached out and gripped the knob, forcing herself to begin turning it as soon as it was within her grasp. She heard the tiny click and felt the familiar jiggle of the loose handle. She started to push.

Like a rubber band straining to its greatest length then snapping back, Leslie felt herself tugged backwards toward the utter, immutable reality of her unmoving body in the bedroom.

She fought the tug. The first few times she had the nightmare, she had given in to that backward pull. Now she knew better. To let herself be pulled back there would be to admit that all this, that every hard-fought movement to get here had been a fool's dream. Once she was back there and realized that, the horror she was trying to fend off would clamp down on her even more relentlessly.

Her hand clenched the knob with fingers as hard and unyielding as its brass surface. She welded fingers to knob and pushed, defying the immobility pulling at her. Open! She cried out, and remembered another cry. A scream. She had screamed in the study. Why? She opened her eyes.

Paul was face down on the floor. Blood was on his temple, more of it on the pale carpet, circling his head like a demonic halo.

"No! Oh, God, no!"

Breathing, but not from Paul. Someone was hiding behind the door! Leslie took a half step backwards.

"Don't run. It will do no good to run", warned a strange voice.

The warning itself did no good. At its very sound, Leslie turned and ran back into the hall. Then her head was splintering in agony and everything was bright flashes.

~~~~~

Featureless white surrounded her. Daylight. The echoes of a scream. Leslie felt so weak and dizzy, she was unsure she could keep standing. She reached out with one shaky hand for a bedside table she had never seen before. It seemed to scoot away from her on silent wheels. A high metal-framed bed was on her other side. Was she in a hospital room?

Before her, just feet away, a door opened. She flinched back from it, nearly falling in the process but she managed to change a new scream into a quiet gasp. A woman dressed in white walked through the door, followed by a tall man in black—in some kind of uniform.

"Mrs. Claridge? My God, look at you! You're standing!" The nurse smiled at her brightly but disbelief flickered in her eyes.

Fighting the foreboding, Leslie forced out a single word, "Paul?"

The woman's smile faded and she glanced toward the policeman behind her. Then the smile was back as she stepped forward. "One thing at a time, dear. First, you need to sit. You know, this is the first time you've moved all week!"

"I'm not lying back down!" Leslie interrupted.

Paul. She tried to push the memory away and knew she couldn't. Pain constricted her throat and burned in her eyes.

The nurse smiled at her again. "Then don't, dear. But you're sitting at least!"

The cop grinned down at her, "Don't blame you. A hospital of doctors and nurses couldn't get me sitting. Not after being unable to move for eight days."

The crinkle-eyed smile faded into intense scrutiny. "Mrs. Claridge, I've got a few questions."

The nurse glowered up at him. "It'll keep for a few more minutes. First, she needs to see the doctor." She gave Leslie another artificial smile. "And the doctor needs to see YOU!"

Leslie ignored the nurse's words. She forced herself to think about that night, to remember, just as she'd forced her body toward that nightmare door.

Settling unto the side of the bed and blinking back tears, she whispered, "What do you want to know? I ...I think I remember everything."

The policeman didn't answer. How could he? He wasn't there.

~~~~~~

The room tilted and Leslie found herself staring directly at the ceiling. She tried to voice a horrified "No" but something in her mouth prevented it. The only sound was the steady mechanical beeping of the monitor by her hospital bed. Above her, a woman's smiling face slipped into her line of sight.

"You're awake early, Mrs. Claridge! Would you like me to sit you up a little bit?"

Leslie blinked yes, as a tear formed.

"How are we doing this morning, dear?"

_I remember! I need to tell you!_

Busy with the bed's button and supporting her back, the nurse didn't see her fluttering eyelids.

_What else? Need to do something!_ She huffed out air, and threw all her will against inaction. Her index finger rose and fell with a forceful tap.

## *Circles*

Edgar Wilson gasped a lungful of air and opened his eyes. The gleaming ball of silver-gold shrank swiftly to nothing more than a twinkle between strands of cloud then disappeared as if it had never been.

He considered sitting up and thought better of it. If the whole encounter had been a hallucination, maybe he'd do best to just lie here for a bit.

The clouds were thickest in the west, their vanguard only a few degrees from obscuring the noon sun.

His left hand sheltering his eyes, Edgar waited patiently for the promised shade.

The sun continued to burn between his fingers.

It was true! Edgar grinned and scrambled to his feet. He stretched his arms up at the unmoving clouds and bellowed out a whoop of triumph. The only sounds were his breath and the throb of his blood. He spun around and looked at the cars beyond the circlet of summer-parched grass in the traffic circle.

Every automobile, every truck, every pedestrian was frozen in place. Every last blessed person caught in the daily East Hollem lunch rush. Except himself.

"They're real." Edgar murmured. The words seemed outsized as if spoken through a megaphone. Eerie. Gripping his upper arms with his hands he swallowed down a dangerous mix of euphoria and terror.

"Gotta get control, here. Gotta think about this..."

The words roared over the rhythmic surge of heart and lungs. Maybe he should keep his mouth shut for the rest of the twenty-four hours.

First, to prove to himself that it was real. Then, to enjoy. And finally, most importantly, to leave evidence that this had really happened—that he hadn't just taken a nap during his lunch break from the library and dreamed it all. Something was actually happening in his life! There was no way he was going to let it fade into doubt and a vague dreamlike memory when the time was up.

Edgar strode away from the center of the traffic circle in a slow spiral, his eyes fixed alternately on the dry weeds and shrubs, and on the silent masses of traffic. Here and there, he spotted an unmoving insect or bird near his path, each one an additional fragment of proof. The bee he struck with his chest was too much. Edgar gasped at the unexpected blow, and then cracked up as the tiny body bounced and ricocheted into a stand of ragweed. He was tempted to wander through the shrubs and bat every insect he saw through the air but he had more important things to do.

It was a busy twenty-four hours.

First, Edgar walked over to Main Street and visited every shop in turn. Pennies disappeared from the bagel shop cash register, finding a new home in the nickel section of the liquor store's machine. The liquor stores' nickels were bumped in turn to the barbershop, while the dimes he found there went to pay a visit to the drugstore.

It took four hours and twenty minutes and many cycles through monetary denominations before he had visited every shop but Edgar knew the effort would be worth it tomorrow. Or rather today. With a delighted grin, Edgar pocketed the twenties from the jewelry store, snatched up a non-ticking watch then strolled back outside.

One task down.

The next chore was the most time-consuming but Edgar guessed the results of his labor would be what he would treasure most. The puzzle of swapped coins would fade to nothing compared to the enigma he planned to create.

Over the next seventeen hours, Edgar gathered Tupperware containers from every house with an unlocked door. Transporting them all with just a food store shopping cart, he piled them high in the shape of a ring until they almost blocked the way between the parking lot and the main entrance. Cartload after cartload trundled down the silent streets, their contents spilled in patient succession just a few feet away from the library's front door.

Edgar tossed container after container unto the slowly growing donut of pastel and white plastic. The job was harder than he had expected. He paced himself as best he could and encouraged himself with thought of the articles that would appear in the newspapers. What conspiracy theories would turn up on the internet? How would the reporters try to explain this? In fact, how would they even describe it? Would the FBI or Homeland Security send agents to investigate?

Edgar stopped and arched his back to ease the pain. How would he handle the FBI's questions? Edgar smiled. What questions? No one would ever think to question him.

No one ever thought of him. The smile faded.

Enough Tupperware.

He slipped through the side door of the library, using his employee key. The daytime circulation manager was in mid-stride, halfway between his office and the front desk. Edgar stared at the man thoughtfully. Normally, he wouldn't even fantasize doing something like this but it was impossible to resist the opportunity. He retrieved the permanent marker from his pocket and carefully lettered "SOB" on the man's forehead in indelible black.

Edgar started to walk away from the bane of his working life, and then turned back. No, that wasn't enough. He had a "moral imperative" to balance the scales more completely.

How fast was Groves walking? He studied the man's feet and, mimicking the length of the manager's stride, he walked down the hall and back. Yes, this should work. He grasped Groves about the waist and then slowly, carefully, began pivoting the man until he was facing the wall. Catching his breath, he sized up the distance between nose and wall. Just about right. Edgar grasped his boss about the waist once more and shifted him over a few more inches. There.

He was tired and sore. And very, very satisfied. Edgar went back outside and walked around to the front of the building for another look at his ring of Tupperware containers. Like a white-glazed donut for giants.

Smiling, he crossed the street, slipping in front of the bumper of a tail-gaiting SUV. It was tempting to teach the driver a lesson about safe driving but he was too tired to come up with anything fast enough or clever enough.

Yawning, Edgar walked back to the place in the circle where he had been when the spaceship appeared. He lay down in approximately the same spot and glanced at his new watch, grumbling to himself when he realized that it couldn't move yet. Obviously he had finished with time to spare. He yawned again and closed his eyes. The sound of traffic would wake him up.

"He still didn't choose a Rolex, captain."

_I noticed._ Sqriggal felt like snarling in response.

From several stations on the bridge, half-hidden crew thoughts pinged at him. They were all weary of circling this rock.

_Enough._

"Resume planet time, Rofat. Call up navigation data to next site, Fligstree. Helm, break orbit when ready."

## *A Garden Mosaic*

Peace is in the dark green rustle.
Harmony beneath the moist tree.
Fecund tendrils coiling herein hide
 And moss protects smooth white root.


I love to smell a whisper of peach
In the prince's garden.
His castle floats in a languid dream
Of petal green spring and flower pink summer.
Bare and powerful he watches me lie near him
As tiny diamonds shine above Moon Lake Mountain.


A sea princess soars
In her gown of delicate spray
As the moon swims
The sky sea.


Listen to the soft wind whispering enticing music!
Scarlet roses twirl in a fiery dance,
Like phantom flame through a garden colonnade.
Behold a lady emerge between two pillars! So lovely
Is she a vision like the flame roses, or is she real?


Light rains on the cherry rose
Like misty dreams in a garden.

Some Leaves I Collected in 2005

## Daisy and the Paper—Mice

Daisy stopped purring and opened her eyes. This was pointless. Her human wasn't talking to her or rubbing her ears, and she smelled strange. Scary, not soothing as she had expected when she slipped up here. The room still smelled of the noisy human. And something else. Wrong. And wrong.

She gave an indolent yawn, and began stretching her tiger-furred body, beginning just behind the shoulder blades and working her way slowly to the base of her tail. A second unplanned yawn interrupted the wash of her messy right foreleg. By the time the preliminary paw wash was nearly done, her former sleeping perch smelled more like the noisy human than it smelled like herself. Wrong.

She jumped down, dragging the sheet to the floor with her, then impatiently jiggling her left rear paw to free the tangled claws. Once on the rug, she continued washing the offending paw. The taste on it reminded her of food. She was hungry but where was that human?

A sound down the hall made her ears twitch. Sibilant and soft. Very enticing. Mice?

The dirty paw forgotten, Daisy treaded to the doorway and peeked out. Nothing in the hall. She crept to the door of the big room and peeked in.

Things were all over the floor. Different, interesting-looking things! And movement—huge and noisy and high up. Not mice. Not birds flicking past her window. That strange human. Her whiskers bristled of themselves and the tension increased in her back. Wrong.

It was looking.

She looked away from him. Wrong.

Her eyes flicked about, studying the corners of the room, soft with shadow. No mice.

There was that good sound again. Crackling. High up. Daisy lifted her head toward the human, noting the swift movement between his fingers accompanied by that intriguing crackling sound. Mouse? She crept closer, her eyes fixed on the human's jiggling fingers.

Paper-mouse, like her own human made her! The uneasiness in her nose and whiskers faded a bit. It was turned away just like her human did just before throwing. Good. Soon now.

Paper-mouse was fun.

Throw it! Quick! Throw!

The paper-mouse came dribbling out of the human's fingers to bounce and roll across the floor. It stopped no more than a pounce length in front of her. Larger than usual, but crinkly.

Daisy crouched behind a table leg, and stared at the paper-mouse intently, daring it, willing it to move, to utter so much as a crinkle.

And then it did. A little snick of sound that tickled the edges of her ears deliciously. Her eyes widened at the secret movement it tried to hide but she had seen it! Alive!

The coiled springs of her hind quarters quivered, as she checked their readiness, and then exploded with precision and power. The leap. Breathless adjustments of eyes and mouth and front paws in mid-air. Exhilaration as her front paws made contact with their prey. She clenched her toes, grappling for a hold, her mouth open and biting at the intriguing little curl at the top. The toe clench firmly in place, Daisy bit down hard on the paper-mouse neck.

Taste. Strange taste, like her paw, like the stuff on her human. Like mice. She got the paper-mouse firmly under control, and then flopped to one side. Clutching it to her, she began kicking it, her mouth simultaneously worrying the mouse neck. Her human never made paper-mouse neck taste like caught mouse. It was crinkling again. She gave it a furious double kick with her hind feet. When that didn't stop its struggles, she kicked it again.

Did it need a third kick?

A noise—much louder than a crinkle—made her jump and lose her grip. Strange human's voice. Not calling her. Not saying 'food' or 'toy' either. At least not ear-hurting like when it had been with her human before. Excited and pleased. She glanced around. No prey.

Clumps of paper-mouse tumbled from the table-where-she-wasn't-allowed. Too many to hunt. Just plain too many.

Daisy scrambled under the table-where-she-wasn't-allowed and looked out. Crinkling from somewhere in the clump. But where? Encouraged, she looked toward the strange human's legs.

He walked away from the table-where-she-wasn't-allowed. He stared at one of the flat, uninteresting bits of paper-mouse, and then hid it away. Seconds later, fresh cracklings came from his hand.

She tensed. She stared at his fingers, anticipating the toss.

This time he was better at it. The paper-mouse ran to the soft-chair-for-sleeping, and then suddenly changed directions.

Tricky! But not tricky enough.

Daisy put on a burst of speed and just avoided running into the wall. She twisted sideways with her front paws and grabbed at the paper-mouse. It bounced away. A frantic burst of speed and she had it!

Grrr. That had been a good one! She chomped furiously on the crinkling neck and killed it again, just to be sure. This human made wonderful paper-mouse. Fast. Sneaky.

He was coming back into the room. Perhaps, he would make more?

She turned toward him.

Fah! What was that smell he was making?

Daisy retreated toward the stairs leading down to the outside door. Sometimes, when her human made bad smells, she would go down to the room with the water, then come up and make things wet and make a new smell. The new smell would be wrong too, but not as wrong.

Would the human go down to the water room next? Top-of-the-steps was a good a place to wait. Where would the human throw the next paper-mouse?

She waited.

Paper-mouse-on-steps were the best. Perhaps, he would see her. Perhaps if she told him. Paper-mice were such fun. She didn't like asking for another tricky paper-mouse but she voiced a tiny mew anyway.

The human was coming this way. He glanced around him and back over his shoulder as he walked toward her. The 'wrong' smell was very strong.

Daisy looked where he was looking. No prey.

The human had paper in his hand. He was nearly at the top of the steps. Daisy slipped down to the second step, her eyes on the maybe paper-mouse, her muscles tensing in anticipation.

He turned his back on her so she couldn't see this one.

Tricky. Good! Throw!

Fire smell! Daisy's back ridged.

Her eyes were fixed on what she could see of the room, beyond the human's huge feet and legs. Would he throw it down this way or up that way? So exciting not to know!

The whisper of cloth. Movement high in the air.

Up it went! Back into the room.

Eyes wide with delight, Daisy exploded into movement—only to be struck a body-numbing blow by the human's ankle against her side. Her legs were out of control! She twisted in mid-air, her eyes raking the steps below her for a landing spot.

The human was blocking her view. His great limbs were everywhere. So were the sounds he made—high--and shrieking like a bird, then loud thumps reverberating up and down the steps.

The step she landed on quivered with the sound. The shriek was still hurting her ears.

Her claws gripped enough for her to turn around and streak back up the stairs.

Terror greeted her. Fire! She was barely in the room, before she found herself fleeing it back down the stairs.

Her ears! Something LOUD was in the room, something even shriekier than the human had been on the staircase. Or than her own human had sounded, before. She needed to get away from it before it ate her ears.

The human was scattered and spilled all over the steps but she found a way past him.

Her heart pounding, her ears in torment, Daisy raced into the water room and hid between her litter box and the cold-wet-thing-that-sometimes-made-noises.

The narrow crack was dark and welcoming but the sound didn't go away. Daisy crouched back further, until her haunches were hard against the cool wall. She flattened her ears against her head as hard as she could make them. She wriggled but there was no room to puff her fur and scare the sound away.

The LOUD still shrieked out in the passageway. Daisy shivered in terror of it and at the horrifying smell of fire. Her eyes burned and watered. All the other smells had gone away, even her own.

Up above her—outside where the birds were—came the answering shrieks of new LOUD monsters. She pressed herself a little harder into her hiding place and waited for the creatures to go away.

Large crashing noises! Shatter-tinkle of glass. Water dripping somewhere close by. None of it louder or scarier than the beating of her own heart. Voices. Strange voices, mixed with an odd crackling. Nothing like paper-mice.

Didn't want paper-mice! Wanted her human and quiet.

Someone coughed.

"Oh, God! This one's bought it. Broke his neck on the stairs."

"John, got one alive up here! She's coughing! Ambulance yet?"

"No. Yes! I think I hear it. Need more help, Christine?"

"No."

"Fire's under control. Get Ray to radio we need a marshal."

"You're kidding! Arson?"

"Yeah. I think I smell an accelerant."

"Humph! Too bad these folks didn't have a watch dog."

Unfamiliar feet treaded into her hiding room. Water was dripping somewhere very, very close! Fire smells tormented her nose and burned in her eyes. The smells of many humans, all strange, blocked the last trace of her human's scent.

She shivered. At least the LOUD was gone.

"Litter box here. Anyone seen? Never mind. Here, kitty. Here, kitty, kitty!"

Daisy sniffed the strange human. Didn't like strange humans! Her paw was dirty. She licked it properly clean as she waited for the right moment to investigate this human. He made sounds that promised food. Didn't want food! Wanted her human holding her, making the right sounds and patting her the special way her human patted her.

Should she wait until this strange human produced a paper-mouse? Didn't want a paper-mouse!

He was wiggling his fingers. If she walked toward them, would he give her tummy rubs? He smelled unfamiliar. Tummy rubs were soothing. Strange smell. Tummy rubs were better than paper-mice.

She got to her feet, and gave herself a thorough stretch. A second stretch that came of itself. A sniff. A pretend yawn...

Now.

Daisy strolled forward, claiming the edge of her litter box with a swift head rub as she sauntered toward the human.

Faster would be good.

But she was a cat.

## The Windowed Door
### (a prose-poem)

Before anything, there is the door. At the bottom, it is yellow the color of dandelion flowers brightened with finger-lets of sunlight. Frames within a larger frame of spring sky are at the top. Within each blue frame bursts and ripples of colors change each into another too swiftly to see, far too rapidly to count or remember their marvelous hues.

Pictures, lives, worlds spring up and exchange places in the shiny squares as numberless across as leaves of grass, beyond counting as stars above and below. Myriads of inviting squares, not one echoing another, none ever the same as itself for two minutes together.

I sit on the floor and gaze at the pretty window pictures until my eyes are weary and my head tips down. The dandelion petals soothe me to sleep. Sleeping, dreaming of flowers. Of gentle beings whispering and singing. Of colors glimpsed through clear sparkling walls. Colors beckoning me to wake. To come and play with them.

One day. The fifth. The fiftieth. The secret number day only the dandelion knows. I wake and lean and my hands touch the yellow. Its petals tickle my fingertips, tug on them gently. Lift me up. And up. A bit and a bit more.

Many colors—playing in shiny blue frames the color of cornflowers—surround me. I touch the first square picture and then the next—across and then up—tasting the hues. Hearing the humble notes of violets holding aloft tiger lily twitters and lemon blossom lilts.

Should I be scarlet poppy or rusty mum, green oak leaf or lavender hyacinth? Perhaps none of these. Beyond them clambering and flying, swimming and striding are those of other worlds not so bright but equally wondrous.

My trembling fingers reach for something beautiful beyond imagination but it is gone before I can touch its clear door and enter in to dance with it. It doesn't leave. It flirts with me, now peeking out of the corner of one square, now engulfing another so fully that the transparent door glass glistens with joy. For a moment, it is spinning on its rim like a great sunflower, and then bobbing gently like a snapdragon in a gentle breeze.

I laugh. I reach.

Five and fifty and the number only the dandelion knows. The dance is nearly over. I look for the door on tired wings.

## *The Luckiest Hunter Ever*
### *(Story-telling guidelines follow. Just add children!)*

### Plot Summary

1.        Kup-Ah-Weese wakes up hungry and asks his wife if there's any deer stew left over from the previous night.  She says no and strongly hints he should go deer hunting.

2.        As Kup-Ah-Weese prepares to leave the lodge with his bow and quiver of arrows, his wife gives him a ball of twine made from the last of the deer's stomach, saying that he might find it useful to use in repairing his fishnet.  So, Kup-Ah-Weese decides to take along his net as well, grabbing it up when his wife isn't looking. Fishing is easier than deer hunting.

3.        He goes fishing, but he just sits on the bank of the river with the net in the water.  Falls asleep.  Wakes up abruptly thinking he hears his wife approaching.  He jumps. The net goes flipping up and behind him. He ends up in the water.

4.        Holding his breath and swimming, Kup-Ah-Weese sees geese feet above him.  He uses the twine to tie a goose's foot. It goes so well, he keeps at it until he's tied one foot of each of the twelve geese.  Running out of breath, Kup-Ah-Weese swims to the surface.

5.        This scares the geese and they take off. Kup-Ah-Weese is tangled in the twine and goes up with them. Unfortunately there's a steep bank on the far side of the river. Dragged down by his weight, the geese are flying too low—right toward the bank. He calls to his totem spirit, King-of-Night, and asks that Owl Spirit teach the geese to fly better.

6.        They do! Hurrah! They fly straight up! Ulp! Avoiding the cliff edge, the twelve geese all land in the top of a tree at the edge of the cliff, with Kup-Ah-Weese (still tangled) barely making a safe landing on one of the lower branches.

7.        He feels something under one leg - the tail of a raccoon? Kup-Ah-Weese ties his new prey to the last bit of twine.

8.        The only way he can safely become untangled is to cut himself free, which means falling into the water from a great height. He takes a great breath and cuts the twine from around his wrist, and falls down feet first into the water. He lands on something--not water and not land. Whatever it is, it seems to give way when his feet strike it, which gently breaks his fall. Whoa! That was close!

9.        Kup-Ah-Weese swims up to the surface and searches the river water downstream. It's a gigantic fish! He must have stunned it when he landed on its head feet first. Little by little, he swims toward shore, dragging the big fish by its tail—first with one hand and then the other.

10.        It's so huge, Kup-Ah-Weese wonders what such a big fish eats to get so big. Kup-Ah-Weese cuts the fish open and discovers a bear inside! Never before has a fish eaten a bear instead of a bear eating a fish!

11.        Kup-Ah-Weese retrieves the geese and the raccoon from the tree, hauling them up the embankment toward his village and his family's lodge.

12.        Suddenly he remembers that he had his fishnet with him. Finding it along the shore, Kup-Ah-Weese discovers that there's a wild turkey tangled up in its cords. He hides the turkey with the rest of his catches against the far side of their lodge. Kup-Ah-Weese motions for his curious children to be quiet.

13.        When he enters the lodge, his wife is sewing furs into a blanket. She follows him outside and around to the back side

of their home. Their children follow after them, laughter in their eyes and hands on lips to keep the laughs from escaping.

14.        Kup-Ah-Weese proudly shows her all that he has caught. There are 12 geese, a raccoon, a giant fish, a bear and a wild turkey.

15.        His wife looks at it all and says, "Good hunting, Kup-Ah-Weese! Twelve geese, a raccoon, a giant fish, a bear and a wild turkey!  But where is the deer?"

## *The End*

## Note
"The Luckiest Hunter, Ever" is based on "The Story of Kup-Ah-Weese", as collected in "Legends of the Delaware Indians and Picture Writing", by Richard C. Adams, published 1905, reprinted 1997)

During my time at the Delaware History Museum, I created "The Luckiest Hunter Ever" to help teach our unit about the people who lived in what we now call Delaware. My DHM supervisor thought we might publish this but we never did. Now, almost fifteen years later, here it is!

Back then before I told this tale, I showed school children hand-crafted artifacts from our reconstructed lodge and describe bits of Leni Lenape culture. Photographs or drawings of animals, birds and fish indigenous to the Mid-Atlantic coast were very useful. While everyone was looking at the pictures, I suggested that the children might want to make animal sounds any time I mentioned an animal while telling the story. Warning: Toward the end of the story, there will be a lot of animal sounds!

You may want to make adjustments befitting your own region before telling this story. Enjoy!

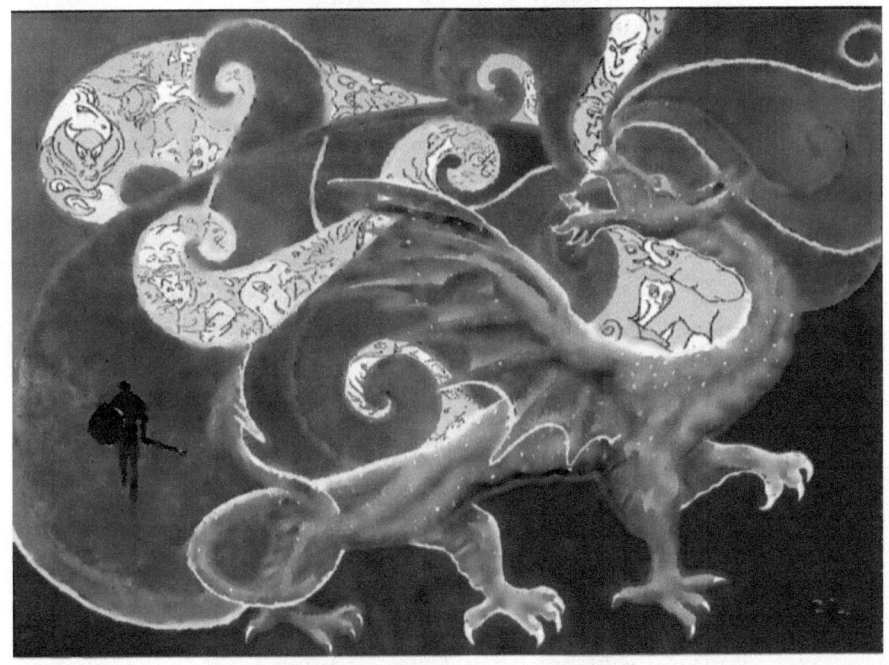

## The Dragon's Tail Tale

Geoffrey was still waiting for his first ale in the Dragon's Tail, when he noticed something odd up at the barman's counter. He was tired from riding all day and he had brought in his saddlebags which he had a mind to still be owning by the time he left, so it took curiosity turning into perplexity to make him get up, heft his belongings and walk over to the bar.

The barman looked up from the conversation he was having with another traveler and nodded. "Sorry! Coming right up, sir."

Geof nodded back but his attention was fixed on the peculiar object on display in front of him. A stoppered glass cylinder rested on the scarred and sticky countertop. Judging from the congealed globs of black and brown substances about its base, it had either been leaking at one time or it had been glued to the counter using a variety of concoctions. Faint unpleasant smells drifted from both the glue and the contents of the cylinder.

But the contents—that was what had drawn him from the comfort of a chair with a leather cushion to perch on a rickety stool. He could make nothing of the gelatinous-looking stuff inside the crystal-clear glass receptacle. Most of it was a murky green. Caught within the goo—like flies in amber—were putrid-pink fragments that reminded Geof a bit too much of spilled guts on a battlefield. His eyes caught a twinkling something, glanced toward it and lost track of it.

A tankard of frothing ale slid under his nose. He looked toward the barman and gave him a preoccupied nod of thanks. After a deep drink and a sigh of utter satisfaction, Geof went back to studying the cylinder. The glop inside seemed to have moved, as if stirred by the wooden spoon of an invisible cook. The pink fragments had migrated to the back side of the container. Closest to him now, replacing them, were huge ragged flakes of something like dirty mother-of-pearl.

Something twinkled. This time he was able to catch a glimpse of its source. Not to say the view made any sense. It looked to be a dying ember with a golden-white flame at its center. Within the space of two eye blinks, it was consumed with a flame that could not exist inside all that hellish gelatinous liquid. All that remained was a tiny ember, dead and powdered with white ash.

He shook his head and turned back to his ale. It was a strong brew and for a minute he grew suspicious of it. But no, he had been seeing odd things inside that cylinder even before his first swallow. Besides, he was too dry and the rich taste too good to stop. He drained the tankard. Finding the barman walking back into the room through the kitchen doorway, he lifted the cup and nodded.

"Want dinner? Back over at your table?" The balding man gave him an ingratiating grin, which pulled taut the shiny pink burnmarks along his right cheek, and extended into his gray-brown hairline like wandering paths.

Geof hesitated. He didn't look at the cylinder, and wasn't sure he wanted to look again. And yet, from the looks of all that glue, it wasn't going anywhere in the next hour.

Two men were sitting a couple of stools away on his right side. Both were grinning but their eyes were fixed on the froth topping their latest drinks.

A fat barmaid came in from the kitchen and plopped down a tray of clean mugs with a clatter. She looked toward him, and smirked, then turned away and scuttled over to a patron on his other side, asking loudly if he was done and ready to pay.

The whole tableau left Geof uneasy without knowing why. He shrugged and answered, "Yeah, dinner if you've got anything edible. I'll take it at that table." He added the last in a tone that he hoped sounded like the location was entirely his idea.

He took his time picking up his saddlebags. Pretending to struggle with a buckle and peer into the contents of one of the pouches, he gave the cylinder one last glance. He thought he could make out something like a giant thorn through the darker murk. He stood up with a groan, and saw something atop the iron-lidded cylinder.

At first he thought it a salamander. On second glance he decided it was a salamander's tail fastened to the red-gold copper model of a salamander. An odd decoration that might have been attractive once, were it not for the model's tarnished surface and the great globs of glue holding it in place - globs nearly as large as the little model itself.

He walked back to his table, past a couple of merchants and a well-to-do-looking farmer haggling over the cost of pack animals, past a slimy-looking old fighter nuzzling the slender barmaid, and past three men whose scowls warned him to look away. Obliging them with a will, he reclaimed his chair and leaned back.

Many's the tavern had peculiar stuff on display to attract and beguile the traveler but this was one of the strangest. He dismissed it from his thoughts at the sound of heavy rain through the cracked shutters. Merhule! Wouldn't you know? And he had to get to Gulver's Pine by the end of the day after next. Much as he hated to do it, he'd best tell the stable boy to have his horse ready an hour before dawn. Maybe the barman or the fatter barmaid would oblige him with a knock on his door, if he pressed a coin into their palm tonight.

The barman approached, weaving between the tables with a tray held high over his head, entirely supported by his left hand. His right arm was bound up as if from a severe wound or a nasty break. The man called over to a rain-spattered group just finding seats around a table close to the hearth, "Alise will help you in minute!" His foot gave the slender, giggling barmaid a passing cuff on her ankle as he went past. "Back to work, girl!"

When he was close enough, he lowered the tray so that Geof could see its contents. A pot of stew sat on it, a long trencher lined with slabs of roasted beef on one side and with gravy-soaked hunks of bread on the other. A sweating pitcher full of ale to the point of slopping over the top, and two tankards crowded the rest of the surface.

"Help me?"

Geof nodded, overwhelmed by the sight and the mingled scents. "With a will! But what's mine?"

The man gave him a gap-toothed grin that pulled the shiny pink scar to its bursting point. "Whatever you like, lad. I'm eating the rest. Owner gets a break too."

He glanced over his shoulder, and nodded when he saw the barmaid sauntering over to the new arrivals.

Geof lifted down plates and tankards one after another, until the tray was empty. His end-of-day hunger seemed to have turned into the feral starvation of a beast. Right now, he had no idea how much the barman would charge him for his portion and he didn't much care. He'd been frugal enough during his journey. Like the barman, he too deserved a break.

The man dropped into the chair opposite and reached down to prop the enormous tray against his left leg. That done, he reached over with his left hand, saying only, "Maxmilian -- round here, just Max."

Geof clasped the proffered left hand awkwardly with his right. "Geoffrey or just Geof." Spurred by the scent of food to add an extra touch of friendliness and trust, he added, "From Cat's Rook."

Max nodded. He poured ale into the two tankards. "Must be going to Gulver's Pine, then." He glanced up sheepishly. "Not trying to be intrusive, but I know this countryside. Most come traveling through from different directions and with different destinations than you. When I talk to a Gulver's Pine townsman, I guess he's heading Cat's Rook way. And vice versa."

Geof grinned and shrugged. He'd been on edge at Max's guess for a moment but the explanation made sense. Interesting private game for a tavern owner.

Still feeling a bit uneasy about other matters, Geof framed his next words with care, "I'm grateful for the food and for the company! I'll be glad to pay my share for this feast you've brought us but I doubt I can pay back your time with any interesting traveler's tales."

Max grinned again. "In other words, why did I choose to invite myself to dinner?"

Geof could only shrug. He was chewing on a huge mouthful of melting-tender beef and bread. He took a sip of the ale, then got out, "Well, actually..." His mouth was empty now but all he could think to add was another shrug.

"It was your interest in my little display up at the bar." Max gave him a measuring look and seemed to be waiting for a reply.

_Ah, gods of the desert Longknives. Was this some kind of scheme for money?_ He couldn't think of any reason why the man would demand payment for his interest in what he'd seen. After all, it was stuck on the bar where anyone couldn't help but look at it.

He answered with caution, "I saw it as soon as I came in. Curious thing, that. I'll wager there's a way to make money off it."

Max chuckled and shook his head. "Wish I knew how! Maybe it persuades a few travelers to return. Anyway, I did pretty well for myself a few years ago." His left hand strayed to his swathed and bundled up right arm, "Well, good and bad. All's said and done, it's worked out."

"What happened?" Geof nodded to the man's arm, "If it's not being passing intrusive to ask."

The barman gave him a sly smile. "Nah. Just hard on some people to hear. I try to pick who I tell nowadays—not liking to throw out paying customers for cursing or for throwing crockery at me and all."

Geof gulped some more ale, and shook his head, "Edgy tempers. I'll make you a deal. You don't try to charge me for telling your tale and I won't throw a tankard at you." He grinned. "Certainly not a full one. This is good brew."

"Thank you kindly." The man leaned back, stuffed some food into his mouth, and chewed reflectively for a minute. "So what happened to my arm." He grinned and shook his head. "Had a little run in with a dragon, you might say."

Geof blinked at the words. _This is a joke. Gotta be_ "Really?"

"Oh, yes, really." Max looked behind him, finding first one barmaid and then the other with his eyes. Evidently satisfied that both were working, he turned back.

"You see, I was out hunting one day about eight years ago. Didn't own a tavern then. Hunted. Did odd jobs. Had been a soldier a couple of times." He grinned. "But hated the hours, and the wages stank considering the danger." He shook his head. "Thought I knew what danger was in those days."

"Anyway, I'd been hunting and bagged me a fine doe. I was cutting saplings to make it easier to get it home, when I heard this whirring sound overhead. Like nothing I've ever heard before or since. Next thing you know, just as true as the Longknives worship sand gods, there's the dragon landing over the other side of my doe carcass with - if you please - its front claws digging into the belly as if it had made the kill.

"I'm still thinking maybe it was young, didn't know it's manners, it having pale green scales and tiny little horns and being all-in-all not much bigger than a couple of oxen.

Anyway, I yell, 'Get! That's mine! You hunt...'

"The blamed thing opened its mouth and I had a pretty good guess what was coming. I dropped and rolled, before the fire came, and I was mighty glad I did, though it singed me a tad.

"I was still picking myself up, when I smelled scorched venison behind me. That made me mad, reckless mad. I hunkered behind a tree, waiting my chance. The critter dug into the half-cooked meat, ripping pieces of gut and muscle away, and paying me no further mind.

"I pulled out my sword, nice and quiet like, then I waited for it to lift its head and chew, figuring it couldn't make fire with its mouth full. Soon as it was chewing, I burst from behind that tree, my sword arm in front of me and the sword tip aimed for the monster's slobbering mouth.

It saw me in a trice and blundered forward over the last pieces of the doe, taking in a breath and ready to turn me to cinders this time. I shoved my sword blade into its maw and kept pushing, hoping I'd get its throat and not wherever it stored that fire stuff. It was moving too, charging at me, the ground vibrating and its tail lashing trees like a giant whip.

"Well, there wasn't much I could do except keep doing what I was doing. I just kept shoving that sword in deeper and deeper, and the dragon just kept on charging. Merhule, it was hot inside that thing! The Longknives would have cussed that heat. I felt like my arm was melting and that my sword must be no more than glowing steel globs by now.

I was shrieking my head off with pain. Wishing the monster would take my head off, actually, and stop the misery. But all it did was keep on charging at me.

"I couldn't do but one thing. If I pulled out that sword, I'd never make another stroke like the first. If I pulled out just my arm, then the sword wouldn't do anymore damage—and it was pretty obvious I hadn't stopped this critter yet.

I held on and I shoved hard. I figured by now that sword was passing clean through it stomach and was well on its way through its intestines. Boiling hot stuff was clinging to my arm, and I just tried to imagine it was no more than chunks of half-chewed venison. Didn't seem to make any difference to the dragon. He just kept on coming at me.

"I shoved some more. The sword seemed to wobble in my hand. I was afraid I was going to lose my grip on it. If the dragon felt the wobbling, he didn't tell me about it. He just kept on coming. I gritted my teeth until a couple of them cracked inside my head, and I gave one last shove. The sword dipped and something gripped at my sword hand. Then I knew where my hand was. I let go that sword and grabbed for a hunk of tail instead. Dragon grunted, but he kept on coming.

"I got a hold of a boulder with my free hand and I dug my heels in like a donkey. Then I gave that tail a yank for all I was worth. Seemed like miles of it slid through my fingers, while that dragon just kept on coming. The scales ripped into my palm and cut into my finger bones but there was nothing I could do but clench and pull even harder.

"At last I had just the tip of the tail in my hand. I drew a breath like a dragon ready to spit fire, and I yanked! I yanked that tail, knowing this was the end one way or another. I pulled that tail and it finally started to move toward me. I pulled harder, and my arm and that tail tip shot back inside the dragon's body, but I wasn't finished pulling yet.

"Well, yeah, that dragon kept on coming. But now he was inside out and going the other way."

His eyes fixed on Geof, Max lifted his tankard and drained it. "Thanks for listening."

Geof didn't move, didn't say anything. He wanted to laugh, and he wanted to bellow that he was not to be made a fool of. His mouth opened, but neither response came out.

Max nodded, and gave him a sympathetic smile. "I've seen that look a hundred times. While you're still trying to come up with something to say, let me tell you a couple more things."

He gestured behind him with his left hand. "That container is full of all the innards that were stuck on my arm that day. And that little piece of lizard tail? The tip of the dragon's tail I managed to hold on to."

Geof felt his mind and his mouth beginning to work. Fury seemed to be winning, but he still couldn't come up with actual words. A kind of choked hiss escaped him.

"One more thing, before you try to take off my head, son."

Max began unwinding the swathing around his right arm. As the last folds came free, out slithered foot after foot of fire-seared limb. The fingerless hand hit the floor and was covered by a ten inch coil of wrist. Staring at the snake-like length of ruined arm, Geof found it best to close his mouth and concentrate on keeping the feast inside him.

## No Substitutions

The message had enough personal information about them that she knew she had to take it seriously. The last part said, "Be at the corner of Third and Main at 10:30 with the recipe and the child or you will be sorry."

Sighing, Abigail crumpled up the note. It had been too good to be true, though she hadn't expected they would be discovered so quickly.

She looked at her watch. It was already 10:00! She removed her apron, ran her fingers through her straight hair and grabbed her best hat.

"Cathy!"

Abigail hurried into the kitchen and began rummaging. Naturally, it was in the last place she looked – under the pile of tattered sheets and volumes on the little desk by the stove. She yanked the fat book out from the bottom of the pile, allowing the rest of the litter to fall to the floor. Something went plop and then made a skittering noise. Abigail chose to ignore both sounds. She turned off the heat under the kettle with a sigh. The scent alone told her that the brew was nearly ready. Ah, well!

"Cathy! Come in here right now!"

When the child failed to answer, Abigail flew out the kitchen door and down the steps into the back yard. Herbs, flowers, shrubs and young trees hid great portions of the yard from view.

Abigail caught the flick of a net from behind the hickory.

"Cathy! I'm warning you! Count of three!"

"Mommy!" The golden-haired child ran toward her, jar in one hand and butterfly net in the other. "Please don't make me come in. Look! I caught three already."

Abigail started to stoop but the child was already upon her. Dropping jar, lid and net, Cathy scrambled into her arms so quickly that one tiny nail left a scratch on Abigail's arm.

"Ouch! How many times… Never mind!" Abigail hugged the child to her. "We have to go back to the shop. Right now."

Cathy whined, "But I don't -want- to!" She squirmed so violently that Abigail could hardly hold her.

"There's no time, sweetie! We only have a few minutes to get there."

"No!" Cathy growled.

Abigail growled back, "Stop that!" She glared into the child's stormy green eyes until the anger in them began to fade.

"We'll come right back here and you can catch more butterflies. And I'll give you a treat."

"I want a treat now!"

"And I want to be young and beautiful." Abigail chuckled.

She settled her hat more firmly on her head and hurried toward the front lawn. Belinda was already out at the curb. Leo was curled up beside her, sound asleep. Belinda had all the luck!

"Thought we'd carpool."

"Thanks, Bee!" Abigail gasped. She climbed in behind the others, with Cathy still squirming to get free. They were barely settled before Belinda started forward. The convertible zipped down the street in a rush of air.

"Do you think she knows about all of us?"

Belinda nodded, her black eyes fixed ahead of her, as they sped downtown.

"Look around you, dear. Everyone's heading toward the shop."

Belinda pulled back on the stick. The carpet plunged toward the intersection, converting into automobile form just as it landed in a parking place.

Cathy stuck out her tongue and stared up at Abigail.

"Oh, no!"

Too late. Half-digested tuna salad landed on the new leather seating. Cathy backed away from the mess with a wrinkled nose.

"Bee, I'm so sorry!"

"It's OK! This new one's self-cleaning."

Belinda scooped up Leo in mid-yawn, and jumped out. A yellow cloud was pouring through the pet shop door, chasing out the last of the customers.

Secure in their invisibility, Abigail and Belinda ran through the last tatters of rotten-egg mist followed by several of their friends.

Mrs. Balustrade stood by the pet cages, tapping her foot. Her pointed hat was crushed between her crossed arms. She glared at each adult and child in turn, counting under her whistling breath.

"Eleven. Twelve. Thirteen. A disgrace! Three whole litters! Otto, I don't want to hear about it. You all know the rules." She waggled her bony finger under the nose of the misty-eyed man. Pointing to the largest cage, she commanded, "Put them in there, and find your recipes."

Abigail gave Cathy a kiss and a hug, followed by a little push toward the cage door. Blinking back tears, she looked for her recipe.

Beside her, Bee muttered "Bitch!"

Abigail turned to caution her friend.

Their eyes met. Swift as the flight of a bat, an idea passed between them. Abigail mouthed three words, "cage" pointing to herself, then "ingredients" indicating her friend, followed by "recipe" again pointing to herself. Not waiting for a response, she took a step toward Mrs. Balustrade and the cage.

"Gertrude, please! We were lonely."

Their leader snapped, "Another word, Abigail Cornbottom, and you'll be a mouse. Find your recipe and start reciting. You can go first!"

Mrs. Balustrade's eyes glared red. Abigail backed up a step and curtsied. Simultaneously, her index finger twitched. The cage door drifted open.

Across the room, Belinda was shoving something into a fish bowl. She nodded.

Abigail flipped to a page in her book and began chanting.

Behind her, children spilled through the cage door. Several ran toward the fish tanks, live cricket box or the mouse cage. Others ran off in the opposite direction, seeking out rawhide bones, balls and treats.

"What? Stop them!"

Mrs. Balustrade lunged for the closest child. Her sharp nails touched the boy's shoulder, just as Belinda dumped the contents of the fish bowl on her. Thunder clapped. Mrs. Balustrade fell forward on hands and knees.

"Hee! Hee! Hee!"

Amidst cheers and cries of relief, Otto and Warren cornered the transformed Mrs. Balustrade. Buckling a collar around her hairy neck, the men led her out the pet shop door.

"Abigail!" Belinda chided. "You made her into a hyena, instead of a poodle!"

Abigail giggled, "No, you did! You couldn't find dried newt eye, could you? Of course not! What did you substitute—a live salamander? See what happens when you play hob with the traditional ingredients?"

Belinda shrugged. "My bad. Still, you know this is more fitting."

Abigail picked up Cathy and hugged her. "Want to go to the zoo?"

## WINTER'S SEASON

Dawn. A good time to stand high amidst the Nala Hills and watch the sun transform early snow to pearl and crystal. Oneida stepped away from her place on the cliff wall and looked down.

Wind caught at her thin gray cape, making it dance about her then snatched at the folds of her silver gown. She ignored its play until it began flinging handfuls of her own hair into her face.

"Stop it! I can't run tag with you. Someone's coming."

Oneida gestured with one hand and, when the wind retreated, absently brushed strands of silver-blonde hair out of her eyes. She knelt on the icy edge of the path and looked down for any sign of the supplicant coming to visit her sisterhood. A pity one would be arriving on the first day of winter. Usually she spent her first day on watch exploring the paths branching from the cavern near here, or playing games with the wind.

But not this first day. Oneida sighed. A change was coming, climbing its slow way up the hills. Change. A word she and her sisters rarely used. A mortal word. Mortals invariably sought for change when they came to visit. The ancient mortals had envisioned the Nala as agents of change. Unlike her sisterhood, they truly believed change was possible.

A wave of unease swept over Oneida. Unlike the ancient mortals, the Maker hadn't believed in change either.

Enough fretting. Change was coming—and in the guise of a mortal! Mortals as agents of change? Just the thought made the headache caused by Spring's avalanche return. Throughout Summer and Autumn, she had been able to forget it but now she felt as if the cracks near her place in the cliff were starting to split open inside her head. Better to banish such nonsense from her thoughts, and enjoy the day before her.

Oneida allowed her long fingertips to stroke the translucent gray white hummock by her knee. She loved snow, but ice was her special delight! She drew comfort from the hardness, the crystalline density, the stubborn endurance of it!

Her first memories, aside from the forming thoughts of the Maker, were of snow-burdened skies and gray rock glittering with ice. Her sisters hated ice. They whispered of black frosts and pitied her for her assigned season. She smiled. Pity her? She who saw the sparkle of ice crystals in the snow and the giddy swirl of newborn snowflakes in the playful wind? If there were any flaw in her existence it was that her duties didn't permit her to walk about at night.

Struggling up the path only a few hundred feet below, was the visitor. She gasped. She wasn't even inside the cavern. Oneida gathered up her skirts in preparation for running along the cliff edge.

What was the stranger doing down there? Dropping her hems, Oneida crept closer to the edge, her head cocked to one side to get a better view. He had stopped near a cluster of icicles and was staring up at them. Perhaps he thought they might crack apart and strike him if he proceeded? No. Oneida watched thoughtfully as the man tilted his head to one side and then the other.

Ah! She remembered that spot. Dawn light refracting through newborn icicles created the most exquisite rainbows in that very place. Often, she would stand just so…

After a final swift caress of the largest icicle and a sigh, the stranger resumed his upward journey.

Oneida jumped up. Now, she was even later than before. She whirled about and ran along the cliff edge, slipping and sliding expertly across the ice patches to hasten her speed. Her actions were instinctive, her thoughts on the stranger. So different from the ones before him. If a mortal could be a change, what kind would he be?

Once past the cavern mouth, she sprinted directly toward the first fire cistern. Already the cavern was too warm for her comfort but that made little matter. She lifted the huge stone urn, dumped coal on the cistern's tiny banked flame and then moved toward the next.

Once she had protested about the cavern's warmth to her sisters, only to have them piously repeat ancient beliefs. The fires, the underground springs, everything was there for the convenience of travelers, not for the humble watchers.

Back when she had complained about the fires' heat, their explanation for it had seemed a worthy one. Not now. As soon as she'd awakened today, she'd seen the flaw in their words. Obedient to the Precepts of the Maker, her sisterhood cared nothing for the ultimate welfare of the occasional suppliant. So then, why were they always so concerned for the guest's physical comfort?

A dim glimmer of memory, older even than the thoughts of the Maker, provided an answer. It was not the Nala who were concerned about mortals. It was their first worshipers, the ancient mortals, who envisioned the Sisterhood's concern for those who worshiped them.

Oneida dutifully dumped a double handful of coal into the last cistern, and glanced around. Nothing else needed doing. Lacha had been her usual efficient self yesterday. The stone benches were in place, the white furs clean and carefully piled over the chest, and the porridge was simmering as it always did.

She, on the other hand.... Her hair was damp at the nape of her neck and she could feel a telltale trickle down her spine. Coal dust coated her bare arms almost to the elbow and clouded the glimmering surface of her dress. She gestured and muttered, "Depart to your place!"

A fine mist of coal dust floated away and swirled into the flame of the nearest cistern, immolating itself.

Now the moisture. It was so hard to get dry once one was wet. Converting the bits of water clinging to her into ice crystals was not permitted, since it seemed to disturb the visitors. Oneida unlaced her cape and started to tug it off.

Footsteps at the cavern entrance.

She sighed and began drawing the cape back into place, then shrugged and cast it from her anyway. She was hot, her head ached and her sisters weren't able to see her unseemly attire. There was a glimmer of protest from the Maker's thoughts but it was mild and she ignored it.

A courteous male voice murmured from the cavern mouth, "Priestesses of the Nala, may I enter?"

Oneida answered with the first line of the ritual, "Enter at your peril, stranger."

"What peril? I come seeking the aid of the goddesses, not their wrath."

The owner of the voice stepped into view with the last word. It was a young man this time, not more than thirty, with black hair and a thin beardless face. He was clad in a green, fur-lined cape, woolen jerkin and trousers and high riding boots.

Oneida inclined her head and continued the ritual, "Since you insist upon entering, I must bid you welcome. But you enter at your peril."

The man chuckled, a sound that ill matched the grief and fatigue in his eyes. "I've heard the Daughters of Nala give less than a warm reception." He unlaced his cape and tossed it onto a stone bench. "Speaking of warmth, why is it so damned hot in here? Feels like the Ninth Pit of Merhule!"

Oneida protested in amazement, "You like it warm!"

"Me? What would you know of my likes and dislikes?"

Oneida thought both his tired grin and the expression in his brown eyes impertinent. She suppressed a weary sigh. Perhaps he was one of the rude ones with no respect for the goddesses or for the ancient Precepts to which she and her sisters had been bound from the beginning. Visitors of that kind made her feel faint.

A moment or two more and she would know. Such visitors revealed themselves all too quickly. She picked up the thread of their conversation.

"You don't like it warm, either? I don't understand. I thought all..." Careful. Mustn't reveal she wasn't flesh and blood. Her hand reached up absently to her left temple. The pain was intensifying.

"Warm, yes. Not the fiendish heat of the pits!" he said. "Oh. Please accept my apology, priestess!"

Oneida gave herself a little shake. The next words and gesture were... She remembered.

She stepped forward with her hands outstretched. "Give your weapons into my care until you leave this place. It is forbidden-"

"I know." The stranger lifted his arms to show that his belt bore only a telltale worn mark in the place from which his sword should have hung. "I left sword and bow at the foot of the path as required." He smiled sardonically. "I found that a harder task than climbing the path. Many tales have circulated about the perils of approaching your goddesses and not many of them are pleasant. The few scrolls about the Nala are even worse. They warn the reader to come here unarmed, and then hint that it makes little difference."

"You..." Oneida frowned and bit her lip. What was the next question? He kept saying unnecessary things that confused her. "You carry a weapon concealed? A dagger, perhaps?"

Her visitor shook his head. "Do you think me mad, priestess, to bear a forbidden weapon into the sacred places of the Nala?"

"Nearly all others do, male or female. They fear the watchers."

"But it's forbidden!"

The watcher laughed. "That has never stopped the greater part of our visitors. What is your name, stranger?"

"Fendark na Ferilin, of the Charin tribe. And yours?"

"Oneida."

What came next? Oneida glanced toward the simmering pot. No, not that. Why must she get a confusing one her first day back on watch? Ah, the Testing! That was it. She turned abruptly and started toward the cave mouth.

"Wait! I haven't told you why I came. Would you dismiss me so swiftly?"

Fendark grabbed up his cape and started after Oneida.

He added, "Aren't you pledged to aid me if I ask it? I thought your sisterhood had an obligation to at least provide food and shelter for the suppliant, and to hear him out. Where are you going?"

Fendark reached forward and touched Oneida's elbow from behind. "I came on an urgent errand and I demand to be heard. If not by you, then by others of your order. Where are they?"

Oneida shook off his grasp and turned around.

"You must deal with me, Fendark son of Ferilin. Only one of us watches at a time, and the winter season is mine."

She paused and looked up into Fendark's desperate face. Words poured from her, despite the Precepts. "Why don't you go away? You haven't broken any of the rules and I've warned you. Are you so very foolish?"

"Foolish? No, priestess. Desperate."

The quiet words tugged at her heart for a moment. Then her jawline stiffened.

"Come, then. Let me show you the carvings along the path and on the cliff wall. That is the next thing."

"Why? I saw them as I climbed to you, if you mean the bas reliefs of the Nala. Looks like there's been a bit of a landslide recently though..."

At the mention of it, Oneida drew a quick breath.

The suppliant noticed. "You're unwell, aren't you? Let's go back to your cavern, and I will tell you of our needs. If I do it at once, you can rest the sooner. You look about to faint!"

Oneida shook her head. "I have a duty, and you have until an hour before sunset before you must leave. So, we have hours to do all that must be done, and say all that must be said. All of it is required.

"Now, come look at the carvings and the gemstones. The Maker tells us that this is the next part of the rites. All must be done by the thought of the Maker. Showing you our gifts from previous suppliants is next. There will be time for your tale and my decision after that."

"But why?"

"Hush. Obey the Maker's thoughts with me." She reached for his hand and tugged him forward, along one branching path, then through a crevice in the cliff wall.

"What maker?"

"Hush!" Oneida gestured at the traceries of gold and precious gems peeking through the encrusted ice on the walls about them. "These are some of the treasures of the Nala: rubies and garnets, great quantities of moonstone. Look about you, and wonder at the wealth of the goddesses. Hands such as your own have given us these gifts, just as the Maker envisioned."

Fendark pulled his hand away long enough to huddle into his cape.

"Aren't you cold? You came out without your cloak."

Oneida smiled. "I like cold." She pointed just above their heads, and to their right. "That reddish glow behind the ice is a cluster of rubies shaped like Summer's Firestar."

"Beautiful," Fendark responded absently. His eyes were on the priestess.

Oneida answered, "They are. Do you wish to touch them? All you need do is shatter the ice covering them with a large rock-"

Fendark laughed. "What now? Are you trying to tempt me to steal your own goddesses' treasures?"

Oneida answered with only a shrug and smile.

Fendark snorted. "Come with me, priestess."

He ducked through the crevice and then started up the path toward the cliff itself.

Oneida followed him. "Where are you going?"

"To your goddesses," Fendark called back. "Come on!"

They walked up the path until they stood under the cliff wall where several bas-relief statues were incised in the wall. Most were muffled by moss, age and snow but the figures of three women draped in flowing garments were prominent. Their gazes seemed to rest on the valley below.

Around them clustered a variety of stone animals and birds, some cracked or shattered by the fury of the rocks which had fallen from above. The women's arms were stretched out toward the animals although whether in benediction or in alarm at the plight of the carved creatures was unclear.

Fendark pointed up at the statues. "These are symbols of the ones who might aid me if you intercede. My people need the power of those they represent. I ...my people have no use for your rubies. I beseech you humbly, priestess, test me no more! Only listen to the tale I bring!"

"You pledge then that you didn't come for our treasures? Speak truth!"

Fendark opened his mouth, and there was fury in his eyes. He stared intently at the priestess. "Upon my honor, I seek what might be deemed "treasure," but it would be nothing you would leave carelessly on display along these walls."

He turned back to the statues, adding thoughtfully, "Rather, something you would hide behind a secret door, like ...that one!"

He pointed to a bare patch of stone and ice between two of the statues and then glanced at Oneida for her reaction.

Oneida laughed. "Your 'door' is where we had our little avalanche this spring, at first thaw."

In spite of herself she shivered and pressed one hand to her head. Cruel, cruel pain. The blurring and distortion of the Precepts, of the thoughts of the Maker.

"I don't want to talk about it." She whispered half to herself, "Aren't the carvings perfect? I wish I were perfect. I was until a few months ago, but-"

"They may be the goddesses of Nala but you're as perfect as any of them."

"But I'm not! I'm..." Oneida stopped speaking abruptly.

One thing she and her sisters had learned over the long years—not to speak about themselves. And what good would it do? He couldn't begin to understand about her, much less about the devastation the avalanche had caused. Everything used to be so clear but now older memories were intervening, contradicting the sacred Precepts...

"They can hear us!" Fendark whispered, and gestured circumspectly toward the bas-reliefs of the Nala. "Can't they? Are they so jealous of their priestess's beauty that you daren't let me speak of it?"

Oneida pursed her lips to keep from smiling. The same error, time and again! And she had thought him different.

"The goddesses are perfect, just as the Maker envisioned them to be. And I know why you flatter me. Like all the others before you, you praise us and seek to turn our heads, that you might gain our ...their treasure."

"So you believe you've heard this tale before? Perhaps, this time, you'll find more sincerity in the speaker."

Oneida looked away from the warmth of his eyes and shrugged. "Perhaps. Let's go back to the cavern. You should eat now and then tell me your tale. This is what is ordained as..."

"A moment."

Oneida had started to turn away. When she looked back, the man was kneeling in the snow and whispering to the carvings of the Nala.

"Good my ladies, greeting. Uh... May your blessing be upon me and upon my house. And if I may serve you, let your priestess tell me how."

He knelt a moment longer and then rose and brushed snow from his boots and trousers.

Her thoughts all wonder and confusion, Oneida beckoned him back to the cavern. Never in her experience had anyone given such worship to the Nala. Flattery many times. Attempts at theft, yes. But such worship never. What should she do now? The Maker's ancient thoughts seemed inadequate to the situation. But that could not be!

Behind her, Fendark asked, "Why did you not do obeisance to your goddesses?"

Oneida was relieved that her back hid her expression from him. How could she begin to explain? Whether it could be called obeisance or not, her obedience dwelt deep within her. It was part of her—or had been until this past spring.

"Then answer this: Why did you lead me out of the cavern if not that we might worship the Nala?"

Oneida essayed a laugh. "To cool off. I merely..."

She looked back from the path and into the stranger's eyes. Something in his gaze, in his manner, prompted her to admit, "No. That is not the truth. I must take all travelers out to those treasures. You were right. We do it as a test of our visitors."

She whispered, "It has been so long. I don't remember why exactly."

"So long?" Fendark scowled at her in bewilderment.

"Since the beginning when the Precepts were set. Since..."

Every blow of the chisel and mallet a Precept. Hush. Mustn't say that!

But the chisel and mallet hadn't been the beginning. The supplications of multitudes of worshipers, their echoing thoughts dizzying...

She reached toward her temple and dropped her hand. The pain was the pain not matter where her hand was.

"Come talk with me. We have hot food and wine, here. And I delight in talking with my few visitors. Tell me why you need the resources of the Nala while I serve you."

Fendark reached out and gently grasped the priestess's wrist. "My lady, if it's permitted. I think I'll serve myself and you too if you're hungry. You look like you're about to faint. Sit down on one of the benches."

"But I must serve you!"

"Do your goddesses watch you when you are in here? Do they know what you do or what you omit?"

"No, but the Maker..."

"Good! Sit down!"

Oneida smiled. "I'll get the wine. There are bowls and utensils on that shelf."

They ate in silence. Or rather, Fendark ate. Oneida sat beside him, her eyes nearly closed, her fingers toying with the rim of her stone wine cup.

The instant the warrior was finished, she knew it. She sighed and opened her eyes.

"Now tell me your tale. How did you come to us? What need do you have for our resources that you would venture into such peril?"

Fendark smiled though his eyes remained sad. "Again, 'peril.' I've still seen no peril here—unless you are the peril."

"It exists. It's all about you and I hold its key for a time."

The warrior shook his head. "If you say so. Your eyes seem the key to a peril I might regret. Already I've tarried here longer than I'd planned."

He gazed at the priestess thoughtfully.

"I've heard tales. Some, that no one comes from this place unscathed. In fact, some ancient writings say that no one comes from here alive.

"However, a man at Staghound Inn swore he had been here and brought forth a great ruby, only to lose it to robbers. I thought that a drunkard's boast. Until another said he knew of a woman whose mother wandered here gripped with the fever, and she was healed."

"Strange tales. People lie about us all the time, you know. I'm not sure why. Surely, we've never changed since the beginning."

She frowned. Which beginning?

I thought as much," Fendark responded, with a relieved smile. "I found it hard to believe all the whisperings of inevitable doom."

"I meant- Nothing. Tell me your tale. I love tales. Why do you need our treasure?"

Fendark stared at the cavern's barren walls and frowned. "I don't think you have what I need. If only common rubies and moonstones pried from a rocky wall were sufficient! But if you truly lack what I need, perhaps you can offer me guidance in my search."

"So. My tale then." He sighed.

"My elder brother, Darsis, the leader of our tribe, is being held for ransom. Meeson, lord of the Ashtor, will take nothing but the Stone of Naalar for his life. Rumor says he read of it and lusts for its ancient powers, but fears to seek after it himself. So, perforce, I seek the Naalar stone in his stead."

Oneida put down her cup. "What a strange errand."

"You must help me. He's my brother. My only family! Can't you see...? He's my brother."

He shrugged and looked away toward the nearest fire.

Oneida stared at him, bound mute by her own incomprehension. Here was a love stronger than she had ever experienced. She could feel it through him. It warmed her but not as the fires did.

"It was a vain hope. Thanks to your test, I see now that your goddesses' treasures are of more ordinary kind than what I seek. In fact, I begin to suspect the Stone of Naalar only a myth. Even if it exists, I was a fool to think that 'Naalar' and 'the Nala' bore any relationship one to the other. But desperation has the power to make men believe strange things and take terrible chances."

"I've heard that. They will kill him? When?"

Fendark shrugged. "Two weeks and a day from tomorrow's dawn. Unless you or your goddesses can save him. Do you know of the Stone of Naalar?"

Oneida's hands slipped up to her breasts and clasped together. She shook her head. "I can give you no treasure, Fendark. None of us can. But, perhaps, I can give you hope."

She stood up.

"The Nala know of the Stones of Naalar. They were once the Maker's own, perhaps the source...."

Oneida shook her head. "Forgive me. My thoughts wander."

Fendark leaped up as well. "Complete your thought! I heard you say 'stones!' So, there's more than one. Priestess, I only need one to save my brother's life. Let me take but the poorest of these stones. Or tell me where I can find them."

A tear slid down Oneida's face. Her lips trembled with the effort to hold in others like it. The trap was nearly closed, and she felt only grief.

"You are sure you wish this?"

"I wish my brother's life."

Oneida winced.

"Your headache is returning?"

Fendark's hand brushed the priestess's arm. "Have you no philter to ease the pain?"

"No. Fendark, go away. No good will come of this if you stay. No good ever comes of visiting the Nala. Our wisdom is madness. Your only hope is to leave empty-handed."

Sharp pain stifled the rest of her whispered words and stilled even her thoughts. Was this truly the Maker's doing? Or was this different—something perhaps that mortals felt?

"Enough warnings and testing and talk! Tell me where I can find the stone!"

Oneida shrugged. Did it matter? She turned and led Fendark to the mound of furs, casting them aside until an iron chest was revealed.

Fendark crouched beside her, awe in his eyes. He whispered, "Should I look away?"

"Go away, yes. To look away now will not change your fortune." She knelt beside the chest, her eyes fixed on Fendark. "Will you go away?"

"No. Show me what you have for me."

"Touch nothing within!"

The priestess used both hands to force open the corroded lid. She leaned forward and studied the contents: tarnished scroll cases, dark vials, daggers, tiny glittering caskets, weathered maps... Many things, nearly all of them made of stone or metal. All without exception deadly though they appeared innocent.

Which thing for Fendark? She glanced swiftly aside at the warrior's weary face, sighed and reached out. The map. It was plausible and it was the only thing that was painless. She lifted it out.

Fendark's hand shook as he reached for it.

"No! Not yet!" Oneida lay the map beside her and closed the chest. It was done. The decision made.

Fendark whispered, "It's a map to the Stone?"

"If you wish it. You've traveled far to reach this shrine, yes?"

"Yes," he answered in perplexity.

"You will travel even farther."

Farther and farther, without rest or pause, without even knowing it until he loosed the map from his hand. But none ever did that. The spell of the map was too strong for any mortal. Even for the gentle, sad man beside her.

Why had he not heeded her warnings! She knew the answer—for love of his brother. So unlike her sisterhood...

"I should start, then. My brother only has two weeks."

"Two weeks until his death. Fendark-"

She glanced into his soft brown eyes but couldn't hold the gaze. Her fingertips brushed his calloused hand.

"Fendark... If you only had two weeks, what would you most wish to do with them?"

"You wish my earnest answer?"

Oneida's blue eyes risked another glance into his face, to be caught this time by the searching gaze of their brown counterparts.

"Yes. Or I would not have asked. What do you wish before you begin your journey?"

"The answer to both questions is the same."

He bent toward her, one hand brushing her shoulder then sliding down her arm to her hand.

"Priestess, you're kind and compassionate. If I fail in my search, neither I nor my brother will survive. Let me leave my memories of him with you, so that someone will remember him and the joy of knowing him, should we both perish."

Oneida nodded, and he began.

Fendark smiled sadly, and whispered, "Thank you."

Silence filled the cavern for the first time in hours, a silence Oneida loathed. It reminded her of her duties.

Awkward with lack of practice, she reached out for Fendark's hand and grasped it with both of hers. She sought to comfort him as his brother had done so many times, to bring him joy as the two of them had brought each other joy.

As she made the gesture, the moonstone about her neck slid along its silver chain and tumbled from between her breasts. Fendark watched its progress with diffident curiosity.

Oneida smiled. "The only treasure of the Nala I've ever fancied. Moonstones are like mingled ice and snow."

"Like you. I came here for one treasure, only to find another. Oneida, come with me. Leave your duty for a time. Leave it forever."

Oneida gave him a fleeting smile as she relinquished her spot on their bench. She glanced toward the doorway and sighed. "It's time for you to go."

Fendark smiled mischievously. "It's a wonder you didn't chase me from your door hours ago. I fear I've bored you."

Oneida gasped in astonishment. "No! I loved it! I've always liked tales, but this was so..."

She waved one hand, seeking for words. None came that she dare speak aloud. For the first time, she had experienced the love of humankind for each other, had felt it echoed within herself. She wanted to tell him, to explain how much it meant. But she dare not even if she had the words.

"No matter. Come with me, and-"

"I cannot. Would that I could! The Precepts are still the Precepts." She found Fendark's cape and her own.

Close beside her, Fendark whispered, "Do you always obey them?"

Oneida glanced at him and shrugged, then resumed lacing up her cape. "I don't always obey our lesser Precepts, no. But I have no choice in this. Some things were given us from the beginning of our existence. Or taken away. But the Greater Precepts are part of us—the very substance of our sisterhood's existence. This Precept is one of them. You must be gone well before sunset and I must be alone, in order to obey the thoughts of the Maker. Lace your cape! It's cold."

"Even now, you'll just push me out the door without even a kiss of blessing or a token of remembrance?"

His hand drew back from her attempt to touch it. He pointed at her necklace.

"Earlier you tempted me to steal a wealth in rubies. That which you wear near your heart has little value compared to the stones out on the path. I've given you my heart without meaning to. Give me your necklace as a remembrance of you. Better, lend it to me!" One finger touched the moonstone. "And I'll swear that my brother and I will come and bring it back to you."

Oneida's hand closed over his. She smiled sadly and shook her head. "Fendark, I would if I could but I dare not. All the watchers wear these. I cannot relinquish mine. Its absence would be noticed." Her smile grew tenderer. "The kiss I'll give you. And should you ever wander this way." She bit her lip. "I hope you come in winter!"

"I will if your goddesses permit. If all goes well with my brother, perhaps in less than a month." He glanced toward the door. "It is nearly sunset isn't it? You're right. I had best get down the path before full dark. Where is the map?"

Oneida picked it up and handed it to him. Fendark took it from her hand, and unrolled it eagerly. As soon as it was open, he hurried out of the cavern. Oneida followed him in despair. About them, the wind swirled and moaned. Cursing it under his breath, Fendark turned about to protect the precious parchment from its grip.

Oneida lifted her head and whispered, "Stop that! Wait upon the crest."

The wind died.

Fendark spared a fleeting moment from his study to mutter, "How did you do that?"

"The Maker envisioned that the wind would be my servant while I am watcher. ...Fendark?"

"What?"

The young man murmured the word like one half asleep. His feet were already drifting along the dusk-shadowed path. As he walked, his gaze never lifted from the parchment in his hands.

"Fendark!" She scrambled after him, her fingers fumbling for the chain about her neck. "Fendark, here. Take this in memory of me."

Foolish. The warrior gave no sign he had even heard her but she seemed to have no choice. Something as strong as the thoughts of the Maker spurred her toward him. Oneida unclasped the chain and fastened it about Fendark's belt. All the while, he walked forward without seeming to notice her. When the chain was in place, Oneida loosed her grip on his belt and stood still.

"Farewell, Fendark."

He gave no answer.

Fare well? That he could not do. Fare he would in many places and through great lengths of time. But never well.

Oneida turned away from the path at last sight of him, and hastened back to the cavern. Tears crept from her eyes and she let them turn into ice crystals. There was no longer anyone to see and wonder.

It was almost dark, and the light from the cisterns within glowed on the snow by the entrance. She took a last breath of cool air and slipped inside.

First, she touched a place on the wall above the second cistern. An oval crack appeared above her hand. She gave it an impatient shove. The oval of stone retreated and sank into the wall, revealing a small pile of brownish parchments very like the map she had given Fendark. She took out the top one and tapped a new place on the wall. At once, the oval of stone rose back into place, with a soft scrape of stone against stone.

One of the Maker's little legacies, alas. If there were no treasures for the chest then no one.... Hush! Mustn't think that!

Oneida glanced toward the dim light outside the cavern, then walked to the chest and placed the new map within it. She checked through the contents automatically before closing the lid, snapped it shut and locked it. Again, she looked toward the entrance. It was almost full dark. She flung the white furs into place, and hurried outside.

She sniffed quick breaths of icy air and gave a tentative stretch but her joints were already beginning to stiffen. Sunset was only minutes away, its final glory already blocked here by the cliff itself.

Oneida made her slow way along the path until she stood below the cliff wall, opposite the rubble-strewn blankness Fendark had called the door. She knelt before the three statues and murmured, "Sisters, one has come today."

"We have seen him." The voice was merry but very soft, scarcely to be heard.

Oneida nodded, her eyes focused on the blue-gray snow before her knees. "He sought one of the sacred stones, not treasure."

"And what doom did you give him?" A new voice, filled with sadness.

Oneida bit her lip and whispered reluctantly, "A map."

"Another map?" said a stern voice.

"He wanted the stone to save a life!"

The merry voice whispered, "And he was fair."

Oneida shrugged at the ground. "Yes. But, sisters, why is everything in the chest deadly? If we can't dissuade them from their purposes, even if-"

"Come to us. The sun sets in a handful of seconds and it is time for you to sleep."

Oneida looked up quickly. "Thank you, sister. But first, answer my question. He meant no ill. He worshiped us. Why must I do as I did? Why must any of us?"

"You know the answer to that, Oneida, as much or as little as we do. The bowl cannot question the turn of the potter's wheel or the statue the strokes of the chisel. We are as it was given us to be by those who conceived of us..."

"But we're not! Not anymore. Our paths were bent from their veneration and hope."

"Hush! Think not of that "before"! Each blow of the sculptor sealed our fates and that of the ones who come to us."

"But why this fate? What madness-"

"Hush! Speak not of 'madness!'"

"She's becoming querulous. That cursed avalanche-"

"No! The fractures help me see back to the time before. I liked him! I didn't want to send him away. I have sent so many away or to their deaths all these years. Why don't we stop obeying just this Precept? Just because an ancient sculptor—a mortal—thought the Nala deadly-"

"We cannot change as you know full well. We are as he made us to be. If we are not as the Maker thought us to be, then we are not at all."

"Come sleep. Perhaps, another will come tomorrow. You must be ready."

Oneida stood up with a groan and turned her back to the cliff. She was weary and her head felt as if it were cracking in two. She looked down over the edge but could see nothing of the distant path much less any sign of Fendark's wandering form. Behind her, three voices cried out in unison, "Come."

Oneida sighed and whispered, "I come."

Slowly she backed away from the path edge toward the shelter of the wall, her limbs shaping themselves into familiar curves and angles. The wind died as she drew close to the cliff wall, until cape and gown hung limp about her. She pressed her back to the hard rock, and felt its chill seep into the curve of her spine and creep toward head and feet.

For the first time in her life, she shivered.

Beside her, voices whispered, "Come. It's time to sleep."

Oneida answered them petulantly, "I am coming."

The stern voice cried out, "Sister, where is your stone?"

Oneida gave an awkward shrug. "I gave it to him as a remembrance."

"Foolish! He cannot make use of it. He remembers nothing. He sees only the map."

Oneida nodded. She remembered how he stared at the map at the cavern mouth, clutching it against the gusts of wind. How he had shut out her words. How he had barely noticed her even when she stilled the wind.

The wind!

"Come now. The sun sets."

Oneida cried out, "Wind! Come play!" She strained to leap away from the cliff wall but could not. Chains and manacles of ice held her in place but they could not bind her voice.

"Go to Fendark," she commanded her old playfellow and servant. "Blow the map from his grasp! Quickly!"

"Oneida!"

"Please don't do this! You will be unmade!" added the sad voice.

"Sister, the Precepts!" warned the stern one. "Break them and they will destroy you! The one who made you..."

"No!" Oneida shrieked as agony ripped through her body like an icy cleaver.

The wind buffeted her in the face, and then swept past her from left to right in a sudden gale.

Oneida tried to reach up to her aching head but her hand wouldn't move.

"Sister! Call back the wind before it's too late!"

Oneida tried to shake her head, tried to scream. She couldn't see, couldn't make a sound. No movement was within her power.

Only silent will remained to her. She spoke desperately in her thoughts _Open your hand, Fendark! Let it go!_

The wind screamed about her.

Blow it away from him, she willed. Her eyes widened slightly in the midst of a blink.

There! There it went. She was sure of it. Her heart beat once more. Twice.

Sunset.

Dawn.

Sun glittered on the ice of the previous night's storm, encasing the four statues of the Nala. At their feet were new splinters of shattered rock. Three of the statues looked pitilessly down on the fragments. The fourth had no face.

This began as a thought experiment.
What if a mortal had the power to create gods in his own image?

## *The Smashed Fairy Song Cycle*

These are filk song lyrics. Filk is the folk music of the SF and Fantasy community. It's most frequently sung beginning late in the evening and lasting well into the night during science fiction and fantasy conventions. Several conferences here and abroad are dedicated to filksinging or bardic circles: OVFF, Contata, Con27ilkin, Conflikt, Concertino, GAfilk, ConFluence, FilkCONtinenta, etc.

"**ttto**" means the following lyrics are sung "to the tune of" [name of tune or song]

**#1** (ttto Wooden Whistle)
Never go into the forest, the fairies' dim forest
When they brew their acorn brew.
If you go into the forest, the fairies' dim forest
At least bring a book and some glue.


Fairies can't hold their liquor, their antics get sicker
When they brew their acorn beer.
They try to keep flitting; they try to keep flying,
But, when drunk, they really can't steer.


They have keg-diving contests and other such nonsense
When they brew their acorn ales.
They'll dive at you with thistles, to use as small missiles,
Using acorns for maces and flails.


So don't go into the forest, the fairies' dim forest,
Learn at least this much of their lore.

If you go into the forest, the fairies' dim forest,
I fear you'll come out never more.


**#2** (ttto Teddy Bears' Picnic)
If you go into the woods tonight
You'll wish you had stayed at home.
There's acorn ale in the woods tonight
With fairies smashed from the foam.
For every elf that ever there was
Is drinking deep and feeling the buzz.
Tonight's the night
Of the annual Brown Ale Picnic.


Acorn ale and elven wings!
The itty bitty things
Are smashing into the trees tonight.
Dodge them; duck them in their lairs,
And see them party on their moonlit night.
See them wildly fly about.
They sing and shriek and shout.
They think everything's a joke.
By morning light, they're moaning and groaning.
They toddle off to bed,
Cause they're hung over fairy folk.


**#3** (ttto Jug O'Punch)
1) In the fairy realm, there's a night in fall
When the fairy folk have their Brown Ale Ball.
Beware the forest upon that eve,
Lest you too get smashed before you can leave.


Duck the fairy drunks as they flit around.
Don't you tread on ones sprawled there on the ground.
Beware the forest upon that eve,
Lest you too get smashed before you can leave.

2) When each tiny fairy has drunk his fill,
They fly upside down all around their hill.
They'll dive at humans with clubs of twigs,
Once each fairy's had one too many swigs.


Duck the fairy drunks as they flit around.
Don't you tread on ones sprawled there on the ground.
They'll dive at humans with clubs of twigs,
Once each fairy's had one too many swigs.


3) Bring a book and glue on their festive night.
When they fly at you, snap the pages tight!
Press thirty elves just as flat as flowers.
With a little luck, it won't take two hours.


Duck the fairy drunks as they flit around.
Don't you tread on ones sprawled there on the ground.
Press thirty elves just as flat as flowers.
With a little luck, it won't take two hours.

4) And when you're done and your tome is home,
Your smashed fairies sit by your Tome of Gnomes.
Such pretty still lifes to show your peers...
Though, in time, the odor grows rather queer.


Duck the fairy drunks as they flit around.
Don't you tread on ones sprawled there on the ground.
Such pretty still-lifes to show your peers...
Though, in time, the odor grows rather queer.


#4 (ttto Waltzin' Matilda)
Smashing the fairies,
Smashing the fairies,
Please come a-smashing the fairies with me.
Thus we sing as we tote our albums and our pots of glue.
Please come a-smashing the fairies with me.

~~~~~

I've never offered a filk song in written form before. Please keep in mind that many filkers are proud of their independence from poetic scansion. "Scansion? We don't need no steenk'n scansion!"

Special thanks to Brian Froud and Terry Jones and <u>Lady Cottington's Pressed Fairy </u>book for the inspiration.

## Dream, with Joey

Please imagine you see an abstract painting titled
"Dream, With Joey"
about


...


here

Thank you.

I dreamed I was part of a large group that consisted partially of family and partially of very close friends. I'm not sure which people were which. We all began as a cheerful—and maybe shallow—bunch. We lived in a city but not one with which I'm familiar. It was very modern but it had few skyscrapers.

We were wandering around the neighborhood when one of us found a claim ticket from a shipping company. Our relative/friend decided to go to the shipping place and claim whatever it was and we all decided to go with him. Everyone was taking turns guessing what would be in the package—each theory more outrageous than the last.

"A million wishbones."

"You wish!"

"Who would wish that on us?"

"Oh, I get it!"

Tears streamed down my face and the faces of my friends. We were experts at cracking each other up with jokes no one else "got". (and no wonder)

The shipping company's storage area was huge and they had several loading docks, most with trailers backed up to them. The claim office was tiny—we filled the space between the front door and the counter. With hundreds of packages arriving by the hour, I mumbled that most shipments must be sorted by neighborhood and then delivered rather than picked up.

A couple of my friends/family frowned and looked back at the door. What if the package was already in a van or had even been delivered? That ticket might be no more than trash. Well then it was trash. My closest buddies shrugged and smiled.

Someone whispered, "Hundred toilet seat covers. Watch."

"Not watching anyone using those!"

"Chartreuse ballerina tutus."

"You guess'm—you wear'm."

"Roasted rubber duckies, packed in ice."

"That's cruel!"

"Fine. Rubber duckies, hold the ice."

Not yet delivered! The clerk on duty called out the numbers through a grilled door and asked for help.

The claim ticket was for a large number of items, which might explain why the clerk at the counter wasn't surprised by so many of us showing up. One person could not have begun to deal with all of it.

Their people brought out parcel after parcel. When we realized this was going to go on for a while, we began taking items off the counter top to carry for our friend/relative.

Mine was camping stuff. I don't remember exactly what—maybe something like old army-type cots, folded up tightly and strapped together or in a rucksack or something. Most of the stuff was outdoorsy or sporty. Once in a while something valuable crossed the counter top. I don't remember what anyone else's reactions were. I do know that I lost interest briefly when something practical landed on the counter and perked up when it tended toward the elegant. There was jewelry but I didn't get that.

On the other hand, I didn't have the impression that each person would get to keep whatever they were carrying. Even though our friend/relative had just happened to find the ticket, I assumed that all of packages belonged to him. We were all vaguely glad for him and seemed to be treating it as if he had been on a TV game show and had won the arbitrary collection of prizes that they offer.

The next to the last item was a substantial chunk of money, packed carefully in a sturdy box. For some reason a quarter of a million dollars comes to mind. Maybe not. But it was a serious chunk of change.

We were still congratulating our relative/friend on his good fortune, when the clerk wheeled out the last item. It was a huge box sitting on a handcart. Just like in a Warner Bros cartoon, the door came open and out hopped a joey or baby kangaroo. (Xanthorpe, this is your fault! Stay out of my dreams.).

Our mood just deflated. What were we going to do with a joey? We lived in the middle of a city. Suddenly, I think everyone realized that we were in serious trouble. Our friend/relative had just signed for all of that money. He couldn't refuse to take delivery on the kangaroo without explaining that none of this stuff was his.

Scared and wondering what to do next, we trooped out of the shipping office, our relative/friend leading the joey by a rope around its neck. It remained docile the whole time. Okay, as docile as a wild animal is likely to be in the midst of city traffic. We must have walked to the shipping company. Regardless, we had to walk home. We couldn't take the joey on the subway or in a cab.

Everywhere we went people stared at us all trooping down the streets, each one of us carrying packages and, in the midst of us, our friend/relative both leading and trying to hide his new pet. We might as well have been blowing horns and dressed for Mardi Gras.

Eventually we got our home. I guess we all lived together. I don't remember the house. We stowed everything in the yard or in the garage. The place was strangely suburban-looking for in the middle of a city. We were still hanging out in the yard—grilling food and having a picnic maybe—when the joey started growing. And growing. That was it. You can't keep a low profile about stolen property when part of it is pushing 10 feet tall.

The real owner arrived and wanted his property back. He said something to the effect that he would return with a dump truck and some friends to collect it all.

Instead of being embarrassed, glad he didn't seem likely to prosecute, relieved we were getting rid of the giant kangaroo, disappointed that the cash and gems had to go too; we were alarmed because our enemies had found us.

He was "one of them".

The dream grew lots darker really fast! We became the grimmest lot you've ever seen, convinced that the jig was up for us.

We rummaged through everything we owned and all of the stuff we had collected and found guns and ammo. We locked and loaded, as they say. We were ready for an all-out war. It seemed we were already partisans in some long-standing conflict.

The kangaroo-owner would return with his people and slaughter us. It was a foregone conclusion. All we could do was to "take as many of them with us as we could when we went down".

About then the man and his buddies returned, and we opened fire on them. Rubber duckies flew toward them, each shattering into ice cubes and rotten duck eggs wherever they struck.

Our enemies were yelling at us but none of it made sense. Finally they returned fire. Wishbones stung my face and hands. Even more clicked and bounced off the ground. Every shattered wishbone fragment erupted into a chicken so frenzied it could fly. The feathered bombardiers dropped load after load on us. It was chaotic and ghastly and it was never going to stop.

I woke up. Still half-asleep, I realized that the owner and his mates had been yelling "Uspokoenie" and "Glasnost!" and "Mir!". So, they were Russian. Once fully awake I concluded my group thought the Cold War was still going on—rather like Japanese soldiers abandoned on islands after WWII. It all felt very tragic, and I was very sorry that we hadn't listened to what they were saying.

I'm still trying to get stuff out of my hair.

That picture I asked you to supply? I scribbled "dream, with joey" when I woke up and began remembering the dream. Later, the phrase sounded so much like a modern-art title that I wished one of the packages had been a painting.

Now we have one. Thank you!

## A Dream With Bowling
or, Kafka, get out of my dreams!

I often remember my dreams and I usually enjoy it, not that I don't have nightmares.

Last night I had a dream filled with so much tension I feel like there ought to be a story in it. Conceded, there was a plot of sorts but no one explained what it was or who was doing the plotting.

I was a confidential informant working undercover for a detective. They may have recruited me via that tired crime show scenario, where I was the perp and had been caught but the police said they'd let me off if I pretended to be someone, infiltrate a group, etc. I got to infiltrate. Lucky me.

The members of this particular group were bouncers, hitmen, drug dealers, stalkers, murderers, violent bikers, members of the most vicious gangs, etc. They spent most of their time, trying to kill each other or take over each others' territory or drug business. But once a month, they met for a secret auction and their cover was bowling.

Now, don't laugh. Yeah, go ahead. These really nasty people met every month to bid on young children's trading cards.

They may have been very expensive trading cards of a specialized kind but I never understood what kind they were. That didn't help my impersonation as one of them—the smugglers, not the cards. It also didn't help that the other people bidding were all seriously bad--like bikers and hit men. Did I mention that?

They bowled but not American bowling. It might have been a bit closer to the English bowling with the dark softball-sized balls on a lawn. But it wasn't that either.

That was "my thing" evidently. Laughing again? Just wait.

I have no idea how the Brits do their lawn bowling, but I'm sure it's not anything like this!

Within my dream, the official rules said someone would try to roll a ball past you when you were distracted. If you reached down and stopped the ball before it passed, you could roll the ball at your chosen target ball—scoring if you hit it. If the ball got past you, you were stuck trying to sneak the ball past someone else.

These men and women had their own rules. Everyone was seated, except when they weren't. If you grabbed the ball in time, your reward was trying to slip it past the next person. If the ball passed you before you could grab it, you got beaten up by the bowler. Yeah. Told you they were a bad bunch.

I had played the normal game before and I was good at it, which was why I was recruited. I had no experience beating anyone up and I hadn't a clue when it came to the differences in the trading cards. Each card had a codename and I never saw any of them. No one just made a bid. People talked, and slipped their bids into the conversation using combinations of coded words

So there I was, wondering what card I was supposed to bid on and what its code was, meanwhile watching out for a small bowling ball to come flying past my feet. Or I might be guessing how much the last person had bid, in case I wanted to outbid them. Was what they just said even a bid? Did I even want to outbid them? People who had outbid others—maybe—somehow got involved in arguments just as a ball was flying toward them.

I was beyond anxious.

I chose not to bid on something early in the game. My competition seemed to think that very clever, based on the smiles and nods, and the congratulatory cuffs on my arms. (I had skipped bidding because I was having a mini-panic attack.)

My detective was one of the other players but he was undercover and in character. He might as well have been my worst enemy when it came to offering any guidance.

I tried to copy everyone's vicious attitude and esoteric language. I tried not to cringe when someone missed grabbing the ball and got punched. I didn't get beaten up—unless you count the congratulatory punches—but I couldn't seem to win the bid on a card. Or maybe not on a good card. Actually I haven't a clue whether I successfully bought any cards or not.

Then the cop began hitting on me—in the flirtatious way.

My head like to have exploded. Everything was already so convoluted!

I couldn't tell if he was just flirting. Or warning me and, if so, about what? Or asking me to roll the ball past him. Or to bid or not to bid? Or maybe jump up and kick someone's ass?

Speaking of jumping, maybe I should just jump out of a window and run for my life? Okay, that was my idea.

Of course that was only half of it. Whatever he meant to get across by flirting with me, was he doing it as detective to his confidential informant? Or in the guise of murderous biker guy to his competitor?

I was so freaked, I went all catatonic.

That's when I woke up, and very relieved I was to do it.

## The Queen of the Tor Sidhe<sup>*</sup>

Dreamlike through the village pathways
Creeping round and through the doorways,
Elven song floats, ebon flute notes,
Fiery drums throb through the moon haze.

Round our bed it seemed to hover.
Magically it roused my lover.
Music carefree stole him from me,
Like an airborne love elixir.

Followed I him to the Tor Sidhe
With him rustling e'er before me.
Joined he to them, dancing round him,
Circling him to claim their booty.

Proud then came one to their bonfire
Mantled in a queen's rich attire.
Silver and green, she who was queen,
And she joined them playing her lyre.

Humbly there I knelt before her
'From this place I pledge I'll not stir,
Til you free him from our world dim.
Free the mortal, oh my sister.'

'You had pledged to do my bidding,
Gathering for me this small worldling.
Trust is broken. As a token --
Be you one with earth, not stirring.'

Roots now bind me strong as iron rings
As the night curves to the morning.
There the queen goes. Tranced, he follows.
Leaf dew is my only mourning.

Cursed be my royal sister
As am I who did assist her.
May iron gall her, ill befall her,
From midsummer through midwinter.

Dreamlike through the village pathways
Creeping round and through the doorways,
Elven song floats, ebon flute notes,
Fiery drum throbs through the moon haze.

The Sidhe ("shee") are one of the branches of elves, sometimes called, "The
Lordly Ones", "The Fair Folk", or "The Good People". Originally associated
with burial mounds, in time they were also associated with the legendary
Arthurian isle of Avalon.

This poem is a retelling of "Tam Lin" but in my version the traditional challenge
fails.

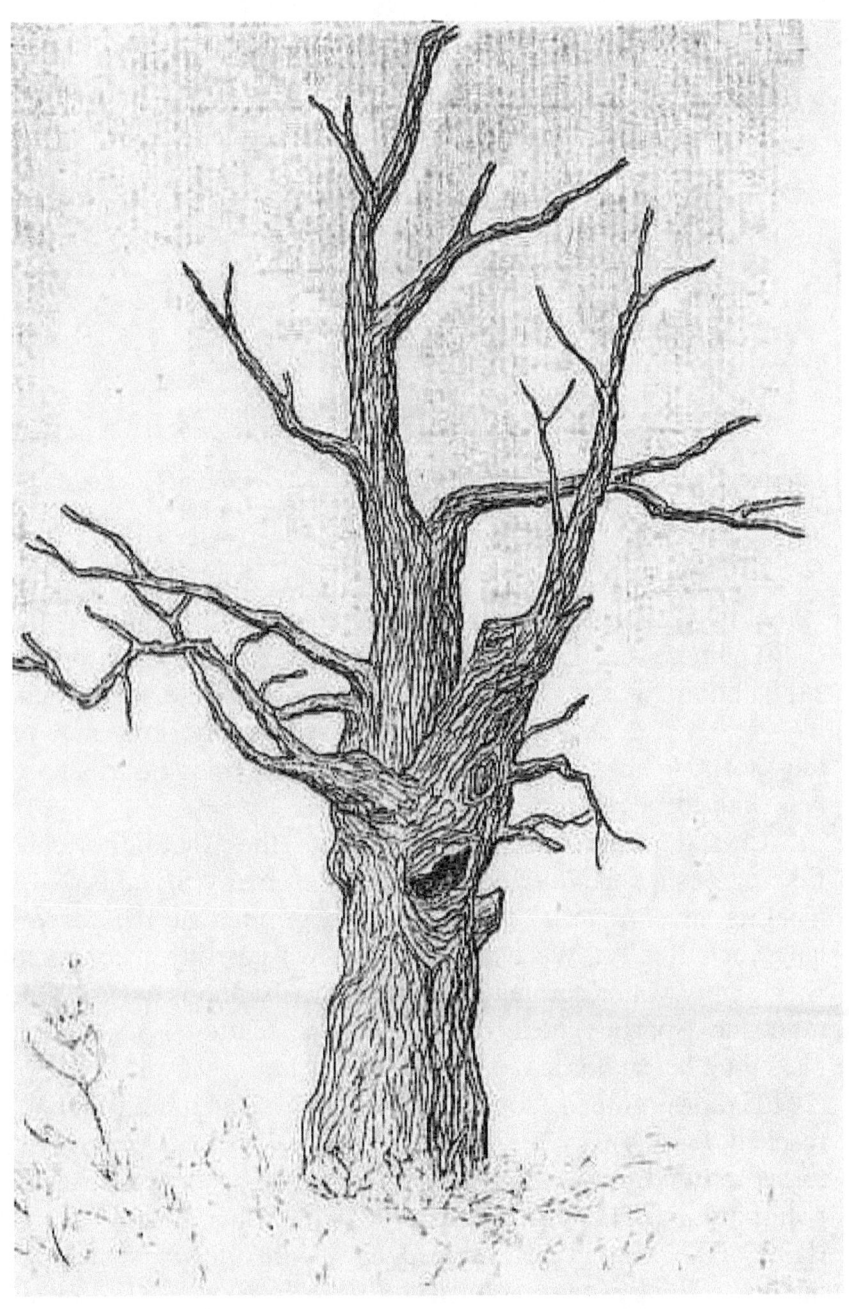

Sketch of a Tree on the Main Towers property, Newark Delaware
(1980's?)

## *Shadow Harper*

(reprinted from UnCONventional: Twenty-Two Tales of Paranormal Gatherings Under the Guise of Conventions. Spencer Hill Press: January 2012, with thanks.

"Filk is the music of the SF and fantasy community."

Thomas tuned out his friend's words. He had heard her explanation for those new to a bardic filk circle for—what was it?—nearly a decade now? No. That seemed too long and yet far too short. He shook his head and rubbed the bridge of his nose. He was tired for it being this early.

Crystal concluded, "Nowadays the bardic circle—or filksing—is a scheduled evening event at many SF cons. No more meeting in stairwells!" The brunette grinned at the responding laughter. "Really! We used to. Now, we get tiny meeting rooms with empty water carafes and coffee urns without coffee! Oh, and mundanes' parties next door." Amidst scattered chuckling she picked up her guitar and settled it on her lap.

Thomas gulped down half a can of Mountain Dew, and reached for his own instrument. Finally, back to music. Crystal turned around to face the blonde teenager in the Anne McCaffrey t-shirt sitting in the concentric circle behind her. "So, Ellie? Is that right?" The young girl jumped as if she'd been smacked, and nodded. "Pick, pass, or play, Ellie?" Crystal followed the traditional invitation with her trademarked "we're all friends here" smile. The girl lifted the sheet in her hand, opened her mouth, and then shook her head.

"Pass this time round. Okay?"

Crystal smiled. "Fine. We'll get back to you in," she glanced around, "Oh, in about an hour and a half."

Several people in the room chuckled, including Thomas. Neos. Imagine giving up an invitation to sing when you might get only three or four chances all night. The Dew was kicking in, and he longed for his next turn. Most of the other strong singers were here now and the neos had begun loosening up. The singing started going around again. . The guy next to him was singing. Howard. Nice chord control. Between measures, his knuckles rapped an elegant touch of percussion on his guitar.

Thomas flipped through pages in his loose-leaf notebook. He searched for the sheet with the chords to "Shadow Harper." There it was, and just in time. He scanned the words and chords he'd scribbled down a few months ago, after waking from a particularly vivid dream. Oops. He'd need the capo. Thomas leaned down and fumbled for it as the previous singer ended his song. Somewhere above his bowed head, Crystal called, "Pick, pass, or play, Thomas?"

"Play!" Thomas straightened. "How many here have heard my 'Shadow Harper?'"

The lights lowered. What was happening? Had some bozo found a dimmer switch? Thomas frowned over his shoulder. No one was standing by the door. Several alarmed comments were throttled by hissed whispers for silence and a soft chorus of "filker up."

Thomas shivered. What was going on? Still, the dim atmosphere suited his song. Might as well go with it.

But someone was already singing.

Thomas scowled and looked up. Some strange man had jumped in on him. His scowl mutated into a glare.

His eyelids twitched the way they did when his boss called him into the office. He blinked.

Men and women in strange costumes filled the small room. Golden candlelight illuminated their faces, as did the warm glow of fire in an ancient hearth. And amidst them all, face shadowed somehow from the light of fireplace and candlestick, a young man sang and played. He was robed in deep green and hooded in black velvet. Bands of silver held his long sleeves back from his wrists.

As he sang, he stroked the golden-lit strings of an exquisite lap harp, agile fingers flickering in the candlelight. His voice, mellow and haunting, danced about the room.

The melodious words seemed soft and far away, hardly to be heard, save in strange resonances mingled with the echoes of whispering voices—though none of those about Thomas spoke. Every word came clearly to him, as if the soft sound bred images and scents and feelings to match it and strengthen it.

The singer's slender fingers coaxed forth the melody, sharp nails gleaming with the plucked strings of gold in fire-warmth, while the sounds they invoked were as muted and cobwebbed with murmured notes as the voice they accompanied.

Thomas listened, half-mesmerized, to the sound of the phantom song and knew it to be almost his own, yet not. How could the stranger have so closely copied his lyrics and melody?

No. A part of him whispered with the song's whispering. This is the original. I am the one who did the copying. I am the one who changed word and note, simplifying and weakening something far more lovely and infinitely more strange.

His song— the song he thought he had written just months ago--didn't have this power. The lyrics swirled around him, born by the haunting, half-heard notes. At times, the words seemed nearly chanted, as if an invocation half-hidden within the tune called to something, to someone, beyond even the singer's ken.

Thomas' thoughts ceased at the lyrics' command, even as those within the song—described by its very lyrics—were mesmerized by the wandering harper in their midst. He bound them to his words and music, causing them to see strange and beautiful things until at last, long hours later, the whole ancient host awoke in the gray chill of morning to find the fire dead in its ashes and the candles melted to wax pools on the embroidered linens.

As the last lyrics whispered into Thomas's ears, stealing into nothingness in his thoughts, the harper looked straight at him.

Thomas blinked at the sudden light. Those about him stirred and blinked also, then looked about. Thomas felt the beats of his heart count out the seconds of a long silence. He breathed in unease from the waiting air.

Crystal whispered, "Thomas? That was wonderful. But how..." She looked away.

Other voices murmured quiet appreciation. No one stole even a glance in his direction. A dim murmur touched his ears—clearing throats, cautious jokes—then people dutifully applauded.

"Uh... Oh. Pick, pass or play, uh, Becky?" Each syllable Crystal spoke was softer than the one before.

The lighted room around him fled away on cautious cat paws. Down the candlelit hall it whisked, carrying its ever-diminishing glow until it found refuge in the glass-trapped flame of a lamp by the outer door. Safely within its crystalline walls, the room shrank in upon itself, coiling for sleep.

"Do you believe me now?" The words whispered in his ear, the warmth of the burdened breath threading deeper and deeper, softer and softer, inside his head, its path as random as a tendril of smoke. Scents crept toward him—braided from wood smoke, amber, wine, and the heady scent of magic—their shared path invisible as they curled about his thoughts and burrowed between impossible memories. Once more, he had been seduced by imagination, his eyes speaking strange lies to his helpless thoughts.

Lies or forbidden magic? The face of the shadowed harper had been his own—but that could not be! He gazed at the distant glimmer of flame in the lamp. Just one more glimpse of that bright room, those strange singers! What had he seen? Where? Who?

"What...?" His tongue was as dry as a crow's wing.

"Look away, Thomas. You have seen all that is needful." Cool palms pressed against his clasped hands. He trembled at their touch. Or did the flame, the world itself, tremble? The floor shifted beneath his unsteady feet. The candlesticks with their restless tongues of flame dipped toward him as if in subtle tribute. No, not to him. To the one with him. He dared not look at her.

Thomas tried to keep his gaze fixed on the distant lamp in which the bright-lit room had chosen to hide. Too late. The inn's noisy corridor, the great lamps of trapped lightning, the strangely clothed gathering, every trace of the otherworldly room melted and pooled about his feet like wax.

No great lamps nor any candles here. Many pairs of silver eyes took their place—one galaxy of warm stars replaced by a colder cluster. A breeze, scented of eternal autumn, lifted locks of his hair and slipped the soft tinkle of bells into his ears.

"What..." His parched lips longed for the cool sweetness of wine. "What did you—what did I see?" Thomas turned to the pale lady at his side, feeling, as before, that he could taste the lush green velvet of her raiment, breathe the mulberry red aroma of her sharp nails, and swim in the silver lakes of her black-fringed eyes.

She smiled.

His throat warmed as if from a draft of rich brandy.

"Your future, Thomas. Your return to mortal lands. As you asked of me and as I pledged. My mirror shows that which will be..." She smiled, a twinkle like spangled fairy dust in her eyes. "...someday. I will keep my pledge. Will you keep yours?"

Future. He frowned, but all thoughts fluttered away like the dusky wings of a moth into wind-stirred shadow.

She held out a slender hand. "The moon is high. Will you not play upon your harp?"

**The Witch's Original Gingerbread House**

## The Pumpkin—Smasher

"It's a lovely old cottage. Quaint is the word. I quite liked it until the pumpkin-smasher came." Oops. I wished I hadn't said the last part. Well, too late now.

The balding, middle-aged man standing just inside my door was sweating into his gray wool sports jacket and heavy-weight chinos. Looking at him, anyone would have thought Mr. Jenkins was a man dressed wrong for a summer evening date. But it was past Indian summer and the calendar was knocking frantically at the door of winter.

"Interesting, uh, Christmas decorations out there..." He stopped staring around the room long enough to slide a too-polite query out between quivering lips. "And in here. Uh. Pumpkin-smasher? I don't follow. Mrs. uh, Leggrease?"

I turned my suppressed sign into the almost-smile of a gassy baby. "Ms. And it's L-a G-r-i-s. Two words. It's French. You turn the i into a long e and just push the s right on into the landfill."

He actually produced a polite chuckle.

I felt my lips curve into a proper crescent-shaped smile in response - both for the common error and for the swift return to courtesy. Maybe I still had a chance. "But you're here for the Open House Tour. Let me show you around."

I waved him into the living room - rather the gathering room as they call them now. Leading him toward the dining room archway at the far end of the crowded room, I began my version of a real estate agent's spiel,

"This is a beautiful, well-kept house. You get solid 19th century cottage-style construction plus every modern convenience." I paused at the entrance to the dining room and added, "Everything has been rewired. All the pipes are new."

I gestured back into the living room. "Wallpaper, chair rail, wood paneling. New hardwood floors and acoustic-tiled ceilings. Plus a few features I wanted."

He turned with her and glanced into the dining room. She pointed to the far wall with the glass picture windows and sliding glass doors leading out into the small patio and huge garden. "That part is brand new."

Mr. Jenkins whistled. "That's quite a view!"

I nodded. Maybe leaving the patio lights on was a good idea.

Before I could launch into the next part of my sales pitch, Jenkins asked, "What is that out there, anyway?"

"Well, the garden," My response was a shade too bright. I tried not to wince. Shit.

"Is that a pumpkin patch?"

I shrugged. "It's my vegetable garden. Flowers in the front yard. Vegetables and herbs in the back. My pumpkin vines happen to be the closest to the house this year."

"Wait a minute!" He turned toward me, nerve-pulsing accusation on his face. "What's with the pumpkin patch?" His eyes made a futile attempt to bore into mine. "You mentioned pumpkin-smashers. I read a couple of news articles a few weeks..."

I finished for him, "You never expected to find this house—smashed pumpkins and all." I waved toward the front door and then toward the back yard and the garden.

"And those gnomes or whatever they are by your gate between the street and the sidewalk. Forgive me, but they're hideous."

I raised an eyebrow. _What's his problem? Gnomes -are- hideous. Ask any fairy._ "You don't like the gnomes? I'm sure that's negotiable. With the right offer, I can ask them to, have them removed at my expense." Liar.

Before he could ask about other matters even less easy to deal with, I said, "Would you like a cup of tea? We can sit in the dine-in kitchen and..."

"I'm relieved to hear you're willing to negotiate about gnome-removal. But—you understand—that's a minor problem compared to the ... uh, other decorations. All that will have to go."

I managed a non-committal grunt.

"I followed the pumpkin-smashing story. What little there was in the papers. Nearly every pumpkin patch in the suburbs was obliterated. Except for yours evidently."

"Over half mine were destroyed as well."

Jenkins talked over my correction. "That columnist, Fowler, theorized it all had to do with the annual Halloween Prize Pumpkin contest."

I shrugged. "It looked that way to me too, at the beginning."

"So, was Fowler on to something?"

I spat, "Fowler's no more than a conspiracy nut! He showed up here a few times. Finally, after Halloween, he let it drop."

Jenkins answered with a sardonic chuckle. "Why's that? A little money in the right-"

"Mr. Jenkins! I suppose he dropped it because Halloween was over and no more depredations were reported. His editor probably told him to get on with something else. Now, I thought you came here to look at the house. Not accuse me of bribery."

Jenkins tried to look abashed. "My apologies, Ms. LaGris. Of course, I wasn't accusing you of any such thing." His probing eyes and cynical smile put the lie to his words.

A burst of anxiety scrambled my thoughts. I grabbed them and stuffed them back into my brain. In my most gracious tone—if not feeling one bit of it—I responded, "My mistake. We seem to have wandered far from our purpose. Suppose we go into the kitchen and start over? I can answer any questions you have about my house and the alterations I've made."

"I would enjoy hearing your theory about why someone spent weeks destroying pumpkins."

"Seed cakes go well with explanations and tea."

That and my grin drew only stone-faced silence.

I imagined Jenkins' legs growing into the planted hind end of a donkey. The normal courtesy during real estate tours had been rubbed away by my mishandling. Or the suspicion Jenkins had brought with him. Maybe I'd sanded my way down to the true Mr. Jenkins. Jenkins, Jenkins. Neither rhyme nor reason produced a connection to what had happened.

What was he? FBI? Ouch. Jack asked me that not so long ago.

I added in what I hoped was a more normal tone, "Look, I agree with you. You deserve a proper explanation. And I was about to offer it. Let's go into the kitchen, and I'll begin with the first pumpkin-smashing and go right on through if you actually want to hear that much. Then we'll complete your tour. Good enough?"

He nodded but doubt clouded any other emotion from his face.

I pottered about the kitchen, opening unnecessary cabinets and showing off as much of the built-in conveniences as I could while preparing the tea and seed cakes.

Jenkins was suitably impressed with the built-in espresso machine but declined having any. He said something about caffeine keeping him awake at night.

I suppressed a laugh. Would that had been the only thing keeping me awake! Lucky man who only lost sleep from a cappuccino.

While I was still preparing our snack, he asked the typical questions about my house. Once I sat across from him, he stopped talking and nodded.

Pinecones and frogs' legs! Well, what were the chances it would slip his mind? I decided to be brutally frank.

"Mr. Jenkins, you're not the first person I've met who followed the mystery of the pumpkin-smashings in the paper. I understand some radio commentator managed to come up with jokes on the subject nightly for weeks.

"Then you come here and see a few healthy pumpkin vines amidst many more destroyed—possibly the only ones intact from here out to the city limits. And you wonder why some of mine escaped being smashed to smithereens.

"That Fowler columnist, even more than the police, made a huge mystery of who was behind it all as if it were a conspiracy. So you would like to know if I were involved in all the pumpkin-smashing. If I were, why would you trust me to be honest about the house I'm selling?"

I waited for his answering nod. When it came I continued.

"As you read, we have an annual "Finest Pumpkin Patch Contest" every year around here. My patch has been declared champion or gained a second or third prize for years. It's a trivial honor compared to others but it's important to me. After the second pumpkin-smashing in as many nights, I was horrified. I was convinced that one of my competitors was eliminating rivals. As one of the better patches, mine could be next. The police didn't take the matter seriously—every year children break up carved pumpkins sitting on people's porches. No one catches them.

"But this was different, Jenkins mumbled.

"Yes. I decided to investigate. That very evening, I went out to search for the culprit." I laughed. "I wasn't more than a block away from here when I realized the foolishness of my errand. I had no idea where the smasher would strike next. How was I to lay in wait for him?"

Jenkins chuckled. "I would have done the same thing!"

"The two previous smashings were nowhere near me. I settled on the finest patch I knew of, closest to the early depredations."

"As you observed, I'm hardly a police detective by nature. Not only did I not plan ahead but I fell asleep in my car two hours after I started my watch."

Mr. Jenkins produced a sympathetic grin.

I shrugged again, adding an embarrassed smile. This was going fairly well.

"I woke up to a sound that I thought was a shriek. Nothing was happening where I was so I got out and ran toward the sound. It had seemed about a block away. The second time it came, it was clearly a siren. Flashing lights were heading toward Ernestine's place. She grows pumpkins too, so I nipped along smartly until I saw her on her back porch, wringing her hands. Several policemen were wandering around her property armed with flashlights. What would I say if they saw me?

"I tried to hide behind a tree only to get tangled in yellow tape but I did see a dark patch between two roots. I thought it was blood. I didn't see anything else for sure. I backed up and edged toward the inevitable crowd of curious neighbors. Just in time to have a uniformed man bid us all back up, as this was a crime investigation. Two other men were putting up more police-tape all around Ernestine's vegetable garden. Waste of tape! Surrounding the crushed pumpkins would have served them better.

"Someone pointed to EMTs and a loaded stretcher on its way to the back of an ambulance. Had a friend kept watch with Ernestine? Had Ernestine attacked the other person when they began destroying her pumpkins? No one could make out who it was. I caught a glimpse of an IV. That was mildly reassuring. Since I couldn't investigate further without drawing attention to myself, I went home."

"The next morning I called Bronwyn Construction and talked to Cole, the construction crew chief who has been doing my renovation work for the last two years. I told him I needed a rush job on the picture windows, sliding glass door and patio you saw in the dining room."

At Jenkins' perplexed expression, I added patiently, "I intended to keep investigating around the neighborhood but if the smasher began hitting places closer to mine, I would to be able to lie in wait for them with a clear view of the whole patch and good bright lights. So, I said I needed a rush job and offered a healthy bonus if everything was installed by the night before Halloween.

"Frankly, I don't quite like the arrangement Cole managed. He had to use pre-made windows rather than custom-sized ones and so on. I expect the best with no exception but sometimes in an emergency you have to compromise.

"I kept investigating at night. Sometimes I heard creepy sounds and a rhythmic noise along closely-connecting streets. It gave me the shivers! I never saw the... uh, perpetrator but I saw lots of his handiwork. Disgusting.

"Once someone ran down the road parallel to this one. His back was to me but he was running so fast I suspected that something had terrified him. I thought about the earlier victim— she's fine by the way, recuperating nicely—and guessed the smasher had tried to hurt someone else. Sure enough, I could hear that horrible rhythmic crunching or smooshing sound nearby. But by the time I followed the sound, all that was left were shattered pumpkins bits and vines torn up at their very roots.

"I ran home and checked on my own patch. Foolishly. As far as I knew, the smasher didn't hit more than one patch a night. Well, not up to that point. That was about to change.

"During the day, I watched over the construction and did anything I could think of to hurry it along. Several times, I overheard the foreman likening me to Lucy Van Pelt. I wondered who that was so I went to our library to find out. When I asked the reference librarian for help, she actually laughed as she told me. I was so mortified—and incensed—I wanted to slap her.

"The construction went well, even after the foreman had his little accident. He was back a day later. I think the workmen were glad of a day's reprieve, even without pay.

"The sliding door and little patio leading to the pumpkin plants were completed the morning of Mischief Night. The night before Halloween, you know. I wasn't sure that I still cared. All the patches around me had been "hit". I had to be next—certainly on one of the next two nights.

"The Patch Prize would normally be awarded Halloween evening but our Community Center had already announced no prizes would be awarded this year.

"I knew I was going to have to sit outside the next couple of nights to guard my pumpkin patch anyway. Whoever, whatever, was doing this obviously had no interest in the contest. All I could think was they, it, hated pumpkins and didn't much like people who grew them.

"Late that same night, I heard what I had been dreading - creaking and thumping sounds out back. The rhythmic noise started up less than a minute later. I crept into the patch with just my flashlight. Foolishly. Here I was in exactly the kind of spot that the previous victims had been. Terrified, I crept back to my new patio. The sound seemed to be following me! I ran over to the light switch and flipped on the floodlights.

"A huge woman was sitting in my patch. Enormously tall and fat. My pumpkins were piled up around her, and she was sitting on a good half of them. She grabbed up a five pound one, cracked it into quarters, bit out the insides, one, two, three, four and munched them. Pumpkin pulp and juice ran down her chin and dripped on to her bodice. Aside from the obvious, there was something surreal about the woman and the whole scene.

"I'd brought out an old cane that belonged to my grandfather but I realized it was a futile weapon against the monstrosity before me. I dropped it on the patio table.

"Multicolored lights flashed just a bit away from the woman. Then, a rather slender man in Regency attire appeared -inside- the flashes of light. I didn't think he saw me. He looked around until he spotted the large woman. I decided that maybe the cane might have a use after all. One too many invaders and this guy was normal-sized—if a bit bizarre in appearance. If I managed to strike him, perhaps the pumpkin-eater would be frightened and leave.

"The man threw off his cape & yanked some kind of cord out of it. It was so bright, it made me blink. Before I could see properly, he ran over to the woman and I think he… restrained her somehow with the cord.

"She called him Jack through a mouthful of sputtered pumpkin fragments.

He tried to wipe pumpkin slobber from his face but his hand was shaking. He corrected her, "I'm Peter. Remember?"

Jack… Peter looked toward me, extremely distressed, and asked, "Are you FBI?"

Jenkins gaped at me.

I chuckled. "That was my reaction. I said no but he said he didn't believe me. Honestly! Do I look like someone in the FBI? Then he asked me if I were a marshal. A marshal—here in the twenty-first century, if you please!

"He told me they were grateful for the witness protection program. That he was trying to keep his wife under control but that it was hard at certain times of the year. He accused me of not understanding. Which was true but his reasons weren't my reasons."

"I don't understand any of this!" Jenkins grumbled. "Sounds like a dream or, well, a break with reality."

I tried to glare at him but he looked away before I could catch his gaze.

"Anyway. He ranted on about the bone-headed idea of using Mr. & Mrs. Peter, Peter Pumpkin Eater as their new aliases. Didn't anyone think about the line, "had a wife but couldn't keep her"? It was hardly his fault, after all!

"Why couldn't they have done something about his wife's eating disorder first? Fat or pumpkins—it was all one! Surely the government should have realized she would give them away with her excessive eating no matter what their names or current location.

"I was flabbergasted and really couldn't think of anything to answer. It finally dawned on me what was so surreal about the pair. They looked like water color drawings! I've thought about it and—

strange as it seems—I think they had entered what was to them an alternate universe but they seemed unaware of it. Or they thought the FBI did it. Yes, I almost believe that! But who knows?

"Peter was furious with me. Well, with whom he thought I was. He was close to both tears and physical reprisal, soothing his wife one minute and castigating me the next. I don't know if he was expecting me to answer him or not. I mean, what could I say? I just stood there about as unresponsive as if I really worked for the government.

"Peter or Jack...or whoever, picked up his wife and draped her over his shoulder. Well, more like lumped her over it. Her head was facing toward me as he started around the house and toward the front yard.

"I grabbed up the cane and went after them with it raised in my hand. When they reached the front corner of the house, I dropped my arm. I remember feeling a bit foolish. Still, I felt like I wanted to hit someone soundly for.... for all this. Whatever. I still do really and now I have even more reason to do it. Just no, uh, target.

"I followed them into the front yard. Mrs. Pumpkin-Eater - Sprat - belched, and out came a lovely peachy-orange bubble in the shape of a pumpkin. It grew as it floated away from her and settled down mostly on the front porch. I couldn't see the bit at the back end. Most of the "bubble" tipped and tilted so that its weight was largely on the ground directly in front of the front corner of the iron porch railing. I didn't pay it any mind for the moment, though I dreaded the inevitable when it popped."

Jenkins started to say something but I waved him to silence.
"Yes, that's what you saw when you arrived. Bear with me. I'm almost done!"

"A slot of light opened like a doorway close by my front gate—just past the gnomes. Peter struggled toward it with his beloved burden. He must have been exhausted! Mrs. Pumpkin-Eater smiled impishly at me, and waved one hand. I thought she was waving goodbye. She seemed sweet, just burdened with a terrible illness. I actually felt sorry for her.

"Then a ribbon of light glittering with sparkles floated from her fingers and drifted toward the pumpkin-shaped bubble. In the blink of my eye, my visitors disappeared. I heard a faint pop behind me. The bubble had turned into a coach with wrought iron porch railing wheels and axles and doors. In the front seat was a driver that looked suspiciously like the Tailors' collie from next door, complete with a furry Russian-style hat. In front of him were two cartoon-like carriage horses for all the world like the ones in fairytale films for children. One horse nodded its head up and down, paused, and then did it again.

"I remember groaning in horror as I watched. The "horse" was just going to keep doing that, over and over. I knew, I just knew I would go ... Well, I just couldn't stand there and keep watching it. I studied the back end of the coach and what was left of my right front living room wall, and I knew that part of the coach must be protruding into the living room like, like a Trek transporter accident. Which it was. Like one, not really one. My baby grand used to be in that corner.

"So, you see, I'm just a victim here. I just want to ..."

"Unload this place on me." Mr. Jenkins sprang up from his chair and strode through the dining room toward the front door.

I hurried after him. "Wait! I'm willing to sell at a loss."

Jenkins gave me a snort of contempt over his shoulder. "What? You're going to pay me to take the house off your hands? Not in a million years. Not for a million dollars."

"But you don't understand. It's not that bad," I gasped as I caught up with him. Honestly, from the back his balding head looked remarkably like a pumpkin.

"The coach never moves at all. Nothing's happened in the garden since that night. And the horses? They hardly move. They eat only shredded paper and they never shit. Please!"

Mr. Jenkins pushed the screen door open. I grabbed his free arm with one hand and the old cane propped by the door with the other but he shook loose and hurried toward the street.

Really, his head looked far too much like a pumpkin. Ridges were bulging from the stem in the center of his bald spot and mole-tunneling down the sides of his head toward his sports coat collar. I hadn't called for the HAW mole-contractor. Something would have to be done!

"Don't do it!" two Norwegian-accented voices rumbled from somewhere around my knees.

What now? I jumped and lost my grip on the cane.

Jenkins unlocked his car and ran around to the driver's door. A roar of the motor and screech of the tires and my latest prospect was gone.

"Thunder, old woman! Is that the way you repay us for sparing you legal trouble?"

Something rapped me smartly on the knee. The cane.

Risi lifted it toward me. I grasped its worn handle, with a ragged sigh. Too late now.

"Did you ever think to ask our help? Why else did you bring us here?" grumbled Purs.

Mute Jotunn favored Purs with an approving nod. Scowling, he tossed a thistle branch at me. It did no harm, falling just short to dangle from the skirt of my dress.

Risi stared into my eyes with a countenance that brooked no deception. "You want to keep this house or not?"

I stared over their heads at the hideous carriage and nightmare horses. Tears hot on my lids, I nodded.

Risi and Purs chorused, "Easy enough if you had merely asked." Jotunn yanked the thistle branch free. Looking vexed he waved it at me. The three turned and hopped laboriously toward the horses and carriage.

"Yes, Jotunn, she's ungrateful but remember she's sheltered us for decades now! You can set the neighbor's dog free. Maybe it will bite you out of your foul mood."

I flushed.

Already about their work, none of the three looked my way.

I hurried to the spotless kitchen and found the mead. Not here in the kitchen certainly! I hefted the heavy crock and managed to carry it back to the brightly lit patio.

## Gajit's Research Expedition

Who would have guessed that any being in their right minds would take an interest in a bit of bent metal in their backyard? What he should have done was allow the transport to burrow under the surface, then polymorph its shape as soon as landing was secure. That way, its upper hull would have blended into the indigenous growth.

But with the environmental maintenance computer shrilling warnings about a possible hull breach and indications of losing atmosphere scrolling across the screen, Gajit hadn't given camouflage a thought. Instead, he was frantically screening through the Owner's Instruction Layout when the ship was attacked.

One time interval Gajit was activating hull repair procedures and shutting down all extraneous systems, and the next there was a massive proximity alert. Then the whole ship was being lifted in the air, over half of its hull surrounded by moist living tissue. The rocking of the ship did nothing for Gajit's sense of equilibrium, as he lurched toward the translation/communication module. Before he could even come up with an appropriate salutation, a voice came thundering through the ship's com-link from outside,

"Aw, Duke, that's not the Frisbee! Now, where'd it go?"

His ears vibrating from the din, Gajit keyed down the volume. The creature wrapped around the hull made great huffing sounds, and then a fresh alarm went off. Gajit scrambled over to the defense display and gave a grunt of relief. The creature was leaking a mildly corrosive fluid from its clutching mechanism but nothing that would do more than tarnish the hull.

The larger organism—one of the humans Gajit had come to study—managed to wrest his ship from the duke creature's grip. Gajit braced himself for a second impact with the planet surface but the human kept a firm grip on his prize. He heard what he surmised was a one-sided discussion between the two beings about the similarities and differences between spaceships and 'frisbees' He inserted a reminder into the data recorder to perform a structural comparison study when he had time.

Speaking of which..."Computer, record all sights and sounds within range of outboard scanners. Mark file, 'Sol Three Culture Data'. Inventory all transport damage, prioritizing life support system damage listing, interlinking with the environmental maintenance system, then giving recommendations and procedures for repair."

"Procedures for repair detailed in Owner's Instruction Layout."

Gajit muttered to, "I know that. I just don't understand them."

"Incoming instructions unclear. Repeat message."

His ears vibrating furiously, Gajit grumbled, "Understand what jettisoning a computer core into a nova can do for its programming?"

"Incoming instruc..."

"Never mind!"

"Incom..."

"Delete computer audio responses!"

He should have tried to make his escape right then though how he would have accomplished it, he couldn't fathom. Well, future eyes can see the past.

Instead, he spent the next two time intervals repairing such damage as had to be dealt with at once--and that he knew how to do. When he finally had time for pausing, and performing some analysis of the data the scanners had been recording, Gajit discovered just how serious his situation was. The human had taken him into a huge living structure. Its opaque walls and complex cubicle arrangement would prevent the navigation module from gathering reliable astronomical data. Not that he needed the data at once. First he needed a procedure to exit this structure. Calculations for escaping the planet could wait.

In the planet turns which followed, Gajit divided his time between scanning the Owner's Instruction Layout and monitoring what was happening outside his transport's hull. If he could have focused his attention just on the latter, he would have been able to refine his earlier instructions to record "everything".

By now, Gajit calculated, properly focused, the module would have recorded and collated all the research data he needed. Strangely, he had become far more interested in getting off the planet that he had come to study than in actually studying it. It wasn't that he didn't want to do the research—he loved research. But analyzing data about alien behaviors while worrying about how those behaviors might damage or even destroy his craft? That was distracting. He first keyed in the more accurate word, "terrifying" and then deleted it. Distracting was more seemly should someone from homeworld find his report next century. If he survived, Gajit pledged to himself that he'd reinsert "terrifying".

Events recorded earlier by the outboard scanners weren't encouraging. The human who had captured the transport gave it into the care of another of his species known as 'Kurt'. Observing that, Gajit had some hope of morphing the ship and escaping when the second human carried the transport outside. He hovered over the controls awaiting his first chance. But the human surrounded the ship with a dead vegetation and hydrocarbon derivative blend—something the ship named a 'sweater'—and carried him, transport and all, to his own living structure.

They were already through the entrance of the other building before he could find the polymorph instruction screen; much less identify an escape pathway out of sweater.

Once more, his way to planet surface was blocked. Still no view of the star field so no way to ascertain mothership's orbit. And no way to take off—even if he were sure the ship were ready.

Over the next four turns, Gajit worked with little rest to prepare his transport for departure at the first opportunity. He spent whatever time as he could spare absorbing the intricacies of the morph programs until he felt he could envision, key in and enable a change of shape for his new ship in just a few breaths.

All that remained now was to study the species a bit more and store minimal specs for the kinds of things humans expected to see around them. As long as he were careful about his choice, humans should pay no attention to his ship as he piloted it through this maze of cubicals to the structure's exit.

Once outside in the planet's atmosphere, he could gather the astronomical data he needed and set course. Once out of planet atmosphere, the emergency beacon signal would be strong enough to alert either mothership or their satellite.

Round trip search and rescue from their satellite would cost him more than he cared to think about. Maybe he would get a research grant to work on the recorded data. After all, that was what had prompted this disastrous theft and excursion.

With critical internal repairs completed, Gajit began fast-scanning through the data his transport's sensors had been recording for the last few turns. His ears vibrated in dismay. Now he knew why the gaseous atmosphere emitters kept clogging up! Kurt seemed intent on drenching and encrusting the transport in various kinds of hydrocarbon derivatives, first pigmented ones and then, apparently during this most recent turn, with a thick clear one. This one the environmental maintenance computer predicted was going to harden to an extraordinary degree, possibly sealing him permanently inside his transport. Why the nova did these creatures set such store by hydrocarbons!

Ears a-twitch with consternation, Gajit worked out a possible solvent, noting in dismay that his ship's stores wouldn't permit him to make much. He'd have to save it for the hatch, ventilators and sensor arrays. The rest of the ship looked like it was doomed to remain silver and black, until ...well, until maybe supernova.

Gajit hissed wearily and groped for another pain-killer patch for his aural cranium. He croaked, "Environmental computer: analyze transport atmosphere."

"Transport atmosphere 58.34% inert gases. 12.37% toxic..."

"Cancel."

He continued scanning through the gathered data, grimly noting that Kurt seemed to have a number of other captive transports in his sleeping chamber, none of which looked like they were particularly space-worthy. He wondered morosely if any of their pilots had survived. Or were they perhaps sealed inside with hydrocarbon derivatives?

...Though there was one which looked remarkably like that huge white transport the humans used to fling around their planet. If he remembered correctly however, it never seemed to get much further than a few thousand orbits about their planet, before they had to bring it back down.

Hmm. Well, so much for trying on his atmosphere suit and slipping over to Kurt's miniature version. He'd probably be better off where he was. Who knew, after all, if he'd even be able to follow the directions in the other transport's Instruction Layout? He turned back to the rapidly scanning data terminal. After a bit more analysis, Gajit snicked in delight.

It seemed that the previous planet turn when he'd been deep in fuel emitter repair, the duke creature's human, 'Jeff', had come into the room and discoursed with Kurt. All the transports, including his own, were going to be taken to an 'esseph con' and placed on display in an art show. The excursion was to take several days. Surely some portion of it would be outdoors! All he had to do was be ready to slip away from his captor—using the morph software if necessary—and then take off when there were no witnesses! Gajit allowed himself a few bounces of delight. Finally! A way off this deadly planet.

He began programming every shape of transport his sensors could scan into the morph files then he added a few of his own, including that old clunker Rjpe used to have. Moving from one to another of these as he was slipping away to the closest viable launch site should keep the human unaware enough to give him a few moments for an unwitnessed take off. All he had to do now was perfect driving the transport at land speed through Earth-type atmosphere until the ship reached a suitable site. He set to work calling up the instruction screens at once.

When the nova did anything ever go as laid out? Gajit was still in sleeping restraints, trying to recuperate from a full turn of learning land-speed driving when he was awakened by pitch and yaw alarms.

This was the day his captor was to journey to the 'con'. Had they started on their excursion while he slept? Hissing miserably to himself, Gajit turned on local gravity and wriggled his way out of the restraints, hampered by the nauseous odor of hydrocarbon derivatives and the bouncing and tipping of the transport.

He stumbled his way over to the sensors but found, to his alarm, that he could see nothing but a vague grayness. Gajit cried out, "What the nova's wrong with the scanners? I can't see anything!"

"Chronometer reads planet dawn. Therefore, lighting is weak. Transport is enveloped in a dead vegetation derivative called 'cotton'. Pilot vitals read 67.32% standard degree of alertness and health..."

"Cancel! Computer, is the transport currently outside the captor's structure? We need to launch-"

"Launch cycle not recommended. Transport is enclosed in an Earthan land-conveyance proceeding at 117% normal Sol3 land speed west northwestward from transport's landing site. Land-conveyance has clear visual sensors with apertures; however, the largest such aperture in the land-conveyance measures 89.43% of size needed by the current pilot to exit conveyance safely. Pilot reads as 66.92% standard degree of alert and health. There is a 58% probability that the transport will hit an edge of the largest aperture, if the present operator in his present condition attempts to launch..."

"Cancel."

Gajit muttered something to himself that involved novas, cosmic goats and the computer's ancestry, then went in search of a fresh pain-killing patch. He was running low. This atmosphere, he mumbled, always full of gasses...

Somewhere, behind him the computer reminded him that by definition all atmospheres were gasses. Then it added something about starting up the rescue beacon. Gajit mumbled an answer, wishing sourly that it would just discontinue itself. And him too.

All he wanted right now was to be home. Somewhere at least where when you looked out a transport, you saw recognizable star fields, instead of either that weird green vegetative life or the interior of a monstrous Earth structure...

He blinked and his ears sagged sleepily. And where computers and data cubes weren't the only ones to talk with. He swallowed the last of his glak, and sank wearily into the command chair, calling up the forward sensor view and then remembering it was blocked with 'cotton'.

Three time intervals later, Gajit awoke abruptly and stared at the sensor monitor in front of him. "Goat's novas!" he muttered to himself. They must have arrived at their destination while he was asleep! So much for slipping away from his captor while not in a structure or a conveyance!

He attacked the most recent data files but his attention kept straying back to the views the sensors were giving him. There, he viewed things which, frankly, defied belief. Humans were everywhere of course, but such strange ones and in such bizarre atmosphere suits! It was difficult to focus on anything besides them.

The closest objects to his ship were the other transports belonging to Kurt, each balanced at the top of its own thick pole.

Gajit checked a monitor, and found that his transport was precariously balanced on a pole as well. Suppose one of the humans struck their pole?

Beginning with the aft monitor, then moving on to dorsal and lateral sensors, Gajit scanned as much of the surrounding environment as he could. More humans. And more objects but in a variety of shapes. Most of the latter were flat, their surfaces covered with random hues and patterns.A human, obviously destruction-bent human, had dangled these from flimsy walls. Better balancing on one of these poles than dangling from a wall.

Gajit reviewed the various shapes he'd stored in the morph file and then switched to the instruction screens he'd been studying on driving the transport in atmosphere. Photon knew he was as ready as he'd ever be. Now, all he needed was a time interval without anyone around in which to glide off this pole, morph to the first shape in the computer file and guide the transport to the closest open exit.

Hopefully, one existed! This was a public structure according to the conversations he'd monitored and the chronometer read planet evening. Surely the humans would soon be retiring for sleep interval.

It had been a salutary event taking that nap. He was reasonably alert—in spite of what the computer stated. He clicked on a fictional work he'd been reading before the crash and, with one eye on the forward monitor, tried to pick up the thread of the story.

Two time intervals later, the last of the humans were departing. Gajit keyed off the reading monitor just as the lights in the room dimmed. Good! He paused for a breath or two. And then thought better of it and paused for a few breaths more. All of the sensors agreed that there were no living organisms in the room— unless he chose to count insectile pests. Outside it, who knew? He would think about that once the transport was ready to glide into the next room.

Gajit initiated the polymorph program and powered up. As soon as the transport's shape was completely changed, he raised the throttle and keyed for lift off.

The ship didn't lift! Gajit checked the landing gear but it was in passive. He increased the throttle. Still nothing! Not one millimeter of atmosphere between transport and pole! It was as if...

"Alert! Hull breach imminent!"

Gajit keyed the throttle down at once. It seemed Kurt had fastened the transport to the top of the pole. And may the goat fling him through a hole for doing it! With a hiss of resignation, Gajit unstrapped himself from the command chair and started toward the suit locker. Now if he had time enough to suit up, go outside and neutralize the human's fastening mechanism and still get out of here...

"Incoming message."

Gajit fluttered his ears in distress. Now the com-link was malfunctioning. What would be next? He opened the locker and began the pains-taking process of suiting up, warning himself to second-check each step as he finished it. He felt sleepy And a little dizzy.

Half heard behind him, the computer repeated, "Incoming message."

He'd had enough. Gajit turned and went back over to the command modules, his hand already forming a fist to smash off the communications key.

"Incoming message..."

"...Gajit? Are you all right?"

Gajit could only gape at the fuzzy picture on the com-link screen.

"Rjpe?" He scrambled into the seat, the head covering under his arm dropping to the floor and rolling away. "Rjpe! I'm here! I crashed a few turns ago, and now I'm stuck..."

The beloved voice interrupted, snicking its delight, "He's all right! Pjwp, look! There he is!"

A new voice, sibilant with impatience, whispered through the com-link, "More than he deserves, the goat'll warrant! Rjpe, we're going to have to dematerialize you out..."

"No! Wait! This transport's ice new and I just need to unfas..."

Rjpe interrupted him, "Sorry, love! We've already tried to get in. Sensors read both the outside entrance to the structure and the one to the room you're in as sealed tight. Only ventilation openings exist, and they're too small."

"But the transport!"

"Nova, Gajit, we're talking your life!" whispered Pjwp. "Now stand back from the command module, so I can get a clear signal..."

"Wait! My cultural data! At least..."

"I'm downloading it right now," Rjpe answered. "Photon, you've got a lot. What's all this about other transports?"

With a hiss of consternation, Gajit tried to spring back to the module. He'd left the morph program running! He made one frantic lunge, only to trip over his cast-off head covering.

And then reality around him faded and changed.

He was lying on the materialization unit in Pjwp's old station surplus transport. Rjpe was bending over him, the star field display just a few millimeters behind her.

Home. Or at least, one of the best parts of it.

Gajit hissed frantically as Rjpe helped him to his feet, "Pjwp! I left the morph running!"

Pjwp shook his head. "Sorry!" As soon as he'd keyed in the trajectory and throttle commands, he turned to his friend, "Too late, Gajit. I'd already sealed her tight."

Gajit grumbled, "Now my batteries will all be dead when I go back."

"Better than dying from hydrocarbon poisoning," Rjpe cut in soothingly. "You look terrible. Will you stop that hissing? Let us get you linked in to the med-comp before you asphyxiate!"

Grumbling good-naturedly, Gajit followed her.

A few miles down-planet, in one of the human-made structures code-named 'Hyatt', a tiny spaceship model gleamed with a pearly light and began transforming itself into the next shape on its morph queue. The art show judges were in for a surprise. So was Kurt.

## Dingle
### A Finish–The–Story Challenge

Finish this story & your version may be inserted into the Kindle edition.

Critter scuffed his way across the bare, unvarnished floor, sneezing at the dust he'd stirred up. It was colder today than he'd expected. He wrapped his quilted robe tighter about him, and then retied the rope belt. If Magnus didn't come soon, he'd have to light a brazier just to keep warm. And that would attract the Night Watchers. Not something you wanted to do when it was nearly dusk.

He shuffled over to the one window and glared down at the path. Not a sign of Magnus or of anyone else. Maybe, if he went outside and yanked hard on the chain, he could get that blasted shutter to close over the window. Then, it wouldn't matter if he lit a fire in the brazier or not. The Watchers could do a lot, but they couldn't see through wood. At least, not the last he'd heard.

Blast Magnus! Icy air was seeping in the through the window, even though it was on the lee side of the cottage. Well, that was that. He might as well go and try to close it.

Critter thrust his dagger and sheath under the ragged rope of his belt, and crept to the door. He stood a moment with the side of his head so close to the surface that his ear kept flicking. Not a sound, except the tiny ones of his held breath and the soft whoosh of his ear fur against the rough wood. Might as well try as not.

He took a great breath, and slipped through the door as noiselessly as he was able. It seemed a shade brighter outside than it had in but the coming of sunset was undeniable. Shivering from nervousness as much as cold, Critter scuttled to the right front corner of the cabin and peeked around it. Nothing there but the larxs bushes, their stringy leaves black and rustling in the last light of the sun. He crept between the closest one and the side wall. Merhule, the shutter chain was high! Been so long since he'd tried to close the window himself, he'd near forgot...

A sudden, familiar scent tickled his nose. Critter started to turn, but too late. Clammy skin pressed over his nose passages, simultaneous with a strong blow to his midriff. The combined assaults made all the air in his lungs burst from his mouth. He choked, unable for the moment to fight back.

The ghost of a giggle blew warmly into his right ear. The grip about his midriff loosened enough for him to pull away from the hand on his nose.

"Magnus! I'll skin you for that..."

"Not Magnus, imp. What were you doing? Oh, the shutter."

Critter leaned against the wall and gasped in air.

The newcomer reached up and pulled the shutter down and closed.

While Dingle was occupied with her task, Critter considered darting off into the darkness. Before the thought was more than half-formed, it was too late.

Dingle grasped his elbow and guided him back to his door.

"Waiting for Magnus, what?" Dingle purred deep in her throat. "He might not be coming tonight, what. Might not. Might not at that."

She shook her head.

"Get inside, Critter!"

Dingle looked about carefully, left and right, before she closed the door between them both and the outside world.


Your turn!

## *The Last Battle*

### The Old Woman

Everyone was passing me by on the dirt road, gifting me with dust and the stinks of sweat and animal droppings. I was so tired, I woke now and again from a nap the length of a single stride. My feet hurt. It was all I could do to dodge the obstacles on the path.

I stopped and drew a breath through cupped hands, chiefly to look behind and then ahead of me. In the seconds before someone grumbled and elbowed my back, I glimpsed massive sandstone walls proclaiming the proximity of the king's summer citadel. Only the weekly market booths stood between me and the twenty ell high bronze-braced entry doors. Just before dusk, praise to the One!

The light of the setting sun caught on the armor of warriors pacing high above us across the parapet or circling slowly behind the machicolation in the closest towers. Peddlers, customers, gawkers, beggars and weary travelers were shifting into the restless shadows cast by surrounding trees and a handful of outlying merchant tents. Soon, the market would begin its slow plunge into the denser dim of the great edifice.

I limped as quickly as I could into the midst of the market, dodging others where possible or waiting impatiently for a way to clear. Sweaty filthy bodies, bodies choking in a miasma of drink or cloying perfume surrounded me.

A single trumpet sang one golden note. The first of three warnings, or so I'd been told, before guards and draft animals began closing the gates. Already within sight of the gates and hearing only the first warning. I grinned, the movement of facial muscles puffing caked dust into my nostrils.

Hawkers cried out to me whenever I slowed my pace.

"My lady! My lady! Fresh! Strong as iron! Savory... Precious... A bargain..." Their claims blurred into the common plea for a full day's profit.

*Lady.* My lips curved at the word, tugging at skin where splashed mud had dried hours ago. A word only a flattering hawker would use, clad as I was in a mended cape & the piebald patched clothing of a spent fighter.

I blinked and drew a breath.

Cobbler. I was looking for a cobbler.

Would a cobbler have a booth out here on market day? Those with imported satin slippers and tooled leather boots did. Importers, crafters of fine shoes meant for nobles would likely live as close to the courtiers' manses and the royal palace as they could afford. One who lived by repairing shoes and boots might expect his custom to seek him out somewhere in the narrow interlacing streets just within the walls.

I stopped, realized I'd done so again, and limped forward lest the second warning trumpet find me this far from the gates. Newly-massed peddlers and beggars shoved others aside to clutch at me and gabble meaningless words. Buzzards shrieking a warning to any who might disturb their feast.

I grumbled and clutched at the haft of my smaller dagger. Street patter laced with flattery transformed into curses and a couple half-hearted kicks. I snarled and pulled the dagger free. The buzzard-spawn scattered.

Now to get through the gates lest lingering catch me hungry and without shelter. Merchants were thrusting small objects into lined bags. Others, their eyes on the crowds, reached beneath their tables and carts fumbling out folds of rough canvas sacks, even as they kept up a steady patter for one last customer.

I turned and took a few more painful steps toward the gates.

"A moment, my lady!" whispered near in the soft cracked voice of an old woman.

Not a peddler—unless her voice had given way from a day of hawking.

Reluctant to hang back from the gate, I glanced over my shoulder without stopping.

Somewhere bundled within a clashing collection of tunics, trousers, a skirt far too short, a hood and two shawls each claiming a shoulder was a small dark woman. Her black eyes--reflecting light borrowed from the setting sun—were a compass to her features. Too thin, cheekbones too prominent but she was smiling like a doting granny.

I offered the briefest of nods.

Like quiet water reflecting paired stars, the sparkle of her eyes greeted my gaze.

A breeze crept through the torn patches of my tunic. I shivered and shifted a step backward with my good foot. My hand froze between dagger and sword hilts, echoing my thoughts torn between pity and terror.

The woman's face crinkled into a smile. "No danger here, my lady. But peril lies within if you are not careful. I have something for you."

Just another peddler. I allowed my hand to drop.

"Something you will need. Alas, my granddaughter refused my gift and my protection. But you won't, will you?"

My head shook of its own—making a decision in which my thoughts had no part. Already dismayed at making one choice before considering it, I held out my hand. My sword hand. Fool!

She smiled--the smile showing the gap of a missing tooth— and lifted the strap of a small bag from one shoulder. Surely only the russet shawl had been there a moment before.

Blended dirt and old sweat obliterated what once might have been intertwined flowers on the bag's padded strap. Wandering past where the strap ended and the bag began, the intricate design laid gentle claim to the ovoid surface of the silk bag.

The flowers—if they were flowers—were varied in hue, bright then shadowed as if caught in turn by noon rays or misted moonlight. No light varied near us except when vendors and beasts passed with their heavy packs.

The woman turned about and scurried away. Yet her voice came clear. "Open it when they think you sleep..."

A growl and a grunt warned of a brawl about to start. I stepped away from the sound but kept my gaze fixed down the twisting empty path beyond the crowds hurrying toward the gate. Shorn of the sun's light, the garish hues of her clothing deepened into evergreen, violet and the midnight inkiness of the sea on a moonless night. Then nothing.

The second warning rang out over the babbling crowds and the protests of donkeys and oxen.

I hurried toward the city gates, one person caught up in the slow jostling of a multitude. A man clutched my left elbow and forced his way through a gap barely big enough for a child. Had he had a mind to steal the old woman's gift he might have succeeded. I slung the lightweight bag up on my left shoulder, clenching its strap between my arm and side.

A whisper echoed by many whispers crept within my ears. "The cobbler lives in the third street. Turn right at the shrine. Look for a thicket of sticks once a fence and a green light in a window."


### The Cobbler

Once past the well-lighted gates and guard posts, night took possession of the thoroughfare. Wary of any cutpurses, I adjusted my grip on the gifted bag the better to use it as a shield. I probably appeared more threatening than the travelers searching for shelter or the city people hurrying from workplace to a beckoning meal and sleep.

In spite of my new grip on the strap, the silken bag swayed and bounced on its shortened tether in rhythm with my uneven steps. I knew nothing of its value but then neither did any would-be thief. Perhaps small loss if it were taken. Perhaps not. Thieves were sometimes known to incapacitate their targets before they knew what prize they might gain.

No longer in the midst of a crowd, I took note of those behind me and to either side.

Many had taken advantage of the first inn we had passed and departed from the group. I should have joined them. The corner of a common room beckoned in my thoughts. Dozing. Warmed by even the scant fire a tin-pinching goodman would permit. Filled with something warm and soothed by the inn's best brew.

I faltered a step, and blessings that I did! The shrine's roof peeped over a crumbling stone wall on my right. Just beyond it lurked smoky chapel candles in three arched windows. Gentle song—accompanied by the familiar lilt of a pipe—sounded from the darkened yard. I saw no one.

I looked as far as I could see around the corner. Those still hurrying up and down the crossing street could scarce be deemed a crowd. Had I left all the shops and inns behind?

With a second glance about, more careful than the first, I turned right as instructed. Suppose the shop were no longer open? Had all the city's proprietors given up on further profit for tonight? Not worth staying open for custom intent on an inn, tavern or brothel.

Just to my left, firelight flared and heavy boots clattered. I spun toward them. My attacker cried out and backed up, sprawling half in the road and half on the shallow steps he had just descended.

A shadow blocked out most of the light. A woman screamed, "Don't hurt him, I pray you!"

My sword was out. I didn't remember drawing it. Instinct rarely left memory. I took a backward step. Two. And finally remembered to sheathe my sword.

Amidst a flood of imprecations, the man heaved himself back to his feet. The woman, likely his wife, asked if she should run for the watch.

He shook his head. "Back inside! Just a misunderstanding." He didn't look me in the face. Too intent on seeing if my hand would keep its distance from my hilt?

"My apologies, sir! I…"

"…came from the wars recently." He finished for me. "Where were you?"

Scattered memories of our last battle lurked behind clenched teeth. I shook my head.

"Well, we were in Itera…"

"…the peninsula battle? I was up-river. Thanks for keeping them downwind."

The man chuckled. "Wilderness Ward, huh? Actually, I missed it." He lifted a cane and briefly pointed the end at me like a sword.

I thought his leg was intact but the dark and his cape left me unsure. We both drew back another pace—beyond the range of bladed weapons. Twin apologies echoed between us. Why he offered one I couldn't guess. Then he hurried on the way I had come.

I turned.

A flickering pinpoint of light, green as leaves on a summer day, caught my gaze. I limped toward the old woman's promised sign. Only as I approached the green-lit window did I wonder what the cobbler would make of someone asking to have her boots repaired at such an hour. Again, why was I dealing with this first rather than tomorrow after a night's rest?

Oh, well. I was here.

The display window was just at the right height to catch the attention of passersby. Two pairs of shoes rested on the deep sill. One pair of white kidskin fit for a countess, the second perhaps of deep red, double-buckled, awaiting their rightful place on the feet of a captain-at-arms. Within, brief glimpses of hearth fire beckoned. At that sight, the night air grew chiller.

I clambered down a half-dozen worn steps, knocked on the stained oak door and tried the latch. It pivoted down then back in place. A narrow band of warm light slipped past the open edge and with it tantalizing scents of hot food lifting from a hidden pot.

A man seated at a table spared me a glance before resuming his task. He held a partially completed boot, one hand tipping it toward the hearth as he added swift stitches to the fine leather. Soft words came perhaps from his hidden lips. (He faced away from me.) I thought whatever he had said the sounds of a greeting, then realized I'd caught the last syllables of a hastily finished sentence. To whom was he speaking?

Laying down his work, the cobbler turned. A smile of content and welcoming arched his white eyebrows and his lips. I caught a glimpse of teeth between whiskers and a short beard. He glanced aside briefly, seeming to frown as one might when warning a child to behave.

Then he hurried over. Offering a hand, he commented, "Vincent, my lady. Welcome. Surely you are in need to visit us so late."

I considered apologizing in spite of the unlocked shop door.

The moment had passed. Vincent was no longer looking at me. He glanced at my feet, the same glance every cobbler gives. The wrinkles at the corners of his eyes puckered.

"A need indeed. Your shoes are too large, notwithstanding your effort to fill the space with double stockings. Please sit!" He gestured to a sturdy stool. "Blisters surely. I have an ointment," He tilted his head, perhaps thinking. "Why are you wearing shoes that are not yours?"

"Because mine were stolen. These came from…"

*From one of the bodies. All of them are male—every boot is too large. All of them under my command…*

He wasn't listening. Blessings on that. His gaze was fixed on the dangling footwear overhead. Looking at his ready stock for a likely match?

### Clever Mice?

Rustles, bearing no part with the hearth flame crackle, tickled my ears. Light traded with shadow between a pair of slippers and the closest boots.

Had something whisked out of sight just as I turned toward it? Nonsense! I'd imagined there had been a something! Why? Because now there was nothing? I tried to look about without appearing to do so. Rats? More likely, just mice.

Vincent cleared his throat. I turned around and wondered how long he had waited for me to remember him. Or had I just imagined he had looked away before?

We talked over a spicy soup from the open kettle. So delicious I sopped up every bit of broth with my last wedge of crusty bread.

As we neared the end of our meal, Vincent cocked his head towards the far side of the hearth and mumbled. Still facing away, he nodded.

He turned back to me, to utter words better addressed to anyone except myself, "So you are going to take the king's challenge."

A statement not a question, warmed by approval.

Hardly was he finished speaking and I was nodding. Like my hand reaching for the crone's silken bag before I knew what it was, long before I grasped what she was saying.

I still didn't know what the bag was or what it held. Part way through our meal I had thought to open it and then forgotten my intent until this moment. I didn't understand what either the old woman or Vincent meant but now I was convinced they both spoke of the same matter. Were the crone, the cobbler and his invisible lodgers bound by a subtle magic? Could they be manipulations of a sorcerer? We had encountered one of them…

A chill touched my spine. I'd thought returning from combat meant I'd left the arcane back in the wilderness.

And so I had! I drew a great breath. What nonsense I'd been thinking! Harnessed as I was to a great weariness it was easier to nod than make thoughtful decisions. Really, I should have slept a night in an inn even before seeking new boots.

Vincent must have sat silently as I tried to bind the ragged ends of my thoughts together. At least he was sitting so now, by turns glancing toward me and then away.

Giving me time to think? The weeks spent journeying to this city hadn't gifted me with enough time for that. A few minutes more? Pointless.

The king's challenge. Volunteering would take me back out of city…

"Tell me more."

Vincent told me of the shoes and boots sent down every day from the palace—footwear mysteriously worn as from a year's use in a single night. A constant custom for him even if peculiar.

"Repairs are boring and the same ones daily take up half my time. Fashioning new shoes stimulates my mind."

He frowned.

"My mind is more stimulated with dread at what this means. Something terrible is at its roots. It's past time for a person of courage and discernment, someone who has faced the uncanny--to accept the king's challenge. And here you are."

We talked past eating. Past bedtime. How late I cannot say. As minutes blurred into hours, I grew used to the rustles and the glimpsed movements where they should not be. Just mice. Someone in the regiment once had a mouse as a pet, hidden during marches in a small leather bag strapped from shoulder to hip.

Someone… Me.

The chill slithered down my back again. I jumped and glanced behind me toward the dark door—hidden by my own shadow from the light in the fireplace. Just as it should be.

Turning back to my host, I thought to offer an apology or explanation. An explanation of what?

Always kindly, Vincent's eyes sparkled now, perhaps with suppressed tears. "So hard a life! Even the strongest must harbor their share of fear."

I would have protested had it not been for sight of my sword a quarter drawn from its sheath. "Vincent, forgive…"

"No!" He offered a sheepish smile. "Not having been in such danger as you, still I think I understand."

With that, we began talking as close to no matter from when we stopped. Minutes, hours, days passed.

Could the royal challenge be a prank sowed by princely boredom?

Vincent dispelled that wishful thought. By our liege? Certainly not. Most of those accepting the challenge had died because they failed. As agreed by those who took the challenge, their lives were forfeit. Rumor said at the hands of the royal executioner.

A handful had never been seen again since they took up their post. We both doubted these few fled their punishment. Perhaps they alone had solved the mystery and died for their success.

So Vincent and I agreed—a spell or its very caster had slain those who disappeared.

"And you said you faced such a sorcerer once." Vincent drew my eyes to his and said no more.

Yes, I had faced one but not alone.

*Phantoms of hope, of slow victory dispelled by the deaths of comrade after comrade. The last of us—sure of death—casting aside every defense and striking as one…*
*No shouts of triumph. Pain. Bitter tears. Emptiness. The agonized need to forget what had been seared into us…*

I mouthed a silent "yes".

The cobbler's gaze flickered but he didn't look away from me. No pity there, thank the One! Pity would not hold me to his purpose. And I could not have borne it.

"So? Are you committed then?"

"I am." Committed? Truthfully to a madhouse for such folly.

~~~~~

"Anna?"

Vincent found me the next morning, burrowed into my blanket and half-wedged between the hearth's edge and the far corner of the room.

I didn't want to open my eyes, still charmed as I was by a dream filled with tiny pattering feet, small whispers and giggles sternly hushed by an equally tiny voice. Laughing mice?

"Anna! Betimes! The king will order the trumpets sounded within the hour!"

I mumbled an answer and sat up. The silken bag's strap had twined itself about my left arm, even as my body was wrapped tight by my blanket. A twining cloth... No. Not yet

Alarm finished my waking. Was I supposed to have opened the bag before I slept? Too late now.

I stood up, leaving the blanket to return to its dreaming if it wished. My hair felt strange. Clean. Tight to my skull. More orderly than sleep would allow. My questing fingers tangled in a garden of ribbons. Testing one, I knew the knots would not easily come free. Ah, well! I could only hope they hadn't made me look a loon.

A woman Vincent's age came through the door beyond the hearth. She held out a green velvet tunic—old but carefully repaired with minute stitches. Fine enough for a princess to lounge about in her chambers without scandalizing the servants.

Had the woman stitched the night away or had the whisperers?

Vincent walked in carrying a bucket, a bit of yellow soap perched on a brown sponge and a rough towel over one arm. They left the room in silence.

I hastened to remove my clothes and clean up as well as I might. The tunic hem stopped above the knee, forcing me to put my worn trousers back on. Not so much the lounging princess now. I had just finished belting the trousers when I nearly stumbled over the promised pot of ointment, silken foot coverings such as I had never seen much less worn and a pair of dark green leather boots just ankle high. They fit my feet as though I had been measured for them.

I looked about, determined to see the unseen.

A tiny giggle off to my left. To my right, movements like a patch of shadow and bit of sunlight exchanging places.

"Thank you."

An answering silence. True silence that drew attention to the background of tiny noises to which I'd become accustomed.

## The Palace

Day old bread and a small crock of milk sat upon the cobbler's bench. I assumed they were for me. Minutes later, I walked through the low outer door, clambered up the few steps, and threaded my way into the crowds. And minutes after, I was approaching an outlying guard post before the palace gates.

I'd made good time and with little pain as well. I scowled at the boots cradling my feet then looked up hurriedly at a rough challenge from the guardsmen.

When I stated my business, the guards' expressions changed— some to solemn sadness, more to stern measuring, and a few to furtive grins. I blamed my likely-ridiculous hair for the grins.

I surrendered my sword and knives to the care of an old fighter. He and a dozen low-level officers formed a loose circle around me. The old guard barely paused at the silver-laced mahogany doors to whisper a password before we swept inside. Who was he? Not who he appeared to be certainly.

Nor was I. Outwardly I suppose I looked a citizen begging an audience with some magistrate.

The sharp click of the doors falling shut behind me sounded like the death-click of a mousetrap.

No one spoke.

I assumed I was being led to the king to offer my services but they motioned me before them into a tiny littered office. Free of me—neither guest nor prisoner—they left by the same way we had arrived. Retreating mutters filled the space behind me.

The wizened woman inside glanced at me, took some papers from a stacked pile in an open wooden box, and inked her pen. First of her questions, "Next of kin?"

"None." The old pain caught in my chest.

She was on to the next on her list. "Disposal of body?"

I blinked.

"When you fail?"

"I won't fail." Yes, I would.

"Disposal of body?"

I described Vincent's shop.

The woman arched an eyebrow but went on.

Then, waiting. Waiting through the afternoon. Waiting through the long evening. Nothing worse than waiting before a battle. Alone, no comrades to ease the passing of time, nothing filled the mind but unwanted memories, some so sharp the mingled stench of sweat, blood and entrails caught in my throat.

Alone, except for the discreet guards.

The small room in which I was held provided some entertainment. A few scrolls and codices lay upon a fragile table. A pianoforte stood a yard away. I didn't dare touch the keys, though I would have wrenched a wire free had I been alone. Tightly coiled it would have fit inside the old woman's bag.

On a table much larger than the first, parchments, two bottles of ink, soft squares of cloth, a padded leather rectangle wide as the table, and a long but narrow box of rosy wood were arranged in a precise pattern. All writing implements no doubt but of a kind only nobility would have the skill and leisure to use.

The legs on the pianoforte's bench looked as frail as wheat stalks. Facing the windows, two long wire-grilled benches boasted curved supports high enough to ease the small of someone's back. I misliked them as soon as I saw the matching grilled windows opposite them—blocking more than permitting a view of a garden.

The sturdy bench drawn close to the writing table beckoned me as did the box. At first it would not open. Peculiar that. Motivated that much more, I looked for depressions which might conceal a spring, but found slender grooves instead. So it slid apart longwise. Mystery solved, I was on the point of sliding the box closed when I saw something I'd dared not hope for. I hid the treasure with my left hand as well as I might. With the other, I pulled quill after quill from the box, studying each in turn before pushing them back inside. The guards lost interest by the time I pulled the fifth quill free with one hand and the small penknife out with the other.

"And to whom did I think I would write?" My question masked the least whisper of the tiny weapon slipping into the old woman's bag.

Unfeigned tears burned my eyes.

I deserted the padded bench facing the guards, and turned to the hard metal seating and the barricaded windows. There I wiled away my waiting hours—perhaps my remaining life—peering through a window's tiny openings to watch the flight of birds and the antics of two lapdogs. Each pet wore a jeweled collar worth more than all I owned, plus everything I had lost.

I thought more than once about opening the bag but two things stopped me. The old woman said to wait until "they" thought I slept. Opening her bag before then might trigger an enchantment created for just that moment and—if a weapon were inside—I daren't let the guards see it. My own weapons had been taken. This one would be as well. I was fortunate they hadn't seen me take the penknife.

Twice trays of food and ale were brought to me. I could do no more than nibble.

The guards woke me from a fitful doze and marched me down corridors, through marvelously-appointed rooms, deeper and deeper into the part of the palace long set aside for the royal family.

The secretary—or whoever she was—appeared early in our wandering walk. She recounted the rules she had earlier bidden me read. Sole purpose: find out how the princes left their shared bedchamber, where they went and what they did. Bring back proof of what I discovered. Do not attempt to prevent anything they might choose to do. They were royals--I just a soldier returned from defending wilderness villages. Do whatever they commanded me to do unless their orders prevented me from obeying their father's command that I discover their plots and plans. And so on. Each word bound my hands a bit tighter.

_And when the twelve princes think you asleep, open the silken bag and pray to the One that whatever is in it be a weapon of power or a scroll with an enchantment even a lowly soldier might voice._

I admitted to myself if the twelve wanted me disgraced and executed, it would be so. My one hope was to appear no threat to their secrets.

As I entered the antechamber adjoining their sleeping hall, I forced my frown into something like the expression I might have had while watching the drolleries of the royal pets. I hoped.

Speaking of pets, what stirred within the cage shrouded in shadow behind the anteroom's still open door? A baby gryphon? It moved about, the better to stare at me between silver bars.

No. Not...

A staff rapped hard against the floor behind me, signaling the king's approach. The guards and secretary hastened to bow. I turned and followed suit as quickly as I could, feeling a new recruit out of step in the practice field.

Footsteps sounded from a second hallway. Perhaps the feet of a dozen...

"Rise." The single syllable was flat. Emotionless. Could our king be bored?

I gave a fighter's salute without thinking--it had been such a part of me these many years.

The royal eyes flickered with interest. He answered my gesture with the acknowledgement of a general on the field of battle.

Then he turned to his sons.

Beginning with the one who appeared the eldest, each man stepped a pace nearer their father. The first bowed swiftly. Defiance in his staring eyes and the curl of his lips put the lie to his brief deference. Others followed, most with distracted expressions. A couple performed their obeisance with eyes cast below the king's gaze. From fear? Several glanced toward me, their eyes betraying a shared malice.

*Not the promised reinforcements despite their clothing! Crying out a warning mere seconds before they drew blade and charged, I sought for the hilt that wasn't there. How had they stolen-*

Green velvet. The tunic.

One of the princes stifled a snicker.

Their father scowled but said nothing.

For the first time, I truly considered what I had gotten myself into. Danger stalked me every day like a faithful shadow I dare not ignore. Death, most likely tomorrow. But what if I succeeded? Whom could I choose when every one of them appeared soaked in contempt and callous pride? And what after?

My gut roiled as not even a week-old body would have made it react.

Their quiet words were finished. Their liege and father blessed them, and offered the hope that his heirs would sleep well. He nodded.

At once, all twelve filed into the anteroom of their bedchamber.

The king drew a dull iron chain free from within the collar of his dark tunic, lifting its length over his head. Two heavy keys dangled from it.

I barely stifled a snort. If one key could not shut them in, would two? A score?

With his free hand, he gestured for me to follow my charges, only to bid me stop with a flattened palm. All to gaze into my eyes? I had no idea what he saw or hoped to see--only that his eyes darkened with gloom. He shook his head.

Dismissed before I even tried?

"Go within," he prompted me. No, not dismissed. Grieved for.

His sons stood gathered by their inner doorway. Whispering. One laughed.

I turned away from them, longing to ask the king what he saw that had banished hope.

Too late. The armored oaken door boomed closed a yard from my face. Metal grated on metal. And then a second time.

I heard no footsteps in retreat. No sound could penetrate a door built strong as a castle's gate.

### And a Health to All!

Soft steps retreated behind me. Heading into their bedchamber already? The old woman's words suggested that they waited until each watcher was asleep.

The scrape of metal on metal turned my attention to the cage. My fellow captive stretched & clenched his claws. A second time, I stopped my fruitless grope for a weapon.

Pop. Then another pop from the bedchamber. Were the twelve already escaping? A third pop. The scent of vintage wine. Soft voices. Crystalline ting of glasses amid the gurgle of liquids.

Three of the sons walked through our shared doorway and beckoned with their arms in friendly invitation. I dithered. I was supposed to watch over them. Keep them in view. But where could they go?

"Thank you but no."

"Then we shall come to you!" The eldest pushed past his siblings, a bottle in one hand and two goblets in the other.

All twelve filed back into the anteroom, filling it from door to door and from cage to barred and shuttered window. Bottles and wine cups passed from hand to hand. The eldest approached me, his manner a caricature of a servant. Nodding, not bowing, he held out a cup nearly full of wine.

I thanked him and shifted closer to the cage.

The eldest toasted their father and all lifted their goblets high, each drinking the entire contents. Still too short of the cage and water bowl, I lifted my cup with them. Lips pressed tight, I mimed drinking as well. My cup still high so none could see its contents unchanged, I returned their toast, nodding to the man farthest to my left then the next and next, until I faced the crown prince. The twelve eagerly gulped wine in their own honor.

I tipped my cup over the beast's water bowl, then pretended a third and final draught. Their secret drug likely tainted the fine vintage. Gambling on that, I studied the interior of the cup for but a heartbeat. When I looked up, worried frowns on three of the younger brothers' faces confirmed my theory.

New bottles were opened. Several drank directly from them. The younger ones kept to the decorum of using their goblets. One man but not the eldest lifted a half-empty bottle and gave me an inquiring look. I considered and nodded, gesturing with two fingers that I wished only a bit more.

He poured first into my cup then the rest into his until it trickled over the edge and saturated the narrow bands of embroidery on his tunic's cuff.

"Look now! See what you made me do!"

He gulped half the cup's contents and dropped it. Pulling out a fine linen cloth, he pressed it hard against his wet wrist.

*...a medic-sage presses an artery to staunch bleeding, with a red-soaked rag and his bare hands. He needs help! A tourniquet. I take a step, reaching for my trouser belt.*
*Where is it?*

My belt was underneath the tunic and a good thing it was considering the stares. What would they have made of me removing it?

Glances darted from eyes to eyes. Smiles broadened. Doubtless they thought the drug was working. Whispers touched my ears too softly for me to distinguish any words.

The eldest came forward a second time and took my empty cup. He clasped my hand in his and lifted them both to his heart.

"Perhaps, this time tomorrow, we will be wed."

Letting go my hand he turned to the others. "Or perhaps, not."

Even the youngest smirked.

Each man called "Good rest to you!" as they walked through our shared door. Stifled laughter whispered from those already out of sight.

Suppose they were leaving now! No. Wait. Since no door hid them from view, they would first take care to see me fully asleep.

About time then. Enough of being scorned and thought weak. First feigning to sleep. Then rising to the hunt.

I walked the few steps away from the doorway to the bed. It sat closer to the window than the cage, so it was not in direct line of sight with whatever might be happening past the door frame. Had they moved it sometime in the past?

I perched on the mattress edge, wanting with a right good will to be off after them. Best to lie down immediately. I huddled under the frilly thing pretending to be a coverlet and listened for breathing. Still here. I hadn't cut it too fine after all.

I offered them a languid sigh as I kept watch on what I could see of the doorway through slit lids masked by a handful of lace. I clutched the old silken bag with my other hand, half of its small bulk between hip and mattress. Again, I sent up the hope, the plea to the One, that whatever was in it would match my purpose. Oddly enough, somewhere in the palace was someone who knew more of the bag's contents than I did. A low level servant had peeked into the bag and shrugged when the guards were taking my weapons.

The beast was snoring. I considered doing the same but feared a mimicked snore might be my undoing. Silence would do...

Still the sound of many people breathing. They were careful for what I'd deemed a reckless lot.

Footsteps approached. Someone whispered. I refrained from scrunching my eyes tight.

Silence. A minute. Another. A handful of them.

"She's gone."

"Two dozen women have come here and we've bested them all. This one's not even a challenge."

"I told you as much when I saw her hair. Her brains were long drawn away by the ribbons!"

Stifled chuckles.

My face hot, I thought to curse the cobbler's tenants for my be-ribboning. Why had they made me look a fool?

Why indeed! It hadn't been a prank but a plan and it seemed to be working. I should have guessed its purpose before the princes made light of me. Blessings on them!

"Get ready but quietly! Take care not to awaken father's furry spy." Footsteps again, now heading away.

I smiled. That was one precaution that need not concern them.


Hissed words no more than a vapor of sound came to my ears. Multiple grunts. A curse. The creaking of something heavy being shifted.

"Gently!"

A groan and thud.

"You just missed my foot!"

"Dolt! Next time step back more swiftly."

"Quiet, both you, or you'll wake her!"

A series of creaks were obliterated in seconds by rhythmic thuds. Footsteps spaced further and further apart. Near silence, and then dead silence.

How far away were they by now? Far enough to risk a cautious check? I crept to the doorway and looked past its frame. No one.

One bed was tipped upon its side, revealing a rectangular gap in the intricately tiled floor. I approached the edge as quietly as I could. Wooden steps, treacherous from age and rot. Candles in two of the lamps both picked out and obscured chance details of the space below. Perhaps the gleam of a door hinge here. A dark gulf the candles failed to reach there. What might be a decorative curve on a slanted railing beyond these. More steps down?

Time to move! I crept from step to step, seeing no movement, hearing only the whisper of my cautious tread.

Half down the flight, I thrust my hand into the old woman's bag. Something hard brushed past my knuckles—the penknife handle certainly. I withdrew it and—lifting the edge of my tunic—wedged the tiny weapon between belt loop and belt.

Now for it. I took care to look down the remaining steps and listen for footsteps. Nothing and nothing. Time to catch them up before I couldn't track them.

I plunged my hand within the bag a second time. All I could feel was worn cloth and the warning twinge of a fingernail snagged in the lining. The blasted nail wouldn't come free! Nothing but cloth touched my hand and wrist! Where was the weapon?

No time! I grabbed a fistful of the treacherous lining and yanked the bag inside out. In a blink, my fingertips disappeared. Something soft and light, something I couldn't see, slid down the length of my body, past my knees and down my shins. Only my fingerless hand and the tip of one boot were visible. Beginning near my boot the lower steps and the landing were exactly as they had been. I grabbed a fistful of the garment and lifted it. The rest of my boots, the bottom portion of my trousers, and parts of two steps reappeared. Hah!

### Hunting Foxes

Trees with silver leaves lined our path on either side.

Half an hour earlier, I had followed my dozen charges through the trapdoor and then chosen the empty arch—guided only by the distant bob and sway of a lantern. I pled the One that it was theirs yet who else would be about down here besides my quarry? No light or sound had come from either the locked door or the second flight of stairs below their bedchamber.

The time since then I had spent creeping down a score of stony steps linking the arch with a narrow path, then following its turns between trees partially by feel and partially by rare glimpses of their lantern. A bit more light came from what seemed a full moon hiding behind thick clouds. Up in the king's city the moon would be just past its waning quarter.

First true forest then manicured parkland. Now a wider path rose and fell as it snaked around the bolls of silver-leaved trees.

Time to move closer to my quarry. I pulled my hood forward, adjusted the bag's looped handle about my throat and smoothed the crone's cape around me by feel. I couldn't even see the hand that did this. My other hand held the penknife.

Someone—some ones—back at the cobber's had nailed moleskin over the soles of my boots. All through the day and earlier this evening, vendors calling their wares, multiple footfalls and a myriad of other sounds within the palace had masked the silence of my tread. Their precaution might be unnecessary even now, what with the continual thuds from the princes' shoes and the rumble of their voices growing louder as I drew closer. Still, I thanked the cobbler in my heart—or more likely his guests. And the old woman of course for the gift of her cape, without which it would scarce matter whether anyone heard my tread.

Some twenty yards ahead the trees looked different. Warmer? Oh! Our liege had bidden me to bring back proof of where his sons went and what they did!

While I still walked amongst trees with silvery leaves, I caught a low-hanging twig between my thumb and the penknife's curved blade. I tugged gently and then more forcefully. Pain lanced my thumb. Slick blood between thumb and knuckle nearly lost me my grip on a two-leafed sprig. Worse, the twig gave way with a snap like a dry branch underfoot. A hard-won proof for his majesty.

"What?" from ahead.

Alarm bid me flee into the trees. I managed to stand where I was. How could they see me when I couldn't see myself?

"Father is following us! Or that woman!"

Several of the brothers laughed at their youngest.

From the head of the file, the eldest son mimicked his sibling's terrified cry, "Or father's pet! It will eat us for sure!"

"That was the snap of wood…"

"So it's the trees then? Shut up or I'll come back and cuff you, you coward!"

The youngest didn't answer but stared around him—even through and past me.

With that the eldest strode back his way. "Have you never heard an owl catch its prey?" He gripped his anxious brother's arm and hauled him forward. "Walk up here with me! I'll protect your trembling hide."

Several princes grumbled that they would be late and miss the first dance.

Another scoffed, "They never start without us, fool!"

"And what is that about..." turned into a short cry of pain. The crown prince making good on his threat.

_So dancing it is. But with whom? None of humankind lived in huge caverns so far underground!_

### The Fair Isle

The trees ahead were indeed different, sporting soft golden leaves and frail filigrees of tiny flowers. I looked ahead and considered my choices. Better at once while most of them were still amused by their brother's protests. I stood where I was until my way was marked by only the bobbing flicker from their lamp. The path had been easy enough to follow so far.

Always willing to learn from experience, I gathered up one edge of the hidden cape and wrapped it around my sore thumb as many times as I could.

Now my liege's second proof. The cloth caught on the branch tip masking it as well. Eyes closed I felt for the bit I had chosen. Gentler this time, I used the tiny blade to pluck the exquisite bit of foliage and flowers from a low-hanging branch. As before what seemed a soft and pliant stem snapped. The knife cut through only the outer layers of my tiny shield but its muffled edge pressed against the cut. Teeth already clenched I still drew in a sharp breath.

Cries of panic touched my ears. Had I fallen behind for nothing if my latest harvest still alarmed them? I hurried after my charges as quickly as I dared.

Words still spilled from the youngest prince when I drew close enough to decipher them. This time his two oldest brothers bade him act the man.

I began to like the youngest brother. He was vigilant and his theories were sensible, at least given what I knew.

That their hosts waited for their guests to arrive before they began the dance troubled me as well. They were royalty so it was fit to wait for them but they were human royalty. I doubted that their hosts were human.

Freed finally from concealing clouds, moonlight shimmered through the trees ahead, transforming their sparkle to ice on branches after a storm. Or the glittering of a thousand-thousand stars fallen from heaven's vault to be cradled in the arms of crystalline branches. Except there were no stars above us nor was that heaven's vault. Neither was that the moon I knew. Too close to the flesh of a white peach—a blood moon poorly camouflaged?

I hastened forward, I confess spurred as much by fear of the eldritch moon that moment as by the duty to which I had sworn myself. Even in battle with our most devious foes, our true moon brightened ice and revealed the brief warmth of panted breaths. The sun seared us in summer but it was our sun.

Duty demanded fresh evidence of what I saw. A small problem made me reluctant to obey--only my knuckle's pressure on my thumb kept me from leaving behind a trail of red droplets.

Spectral hounds sent out by our foes had traced us many times by blood scent.

The glittering leaves must be diamonds. No description of mine would equal the sight of diamonds hanging like sparkling fruit from a frost-laced tree. One last pinch of the knife, a stifled gasp, and the third treasure joined the others, knotted fast together in a corner of the cape.

New cries sounded ahead. A brief argument. Perhaps a scuffle.

Someone muttered urgently to let it go until later. "Surely that's their music drifting across the lake!"

I glanced toward the source of the sound and saw an isle tangled in a mass of trees and pierced with flickering light. The princes' nightly destination.

Shaped like the blunt of an egg, the isle sat low in the middle of a lake, cinched about by trees too big for its size. Tree tops formed what might in daylight be a green roof. How could any tree live down here where our sun could not stoop to enter?

Gaps in the interlaced branches—sculpted and serrated like a fortress wall—allowed squares of lamplight to shine through as if from masoned windows but no glimpse of stone betrayed hand-crafted walls within the living ring.

Half ancient trees and half fortress. The sight reminded me of my brief visit as part of an honor guard for an envoy visiting the king of the Elven Fae. Perhaps that was what the princes thought they saw.

Even the candle lamps, hung from branches in an arc, were too evenly spaced to be nature's doing—but what here was natural, as humans mean the word?

*...Crouching, we creep toward a small clearing in the forest, too filled now to still be as undisturbed as it was a week ago when we raced through it. We were in such fevered haste to catch our enemy before they dispersed, none of us guessed until now that hours before the coming skirmish, our rear guard had vanished. Would the clearing give sign of them?*

*Comrades we are hoping to find and free are staked in place-- killed swiftly but with many blows. All sharing the rigored faces of horror and disbelief except one who seems to move. I draw my dagger to end his pain, but it's just maggots crawling about, fresh from feasting on a wound that has obliterated his right cheek and eye. I fix my gaze on another victim's body and somehow manage to give sensible orders in a steady voice.*

*Eyes still dry, I turn to my remaining following, chastising them for crying aloud at the sight—loud enough to be heard by any lurking enemy. Reminding them of what we all know—that we would be dead on the instant if those we fight hear the sounds...*

Though shaken by the ill-timed memories, I disciplined my mind to mend my shattered thoughts. Did the princes think themselves dancing amidst those who lived within faerie, on a lawn close by a small castle?

Dancing and dancing, night after night and week after week. Not yet killed or even tortured in all this time. For what other purpose would their captors entice them here?

During my brief absence from the present moment, a dozen small boats had been launched and were floating from the island toward the princes. Each vessel was brightly painted and fancifully shaped, complete with the heads and wings of waterfowl or the fins and tails of leaping fish. No two were alike.

The only sound was the gloop of still water disturbed by languid strokes of a dozen oars. What beings rowed these boats our way? My memories held no shortage of possibilities. Could I, not enamored, see their true forms? I stared at each boat by turns, looking for signs of their inhabitants. In the dim light of this unnatural moon and at this distance I saw nothing that gave me pause.

By the time the boats were halfway to us, the princes had all picked out their own. Several called out greetings across the water. Someone waved—a slender hand and arm bedecked with a bracelet sparkling a dozen faerie tints in the false moon's light. The swiftest boats touched shore. Feminine hands--all adorned in some way--beckoned from each boat. The boats' decorations still obscured their faces from view.

Twelve brothers jumped each into his own boat. Each shared a kiss. I still failed to see a single woman's face. No matter. Now was not the time to ponder over their appearance. Their purpose would serve me better.

All twelve boats turned about and made for the inner shore. Cheerful chatter reached my ears. Good. Less likely anyone would hear me. I shoved the edges of the old woman's cape well into my belt and slid into the water.

Swimming kept my body occupied but it failed to fill my thoughts.

Our enemies must already guess they could keep up this deception for as long as they wished. Were the brothers being used like spies within the palace? Maybe at the beginning, but what more could those on the island glean from the same idle chatter every night? In what other way might their hosts find the princes useful?

Ransom? What would the princes' royal father do if some day he unlocked their door to find the bedchamber empty except for a message?

How long had this been going on? I hadn't thought to ask.

I rose from the water and waded toward shore between two closely tethered boats just in case my cape had shifted and some part of my body was visible. Perhaps unnecessary but why take a chance? I thought of seizing an oar as a weapon but it lacked a sharp point and I lacked a mount from which to wield it. Such a weapon was worse than none at all.

Lively music greeted me—harp, lutes, and pipes each taking their cue from softly beaten drums.

The princes and their bejeweled partners joined hands and swirled into practiced steps. On occasion one pair and then another would grace the music with a duet of lyrics. Many laughed for no reason I could see. Perhaps their laughter rose each time the musicians changed their beat? I knew little about music played for dancing nobility.

Couples danced apart only briefly--when the music called every dancer to form a large circle together, males on one side; women--or whatever they might be--together in their own arc. The great circle split into two and split again until prince and partner were free to join hands. The twelve brothers always returned to the same partner. Were those steps a test? The spell never failed to keep its hold on all twelve guests.

When the drums were at their loudest, I crept from dock to island and took shelter behind a tree entwined with garlands--and as far from any trees bearing lamps as I could manage. No plan had made itself known to me while in the water. None greeted me when I reached the tree.

Must I stand silently and watch the dancers all night, and then hurry back to their bed chamber before them? Well, yes. I hadn't been tasked with rescuing the princes from their entranced entertainment nor had I a plan to do so. If only all twelve returned to their father unscathed! I as well, with my stolen proofs hinting at where they spent their nights.

### Fair? Or Foul?

Mere descriptions of the decorated boats, the subtle fortress-like pattern of the tree branches, even the unnatural moon would not be compelling to anyone who hadn't seen them.

I stared hard at the princes' partners in the hopes of catching some hint of their true nature. Every fighter needed to know what signs to look for that revealed sorcerers or the ones who did their bidding.

The twelve showed every sign of being alive and human. The king would command me to recount every detail I could remember about them and so far I could see nothing out of the ordinary. This wouldn't do!

One thing—the princes could identify their partners from shore even before the twelve boats docked. Each prince always danced with the same partner, likely at the whim of the ones who brought them here. What could that mean?

I tried again to divine a motive I hadn't thought of earlier. What was the point of enticing them here each night, to dance like a dozen marionettes? A night or two of this might once have been amusing but hardly so now. Those who planned this wouldn't have bothered unless they had a larger goal in mind.

Interrogation? Why wait? Execution? Ransom demands? Again, why wait?

What was I missing? The brothers all knew which boat held their partners. So far as I had observed, not one thought of dancing with another.

*"They never start without us, fool!"*

*"And what is that about..."*

No other dancers. No other partners.

Not murder or ransom. What else?

To marry? That could never happen! Aside from young women who set their thoughts on a goal beyond them, who would think they could marry into the royal line? For centuries each generation of our leaders and protectors were told whom to marry by the generation born before them.

I grimaced. A noble burden that even those of royal birth must find hard to bear. How many--their hearts given to another--had chafed at the centuries old command? More than half of the twelve must be betrothed by now, no matter whom else they desired...

But in the war-guarded palace, who else would they have occasion to desire?

No. It could not be!

Once the leader believed the brothers were sufficiently enamored of their paramours, the women might ask them for marriage pledges. Would even one of them refuse?

More likely the princes would join with their eldritch partners by impulse alone. Even tonight. Why should the spell-caster delay when the brothers were so pliant in their grip?

Let it not be tonight, I pleaded of the One. The king and his enchanters could stop this but first we all needed to return safely and then my liege must be convinced.

Would my bits of silver, gold and diamond be persuasive to someone who had never seen their parent trees? All three were as hard as crafted jewels now. The princes would find a way to make light of a soldier's stolen trinkets. What would king and court make of the rest of my tale?

I could show them the door hidden beneath the prince's bed! I snorted. Yes, if it were to be found when I tried to reveal it. Their chambers must have been searched many times. I knew where the door was because the brothers left it open. Probably it was too heavy to lift from underneath.

What else could I bring back to prove the brothers came here every night? I needed something that could not be crafted in our true world or, failing that, something that might betray the nature of its owner.

I circled the festivities, taking care to keep my distance from the dancers, the musicians and the many lamps. The feral expressions of the musicians and the random movements of their hands proved them guards. A musical instrument that was not an instrument but a weapon would be proof but the guards never laid these aside--even now when the dancers drew apart. Enchanted bodies still grow tired just as shoes wear out. But fighters must remain vigilant.

The brothers drank from flame-red goblets. Their conversation was desultory, their eyes ever on their partners across the dancing green. My heart grew sore for their father.

I turned to the women, many fondling small animals and offering them treats. I rejected scooping up a pet at the height of the next dance. The women were chattering—perhaps all saying the same words one after another. Their thoughts were obviously not on the conversation but on their charges. Someone brought them cups on a tray, setting it upon an elegant table which surely had not been there minutes before. I couldn't see the servant. The slender vessels had black surfaces which failed to echo the lamps' warm flicker. What power lurked in their drinks? Surely a different something than in the men's flame-etched goblets.

One musician trilled a note upon his flute. I could well believe he clenched a dagger in his teeth though I could not see it.

Casting aside their drinks, the dancers hurried to the trodden grass circle and resumed dancing. The brothers seemed as refreshed as when they arrived.

A cup might be proof—most likely if it were a black one. I slipped wide around dancers and musicians, staying as close to the boats as I could the better not to be sensed. Strange luck or a blessing, I did not know, but no one seemed to feel my presence. Perhaps the old woman's cape helped in more than one way?

I waited on the far side of the circle until the musicians were playing their loudest, and then crept closer to where the women had gathered. Chained animals gave low warning growls—more like hunting varths than pampered dogs. Black goblets were scattered about, some nearly hidden by the untrodden plants. Not a mark on the ground!

Odder still, all twelve vessels stood straight upon their bases. Perhaps keeping safe the rest of their contents? The table and tray had vanished. I was too far away to see if the princes' goblets were upright. If someone had brought them a table, it too was gone.

The dancers were breaking from the great circle into two smaller ones. From there it would be four circles, then each couple alone. Now! I crouched by the closest cup and picked it up gingerly by just its fragile rim. It would be difficult to secret such a large object within the old woman's cape but I must find a way. The cup began gliding out of my grip thanks to a skim of blood from my thumb. So, the cut had reopened. Well, no matter. I tightened my grip on my final proof for the king.

Tension choked the air to breathlessness. The music faltered and—with it—a slip in the dancers' steps. And then a full stop. Cheerful conversations and laughter ceased. The pets' deep growls and the rattle of their chains were loud in the sudden silence.

The princes stood still, every one of them in the same pose, either agape in astonishment or held fast by a spell.

Still seated in a tight circle, the musicians now looked like guards and their instruments like weapons. Their furrow-browed eyes were on the princes, not me.

Not one of them moved from their place. No new orders? That would be remedied soon enough. Their unseen leader might be waiting to see how its captives reacted to the break in his spell.

Still enamored they would live. Otherwise, ransomed or killed.

*My followers hold to their hidden places in the circle of trees— ready to loose arrows once our would-be captors are close enough for me to give the signal…*

Cursed memories, scattering my wits at the worst of times!

*I am alone, my companions are held helpless by some sorcery a mere blink may have awakened.*

No guessing this time—I remembered none of this from combat. A drop of my blood mixed with the sorceress potion must have weakened its power. I was here wherever here was—and nowhere near that terrible clearing where we had battled to the death days ago. Weeks? Even months?

Focus. What can you see or hear you dare trust?

I risked a glance the other way. The dozen women stood in tattered gowns, faces gaunt and saliva dripping from pale lips. Sorcerers of a kind I'd never seen before. Only one of them looked all around her, even in my direction. Twice her swift gaze crossed my chest and I couldn't breathe. The cape may have turned the greater power of her gaze aside.

So she could move but she couldn't see me.

I stepped forward and dashed my heel against a slender black wine flute. A screech probed my ears and I winced. Ears still ringing, I stamped on the next vessel. Another and another, until I had crushed all those still scattered in the grass.

Eleven of the former women hobbled back a few steps and formed a parody of their dancing arc. Their true appearance turned my stomach. Stabs of frigid agony pierced me from twelve gazes—each lasting mere seconds—as they searched for the intruder.

I stood where I was lest even my soft-soled boots give me away.

The last sorceress—the one whose cup I had stolen—held her ground as well. She glanced toward the guards, no doubt about to give orders.

I held the king's proof in my fingers but what good would it serve if I died here? Clenching stem and base, I ran to the nearest tree and dashed the fragile lip against the trunk.

Just behind me, a shriek gave way to gurgling.

A man cried out, "What is wrong with the moon!"

"Fool! As if that matters! Look at our partners!"

"Are those dead bodies? Who did this to them?"

"Who did this to us?"

"Look at the musicians!"

Groans of horror and dismay.

"May the One protect us!"

"Look! There!"

The last sorceress' headless body charged me. Targeting the soft flesh under the ribs, I swept the cup's jagged edge up as if it were a small dagger. The body fell over backwards. Black-flecked blood pulsed from the ragged wound. And stopped.

*I fix my gaze on another victim's body and somehow manage to give sensible orders in a steady voice.*

*Eyes still dry, I turn to my remaining following, chastising them for crying loud enough to be heard by any lurking enemy. Reminding them of what we all know--that we will die on the instant if those we fight hear the sounds...*

*"Too late!" booms a voice.*
*Shardaki stands at the edge of the clearing, holding our struggling leader by his arms. Everyone else must be dead. Already doomed to die, we charge toward sorcerer and captive.*
*Shardaki yanks on his captive's arms. The body shatters to splinters. Crushing shards into dust beneath his boots, the sorcerer steps closer and lifts a hand.*
*Not one of us slackens pace. The last alive might yet revenge our leader...*

*The world tips, rolls on its head.*
*The forest clearing hangs above me like an ominous cloud blotting out the sun. A vice squeezes my feet together and shakes my body-- a ferret caught in the maw of a hound.*
*Fighters charge toward me with feet up and heads down. All racing to their deaths like flame-drawn moths.*
*My people!*
*"No! Run!" I shout over and over but not one of them listens.*
*Some fall—up and away toward the ground. Out of my sight.*
*I cry out. A warning? A shriek of loss? Rage?*
*The remnant doesn't falter. Every one of them strikes the bloodied ground above me.*
*Shardaki's laughter thunders about me.*

*The pressure on my feet gives way and the ground plunges down to meet me. I brace my arms and try to roll.*
*Blackness.*
*Silence.*
*Pain.*
*I struggle against the returning blackness and lose.*

*My forearms and left shoulder hurt. Feet and ankles, numb at first, throb to waking life.*
*Bodies everywhere. Only a few are the sorcerer's guards.*

*"Shenar needs help!"*
*I stagger to my feet and look for our surgeon mage.*
*Shenar is trying to staunch a woman's wound...*
*I press against his wound with my hands.*
*The blood is cold to the touch and alive with maggots.*

*Blinded by tears, I stumble between the bodies of my comrades, taking someone's shoes and stripping socks off their feet... More socks from someone else... from someone else...*
*To keep the shoes in place.*

*I must stop them from charging!*
*Instead, I turn about to join them.*
*"Too late!" Laughter comes from my feet.*
*Everyone is already dead.*

*"Go! Go now!" commands a soft voice. The voice dissolves both battle clearing and pain.*

Where am I? A forest clearing surrounded by water... An island surrounded by trees...

"Go now!" The same words as before but in a different voice.

"Wake up!" Someone grabbed me by my shoulders and shook me like a ferret. A dream. That had been my feet...

### Cold Iron

"Wake up!" The crown prince shook me by my shoulders. His brothers were gathered around us.

"We need to go now! Show us how!"

The music had stopped. The guards gripped their weapons but stayed where they were as if chained like the beasts. Still no new orders.

Had the "pets" freed themselves? I risked a glance behind me. Yes. They stood between us and the way to the boats. The last sorceress must have given them orders just before she charged me.

One of the brothers shouted, "Look! The guards are waking up!"

So they had been given orders as well but not by the sorceress. Their hidden leader must be on its way to salvage what it could.

The crown prince muttered, "We must take the guards' weapons to use on the beasts, but how do we do that when we have no weapons?"

"If you would listen to me, I just told you!" The youngest son pulled a long sturdy chain & locket out of his tunic without lifting its length over his head. He held it out to me.

"Cold iron?" I asked, already sure of the answer.

"Father gave each of us one and bid us always wear them."

One of the two men that I had finally realized were twins interrupted, "Not that we have a choice—they won't come off!"

The youngest man spoke over his brother, impatience sharpening his words, "There must be a way to do that. Our father removes his chain every evening when he locks us in. But quickly now! I think he gave them to us to use as weapons!

"Yes, cold iron can be used as weapons."

Only the youngest prince seemed to hear me.

Several brothers were staring at the musician-guards, misgivings in their expression.

"Listen to him!" Frustration and alarm together sharpened my voice.

Most of them refocused on us.

I repeated, "Listen to your brother! The movements of our enemies are still sluggish and uncertain! You're sure you can't remove your own chains? Try to remove each other's! I grasped the youngest prince's chain, and yanked it up and over his head.

"Keep talking! What must they do?"

Someone was struggling to pull off his own chain. I ripped it over his head. Seeing the ease with which the twins removed each other's chains, the other brothers helped one another do likewise.

Did the chains and lockets explain why none of them had mated with their dance partners? I glanced over my shoulder. A thought for another time. Our enemies were stirring.

Two of the princes still voiced alarm. "Our father said these were to protect us!"

I muttered, "Don't put those back on! You do need protecting, here and now, and however we can do it."

"Yes" answered the youngest, "They protect in other ways. Evil beings, and those who serve under them, will lose consciousness when touched by any form of cold iron."

Someone protested, "Too briefly to help us!"

"Briefly, yes, but…"

The youngest interrupted me, "Long enough to force our chains down their throats. Even the lockets if they'll fit!"

I interrupted him. "No. Take the lockets off the chains and clench them tight in your left fists. The chains ready in your right to strike them."

"A couple of them are starting towards us!"

"We're ready!" I lied. "The instant that you can, do as your brother said. Strike. Then the chains down their throats. Work together and help each other! Grab the weapons. No one retreats toward the boats until everyone can do so!"

"You have no chain!"

"They're all heading this way. I still have this!"

I lifted my right hand to show them the sharp remnants of the goblet's cup and stem covered with the blood of the last sorceress. A fragment of its base had broken free and cut my palm. Best they didn't know about that. I was clenching the rest of the base tight, to staunch the bleeding and to remain sure of my grip.

"Everyone ready? You've never been in combat. Keep that in mind.-"

"No, but we've had fencing practice every day since we were old enough."

How like their father! Good man! Liege. I clenched my teeth to hide a grin.

Did they understand? "Fencing isn't the same. You've never handled-"

"We use sharps."

One of his brothers interrupted. "If we live, I fear I have apologies to make not just to Father but to my arms master."

"We can avoid that if we wait much longer!" The youngest brother swirled his chain above his head like a herder's lash.

Someone chuckled. Others groaned.

"Let's go!" My leader's grumble fought a rebellious smile and lost.

### The King's Ruling

The first of the three dawn trumpets blew, out at the main gate. Most weeks, he might hear it only once or not at all. Today was different. He had been abed but awake for over an hour, after being up half the previous night reading reports from the field and from his secret observers in the palace, throughout the city, and beyond. Most of his armies had gained precious ground over the last two months or had at least foiled those who tried to break through their borders.

A few regiments reported losing control of random pockets of land—the bits likely taken by enemy commanders with the aid of their sorcerers. Centuries-old maps and other records suggested that these sites had once been seats of power for their enemies. This citadel had been built by his great grandfather on such a piece of land or so his early tutors taught him.

Keeping that in mind he had chosen to winter here, the better to investigate any phenomena that might be a sign of their enemies. A decision he regretted after his sons began to disappear each night and change their dispositions to that of defiant captives. He had thought of moving to their winter fastness after all, the better to protect his sons. But would even distance from this place break the spell on them? Or would they be drawn back here with such power they would return here alone?

What hidden evil might freely take control of this city's people if the royal court and guards left? He and his commanders needed to seek and destroy that which snatched his heirs from his protection every night before any of them dare leave.

Then there were the missing reports—the ones that had stopped arriving in the couriers' saddlebags. Nothing had been delivered from Wilderness in over a month and that woman—the latest volunteer—wore Wilderness fighters' trousers. Her eyes revealed at least as much as the missing report would have and likely more than she could remember.

If she were still alive this morning after giving him her report, he would bid her speak with him and try to tease out anything she remembered between her deployment and her arrival here—footsore and alone. He dismissed the possibility that she was a deserter, that leaving only one logical and grim alternative.

He finished dressing just before his High Steward tapped on the door.

"Come."

He would break his fast later. Right now, he needed to confirm his sons were still alive even if still ensorcelled.

The king walked into the last hall and down its length toward his sons' sleeping chamber. Every morning, he woke eager to see that they were still alive and back under his care. And every time he approached their door he dreaded to see their faces.

He removed the chain and pushed a key into the first of the two keyholes. Pausing before he turned it, he reminded himself as he always did, that his boys were under an ensorcellment. They were not to blame. He was, for not protecting them better.

He removed the key from the second lock, backed up a few steps and nodded. Two of his strongest servants shoved on the door. On either side of him, a dozen hand-picked guards and the old enchanter stood ready.

Standing within were his sons, exhausted and spattered with mottled blood. In the name of the One, what had happened to them last night?

His youngest offered him a tremulous smile.

And the woman? Anna? Behind the others, possibly held upright by the twins. Her smile, equally weak, flooded him with disbelief. He nodded toward her and would have offered her a salute but remembered at the last moment that soldiers saluted first. He shook his head and barely stifled a chuckle.

"Healers first! Then we need to talk." Lest his words be misunderstood, he looked at each one of them in turn and added, "Welcome back! All of you!"

"First before first", Anna mumbled. "The way to their lair must be blocked!"

_Ah. So there is a lair. And my sons so close to it! Forgive me! We should never have stayed!_

"Come out straightway! I'll lock the door."

Answering thirteen troubled faces, he added, "Yes, and post a squad of guards here. Those with me to begin with. Others where we are most vulnerable."

He strode forward and embraced each of the brothers in turn. How good to look into their faces and to feel the honest affection in their touch.

He was not sure he believed his own words but they needed his assurance. "I suspect we're safe from attack for a day or two. By then, a regiment will be blocking our way at every turn and door. When you are all rested and well enough to tell your tales, meet me in my large antechamber. But give yourself time first."

He grasped Anna's hand in lieu of a hug. She winced at the touch, drawing his gaze to the makeshift bandage spotted with human blood that was wrapped around her palm.

"Forgive me! Welcome back, Anna. When my sons visit me, be sure to come as well."

~~~~~

"My liege, your sons are gathered just outside the large antechamber."

The king sprang up from his writing table.

"And Anna? I mean the soldier who accepted the latest challenge?"

The High Steward nodded.

He found a place close to the inner door of the anteroom but just out of sight of the ones entering. A few of them had visible bruises and small stitched cuts. Larger bandages were concealed by their clothing. He already knew about each wound—he had known everything within an hour of each of his boys being treated.

Their expressions were grave. Every one of them seemed older. Not just from pain, he hazarded, but from everything they had experienced.

Anna's right palm was properly bandaged now but stitches and bandages couldn't repair all wounds. Someday, perhaps she would be able to reveal what had happened. In the meantime, he had ordered half a regiment to the Wilderness Ward, and two of his strongest enchanters with them.

They were waiting. He walked in briskly and nodded them back to their seats.

"Before you begin, I want to reassure you about our defenses both here and down in the city. I promised you that we would be tripping over guards at every turn. Walking full into them would be closer."

He turned to his eldest. "Now what happened? Not from the first time but what happened last night?"

The crown prince pointed to his youngest sibling, "Best to ask the one who best knows the details." He nodded towards Anna. "Or rather the two who do."

~~~~~

They talked for over three hours. Halfway through the king sent for the commander of his armies so that he too could hear everything first hand from the witnesses themselves. He had already decided to order a preemptive attack before the sorcerers regrouped but he didn't announce this.

Once they completed their account and the commander left, he spoke the words he had been longing to speak through the long discourse

Neither his sons' cast down eyes nor their cheeks flushed with embarrassment kept him from repeating his delight at having them all back safely and acting like themselves.

He warned them jovially that they would all be subjected to similar words and thanks for a very long time indeed.

"Now to another matter. Anna, have you chosen?"

The ex-soldier shook her head. "I'm at an impasse, my liege. I've come to admire your sons and particularly the youngest for devising a way to escape our captors. But we all know that I am older than even the crown prince—who is surely betrothed by now.

"For these reasons a union between any of your sons and me wouldn't be proper. Is there any other of the royal line?"

Her eyes caught his, only to flee from his steady gaze.

The king smiled.

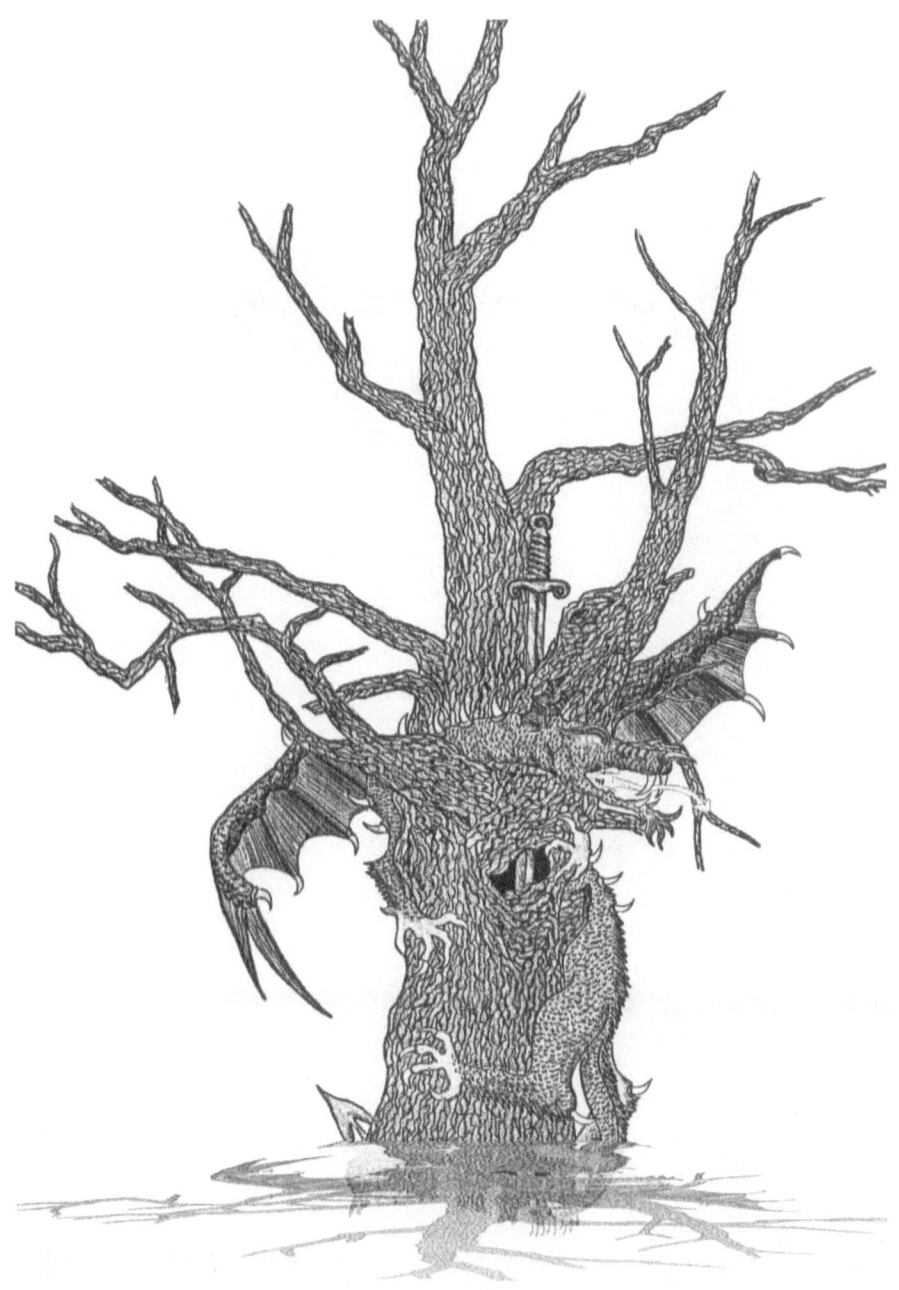

The Guarded Tree, (circa 1986)
(If the tree looks familiar, you've got a sharp eye!
If not, go back and visit the elves.)

*This marks the end of "Fantasy, Mostly"*

# REALITY, WHATEVER THAT IS

*'Reality is that which, when you stop believing in it, doesn't go away."* ——*Philip K Dick*

A Carousel Lion's Head
(sketched while visiting the Smithsonian Museum of American
History; circa late 1980's.)

## *Preteen Girls, Horses and Aliens*

In the mid-fifties, I was a preteen girl beginning junior high and I was in love with RodG and horses. The closest I ever got to dating Rod was sending him anonymous Valentine cards and standing wistfully outside his house. The closest I got to horses was riding one each weekend for a few weeks and reading books about them.

You'll notice that Rod's name isn't in the title, so we'll drop him at this point—the way I used to wish he'd drop his girlfriend, Leslie—and move right along to those horse books.

DianaF, MaryS and I read every book involving horses that we could find in the library. Our favorites were the Walter Farley "Black Stallion" books. Some of you may have heard of them. Farley seemed to share our love of all things equine, but his true focus was on the Sport of Kings. And, since he wrote about horseracing, we dutifully read about horseracing. I can still describe how best to weight the saddle of a horse entered in a handicap race and I know a little about the hoof disease, thrush. In fact, I think two toes on my right foot are suffering from it.

Farley gave the Black Stallion a good run for his money if you'll excuse the expression. Then evidently having grown bored with the horse or his humans, he began a new series about The Island Stallion. Actually, I think he must have grown tired of the humans, since The Island Stallion was really the Black Stallion, now a red bay and stuck on an island. Otherwise, it was pretty much the same horse—the fastest in the world and feral except when a certain teenager was nearby.

So, when is she going to get to science fiction? RSN.

In the first Island Stallion book, Farley had a vacationing family discover an island no one knew about --- one with steep cliffs on the exterior which gave the impression that the place was nothing but one giant boulder, stuck out in the middle of the ocean. The adults found traces of landings hundreds of years before by pirates or explorers. In the meantime, their son found a way through the rocks to the interior of the island and discovered a small herd of feral horses, the descendants of those that the sailors had left behind.

Well, after a book or two stuck on the island, Farley evidently couldn't resist getting that red stallion into a race. There was just one problem. How? No one knew about the horses and the family—now studying the artifacts—didn't have a big enough boat to transport a horse. Poor Farley was in a severe writer's bind, one of his own making.

At last, he came up with the obvious solution.

Aliens.

Yes, aliens. See. I told you we'd get to the SF.

It's been a few decades since I've read any Walter Farley books, so the aliens' reason for landing on a tiny island kind of escapes me. Actually, it probably escaped Farley. In any case, the aliens agreed to help the boy transport The Island Stallion off of his island, and even went so far as to plunk the boy and the horse down at a race track which—conveniently—was about to have a match race between the two fastest horses in the world. As in all the Farley books, The Island Stallion won the race after overcoming nearly insurmountable difficulties. Boy and horse returned to the island, and the aliens are neither seen nor heard of again not even in future books.

That last plot point was a terrible shame from my point of view. Suddenly, between one chapter of a book and the next, I was enamored with aliens and space travel, rather than horses. Specifically, what was it that did it? That old but ever new, "sensawonda" thingy. In a second rate book with a plot that used aliens strictly as deus ex machina? Yup. Let me explain.

It was the aliens' ship that did it. The only thing I remember about the aliens themselves is that they had crystal clear eyes. A problem, if you think about it, both from an anatomical and visual image point of view.

But that ship! Wow! First, it was invisible. There was something about it that made it invisible to humans. Maybe you needed crystal clear eyes to see invisible ships. More important, it was alive! Well, parts of it were alive. Some wall panels or maybe tapestries could react to strong emotions by changing their colors or patterns. In spite of this they weren't independent creatures—just part of the ship. Those panels were my introduction to the concept of biogenetic engineering. I loved it. Time travelers. Aliens. Inanimate objects that weren't all that much inanimate. What next?

I persuaded my friends, Diana and Mary, to read the book. That wasn't hard, since we were all so into horses. And, somehow or the other—the book, Farley or me—we got my friends hooked on the idea of space travel and visiting aliens.

We started a club, just the three of us. We had two main activities. The first was something that, years later, might have been called role-playing. We took turns being the pilots of space freighters and the representatives of Solar System planets and we bargained for dock space and traded commodities. This sounds a lot more sophisticated than it actually was. On the other hand, we–did—discover G7, a planet in the Solar System that no one else knew existed but us.

That was the first activity. The other was more fannish or at least more imaginative and creative. We used to envision what visiting aliens would make of mid-twentieth century culture and technology. Yes. Mary, Diana and I would sit around and muse on what someone from another world would make of American Bandstand or meatloaf.

Eventually, we branched out into discussion of time travel, since it was more fun having our imaginary "guests" marveling at the things in our day-to-day life. Westerns were very popular at that time, and they had horses, so we often envisioned the reaction of people from the 1880's to the mind-boggling tech of 1950's America. All of our guests were male and handsome. Come on! We were girls just reaching puberty. What did you expect?

I moved away from Brookside not long after this, and lost contact with both my friends. The habit of trying to envision alien reactions to common twentieth century human activities remained with me but I learned to not discuss my hobby with others. One time in high school I tried to explain what we used to do only to have someone in my class ask me how George Washington was doing today. Poor kid. He just didn't get it.

The other habit I developed as a result of reading The Island Stallion, I also learned to keep to myself—the habit of reading science fiction. I came a cropper on this pastime while I was still in junior high.

Not long after reading Farley's book, I started looking for books with aliens in the school library. (Yeah. Really. Aliens helped me look for books in the library! Giggle! Uh... Sorry.)

I found a few—books not aliens—but they were hardly classics of the genre since they were written for children. But I persevered, doing better when the family went to the public library in Wilmington. There, I found Bradbury's Fahrenheit 451, The Martian Chronicles and Something Wicked This Way Comes. I gulped down Poul Anderson's Time Patrol books whole. It was like they were made for me! I even tried to write my own Time Patrol stories. I also read Shirley Jackson's The Haunting of Hill House—one of the greatest fantasy/horror classics ever written—scaring myself into not sleeping for two nights running.

Finally, I discovered Nevil Shute's On the Beach and An Old Captivity. And that's when I got into trouble. We had a list of approved books from which to choose for English book reports. On the Beach was definitely not on the list. When I got up and gave my report on a book describing the apocalyptic end of the Earth, my teacher was not amused. Victoria herself would have been more amused. The next thing I knew my report was reported to my parents. I was in even more trouble than when my school sent a note telling them I wrote left-handed.

That restricted my official school reading for a while. I did my book reports on—yawn—approved books from the English reading list. I dutifully checked out historical novels from the public library—and—envisioned what the characters would make of twentieth century America when the government time-travel laboratory in which I worked brought them to my time and town.

But you can't keep a speculative fiction reader away from her favorite genres. I have Aunt Dorothy to thank for that. She used to bring up huge boxes of paperbacks when she came to visit us. Aunt Dorothy loved a good detective story and so did my dad. She also liked the occasional SF book and horror. So, while my dad was gathering up all of the Gardners and Queens, I'd poke around and make off with Ace Doubles like One in Three Hundred and The Transposed Man. Then Dad and I would battle over who got to read the Alfred Hitchcock short story collections first.

There's always a way. Ask George Washington. He knew how to deal with oppression.


Note
I think we're born with a longing for "the other". For some of us, reading speculative fiction of whatever variety triggers wonder—a kind of recognition of something we always hoped existed. Confronted by a story which reflects this, our reaction is, "I knew it!"

## Baffled by the Green Door

The door closes, and I turn and walk down the steps. As I start walking in the direction Marcea's mom pointed, I remember words unheeded or perhaps words I didn't want to hear at the time. The Girl Scout troop was to meet here, and then bike over to the roller rink. Our troop leader said Marcea's was the closest to the rink. I knew that. I should have known they were already gone.

Mrs. Brown knows I don't have a bike. I told her when the troop was planning the trip to the roller rink. Maybe that's why Marcea's mom looked so disapproving. Or, was she angry? Impatient? I'm not sure. I spent the time she was talking to me trying to read her face, and I spend more time now trying to understand what I saw. I stick with my first guess. Mrs. Brown told us we would bike over to the rink, so I shouldn't have knocked at the door and asked her where everyone was. That was why she looked like she did.

I stop and sit on the grass, and look for four-leafed clovers. My fingers explore the plants one by one, but I am still thinking about the situation. I want to be with the rest of my troop. Right now, they're together in the bright magic place of "The Rink". I've never been to a rink. I've heard about them. I conjure a picture of bright lights and laughter.

Then I remember the skating part, and I get confused. Why do I care? I don't know how to skate. The skates I've dropped beside me are used, but not by me. They're from Goodwill, the huge store up the steep hill in Wilmington. I've had my skates for a year maybe, but I can't use them because I can't keep my balance.

The same was true with the bike I got for my birthday. Training wheels were on it and Daddy was eager to raise them so I could balance.  But I couldn't balance. I tried every day after school for a week. I was scared and confused. Why couldn't I balance? Everyone else did it.

At the end of the week, the bike was gone. Mommy and Daddy explained that the doctor had found out, and told them to take it back. I had rheumatic fever and German measles before I was one year old. I almost died of them. Now my heart is scarred and it murmurs.  I know the words - have known them for years and can glibly pass them on to teachers.  It means I can't exercise hard because it hurts my heart. That's why I don't take gym.

But the doctor had said once -- I'd heard him say it --, "She could dig ditches. That was years ago, and she's fine now. ... Okay I'll write a new note."

The doctor must have changed his mind about my heart. Somehow he had found out about the bike, and then he'd changed his mind and warned my parents to take the bike back. I wonder briefly how he found out about it. I am almost relieved that he did. I couldn't balance and, after a week, I'd grown tired of trying.

An old Packard is racing toward my corner, its radio blaring, "Don't know what they're doing, but they laugh a lot...wish they'd let me in." The tires screech as the sedan takes a wide loop to make it around the corner. The next line of "The Green Door" I hear is, "Door slammed, hospitality's thin there." I repeat the new lyrics carefully, until I've got them memorized. They make me think of Marcea's mom.

I get up from the grassy spot with two new four-leafed clovers. We have lots in the neighborhood. Mr. McDaniel says we have experimental grass. I don't care. I'm just glad to have two more four-leafed clovers for my grandfather's New Testament. It is already stuffed and it's getting hard to find empty pages. I put the tiny leaves in my rumpled handkerchief and slide it carefully back into my pocket.

Picking up the skates, I start toward home, then stop and walk toward the shopping center. At home, I'd have to explain why I'm not with the troop, but I'm not sure I know the answer.  Besides, home would be someone arguing, or Uncle Dan smelling funny, or maybe Mommy would be having a headache.  My spirits lift a little. I don't need to be home right now. They don't know everyone left without me.

As I walk, I try to understand. I spend a lot of time trying to understand why things happen differently for me. I already know one reason. Mommy has explained it to me many times. Our neighbors and my friends are OPs. - "other people". They aren't like us. That's her explanation, but I don't understand that either. They look like us. Of course, they have stuff and they go places. But they look like us. Why are their lives so different? Why am I different? Why didn't the troop leader remember that I don't have a bike? Why did Marcea's mom look disapproving? Did I do something wrong? I told the troop leader about not having a bike. I really did. The gleam of the rink fun disappears, swallowed by a surge of guilt and hurt.

It wouldn't have been fun. Don't I know that by now? It's never fun with them. Even my best friends Mary and Diana aren't fun when they are part of the troop. They are all the same, all OPs, all the same except for Hazel and me. That is why I am the one who sits with Hazel while they have the scout meetings. Hazel can't talk properly and she hits. I wonder who is sitting with Hazel at the rink. Maybe … I'm lost for an answer. No one else ever sits with Hazel. She hurts, after all.

Brookside Boulevard brings my thoughts back to my feet. A horn blares as a car flashes by. I want to call out angrily that I was stopped, but it's gone and other cars are taking its place. I try to decide what store I will go to after I cross. I have twenty cents and I need notebook paper, so I should go to the five and ten. But first, I want to look in some of the other stores. I find an opening in the traffic and hurry to the middle of the road, then dart forward again, nearly tripping on the curb as I jump up to it. I can feel the soft throb of my heart, and I wonder what part of the sound is the rheumatic fever murmur I've had since I was one.

Girl Scouts are still on my mind, though. I decide to go to the department store first, and peek at the things in the Girl Scout display. I push through the glass double doors, so heavy I can barely open them, and then slip along the wall past the rows of clothing. Juniors and Misses look boring, with all the same colors on each rack. At Goodwill, the colors are all different on the racks. Everyone at school is wearing brown and tan and a funny green right now, just like the clothing I'm passing. I'm wearing red and a very dark purple. Yesterday I wore yellow...

Salesgirl. I slip around a rack of blouses and retreat toward the wall. I look for an opening to go to the escalator. Now. I hurry over and stand at the top, trying to get over the familiar terror. One foot lifts, but my mind says not now. I wait, as step after step glides away from me. I try again. I feel a nudge from behind and stumble onto a downward-drifting step, my heart racing. I'm scared and mad. That wasn't nice. But now the bottom is approaching and I hastily ready myself, so I don't get pushed again.

No one is at the Girl Scout display. The skinny, grouchy sales lady is with two women at the fancy food stuff. I squat down and look through the heavy glass at the badge display. When will my badges come? I love them. They are so beautiful - tiny miracles of satiny sewing. I've earned that one and that one, and that one over there.

The knot-tying one was my favorite. I used twine to tie all my knots and then glued each one to its own half sheet of notebook paper. Labeling them all carefully in my neatest cursive, I'd twisted the left corners of the pages to hold them together and given them to Mrs. White five months ago. She had made complimentary sounds, and I had smiled.

I wonder why mine are taking so long. Everyone else's sashes are covered with five and six or more badges. I have my pin but that's all. I wonder what badge to work on next. I've done just about all of the ones that I understand. Sewing stuff is out. No one in my family sews. Other badges mean going to other places to do them -- like the horse-riding. I stand up.

Horses. Someday I'll have a horse. I'll live in Ocean City and have a horse in a barn and I'll teach math in junior high like Mr. Fenstermacher. He's a nice man. He told my parents I should go to college, and that made everyone angry. I'll grade my tests out on the music pier. I'll get a big shell to weigh down the papers so they won't fly away in the wind.

"May I help you?" Strange how the woman's face seems to say instead, "What are -you- doing here?"

I stammer, "I'm just looking at my badges."

"You'll have to bring your mother and the troop leader's paper if you want to buy them."

I look at her in puzzlement but I don't ask anything. She wants me to leave, and I want me to leave. I oblige us both. The badges will come - someday. I'll be getting a bunch - all in little boxes and bits of tissue. In the meantime, the escalator is too close for comfort. I dodge away; letting several people speed up the silver stair, then I creep carefully onto the bottom step. It's easier going up - no gulf gaping below my feet.

I walk toward the five and ten, checking my money carefully on the way. Twenty cents. Two nickels and a dime. All I have left of my twenty-five cent allowance. I bought a Hershey bar with one nickel. It must be nice to get dollars like some kids do. Then you can get toys and stuff.

Cookie-selling season is coming soon. Maybe I'll sell lots of cookies and win a prize. I've wanted one of the fortune-telling black balls ever since they showed us the prizes last year. But I only sold five boxes last spring. Some of the girls sold fifty or more. They said their mothers helped, and their fathers took boxes to work. It isn't fair. Why don't my parents help? Daddy works. Why doesn't he sell boxes? But this year will be different. I'll walk all over Brookside. I'll stop at every door. Or, not. I hate trying to sell cookies. Everyone looks at me just like Marcea's mom did. But I'll do it. Maybe I'll do it. By then, maybe I'll be braver.

I open the door of the five and ten to the sound of "Green Door". It's just starting! Trying to crack the code, I listen to the words carefully.

*"Green door. What's that secret you're keepin'?*
*Watching til the morning comes creeping..."*

What -was- behind the green door? Maybe that's where OPs live.

I find the notepaper and sigh. The icky paper with the wide-spaced lines is fifteen cents and the good paper is twenty-five. I shouldn't have bought that candy bar. I don't want the icky paper. Tears in my eyes, I pick up the icky paper and then put it down. I feel the coins in my pocket, feeling, hoping, wishing for another coin to appear. It doesn't.

Someone is coming -- the old guy who owns the store. I don't leave. He's nice.

"What's wrong?"

I blink back tears and shake my head.

He persists. 'Something's wrong. What is it?"

I force the words out, "I don't have enough for the good paper." I reach into my pocket, scattering the handkerchief and a clover to the ground, and bring out the three coins. The other clover comes out too, sitting on the base of my thumb.

"Yeah, but look! You've got a four-leaf clover there!"

I shrug. He might as well have said I was breathing.

"Tell you what. I'll buy the clover from you for a nickel. Then you'll have enough for the college-ruled."

I stare a moment to make sure he's serious. His warm brown eyes stare back from his crinkled face. Other thoughts flit and are dismissed. What will my grandfather say? I won't tell. They'll never know. Mommy will have a headache or something, and they'll never know. Elation floods me, but I hold it in, taking care first that I've thought about everything that might happen. I'll come in through the carport. I'll hide the bag when I come in the door. I'll put the paper into my notebook when no one is looking. And it will be the good paper. I nod.

"Deal." He smiles and waves me to the register by the wall.

As he rings up the sale, "Green Door" ends on the radio,

*"-- someone laughed out loud behind the green door.*

*All I want to do is join the happy crowd behind the green door."*

I'd forgotten to listen to the rest of the words. I still don't know what is behind the green door. The man hands me the slim brown bag and picks up the clover from the counter with a moist fingertip. As he studies it, I ask, "What's behind the green door?"

He glances at me and shakes his head. Then, turning back, he rests his forearms on the countertop and studies me. His eyes are still kindly, and I don't mind. "Kid, the boy in that song would be real disappointed if he ever got inside that door. It's like the grass is greener, ya'know? Nothing special, except imagining it is."

I nod, sort of getting it. He nods back and grins. "Good. Enjoy your paper!" Then he walks away.

I start for home, imagining how I'll use the first sheet of paper. Probably I'll draw a horse - the one I'll have in Ocean City. And I can write down all the words I know from that song. Maybe I'll see a clue. The five and ten guy is wrong. There is something special behind the green door. The singer knows this, and so do I. Someday, I'll find out what it is, and why the door is shut.

## The End

Note

    I wrote the scenes and the narrator's thoughts in "Baffled By The Green Door" as if they all took place in less than a day. That isn't accurate. After all this time, I don't remember how much time passed from the first of these experiences to the last one. I do know that I recounted every event and every thought in Baffled as accurately as I know how—with one exception. The large department store wasn't within walking distance of the five and ten cent store. To simplify my account I resorted to some geographic jiggery-pokery.

(circa 1956)

# Fandom 101

Here's my attempt to recall the events which brought me into fandom some time back in the early 1980's. I don't remember the exact year I found out that there was such a thing as SF conventions, and I can only name one person who was at the first convention I ever attended---probably because that person was the GOH (Guest of Honor). In spite of this, I hope that someone out there might find parts of this mildly entertaining.

Back then, whenever it was, I had been reading SF and fantasy for quite a few years, but I knew only two or three other people who read anything in the field. Didn't know from cons, didn't know from fans, and didn't know from fanzines. Then, one day, I bought a copy of a magazine called The Science Fiction Chronicle. It had a cool cover illo and lists of lots of SF books in it. It had a Writer's Marketplace (alas, a feature which no longer exists in its original form). And it had a list--way in the back--of upcoming conventions.

Conventions. What a concept. The only conventions I'd ever heard of were the ones for librarians and the ones the Shriners had each year---these not being as different from each other as you might suspect, at least not when it comes to evening activities.

## I.

I registered for the convention called "DarkoverCon" partially because they were holding it only 11 miles from my home. And the local chapter of the Mythopoeic Society (fans of Inklings: CS Lewis, JRR Tolkien & Charles Williams) met in the same hotel at the same time. Not as laid back as the rest of the con, the local

Mythopoeic chapter meetings focused on my favorite authors! People met to talk about the Inklings! Who would have guessed!

On the first day of the convention, the day after Thanksgiving, I turned up at the hotel. I was ready and prepared. After all, hadn't I attended a decade's worth of Delaware Library Association Annual Conferences, plus two one day visits to the national ALA Conference?

People in business suits were streaming out of the hotel lobby as I came in dressed in my dress-for-success dress. I felt like I was going the wrong way---were we being evacuated? But it was only the power lunch folks, trying to get to their Market Street offices before the Thanksgiving Day parade started, and they <gasp> found themselves blocked from getting back to work.

A Thanksgiving Parade the day after Thanksgiving: another new and amazing concept. But in a tiny city like Wilmington, if you have the annual parade the same day that New York has the Macy's parade, no one is going to come watch, not even the mothers of the kids in the marching bands.

I went to the registration desk and found out that I couldn't check in yet, so I checked my suitcase & wandered around rather forlornly until I heard the sound of marching band music. For lack of anything better to do, I found the front exit and settled in to watch the parade. After a few minutes, an odd thing began to happen. Once in a while someone would dart right through the parade from the far side of the street to my side, suitcase in hand. Odd. Very odd.

Never doubt my powers of observation. In no less than a half hour (ok, maybe three quarters of an hour), I guessed the identity of these parade crashers. They were people heading toward my hotel (the Radisson) and to DarkoverCon. It took me a while to make the connection, because they were none of them "dressed for a convention" and they seemed to be enjoying themselves.

Having seen my umpteenth marching band and political candidate, it seemed like a good time to go see if my theory were correct. Were these strange folks my fellow conference attendees? I walked back to the hotel.

There was a line at the desk, and a couple of people in t-shirts and sweatshirts were hastily stapling pieces of paper together at a table down the hall. Something was certainly up. I got into the hotel line, did the registration thing and dumped my suitcase in the room. Then, grabbing my clipboard and pen, I scooted downstairs. Ok, Ok, so I waited impatiently and with much puzzlement for the blessed elevator to re-materialize.

Prompt elevator service at an SF/Fantasy convention was documented once by three physicists attending the science track of the con. A year later, the three jointly published a paper cross-correlating their documentation with worldwide observatory tracking of black matter and black flow encircling the Phuree Nova. The paper's title runs ten lines and I could make no sense of it. Fortunately their Conclusion is succinct, "Another anti-matter gerbil nibbling on the space-time continuum." Hate that.

By now, the lobby and its environs were well on their way into metamorphosis. People were everywhere. Nobody was dress-for-success, and the only one with a clipboard was sitting behind a table, looking harried and being besieged by a line of folks in hats, t-shirts & armor, --some of whom seemed to be speaking in foreign languages. I approached them with some trepidation. The closest ones at the back of the line came to my assistance (kindly over-looking the dress and the clipboard). Yes, this was the registration line for DarkoverCon. More people were coming to help, but they weren't there yet, so it didn't matter for the moment that I was pre-registered. So, hi! Might as well hang out with us!

I did. As I said earlier, my powers of observation are quite considerable when I put my mind to it. It didn't take me long (pretty much by the time that I reached the front of the line) to realize that the people around me were friendly and funny and warm and very, very well-informed when it came to SF. In fact, I went from briefly gabbling like an idiot, thanks to finding "people like me," to briefly being completely tongue-tied with awe at how much everyone knew about every author, book, legend, scientific discovery...you name it.

I got to the front of the line, and told them who I was. The people at the desk (there were three of them now) still looked a bit harried but they were several orders more pleasant than the people who do registration at Delaware Library Association Conferences. Meetings wouldn't begin until 6:00, and I felt at loose ends. Could I help? Sure, one woman said. You can write up people's names on their badges for them. I dragged over a chair. Ten minutes later, I found out (from a Nordic barbarian, I think) what a "badge name" was. I was crushed and disappointed---my own stupid badge now had "Sherry Thompson" written neatly across it in imperishable magic marker. Had I but known, I could have "been" my D&D non-player character, Zeerik, all weekend! Oh, well, next time.

**II.**

I abandoned the registration people in time to grab a bite to eat and to run up to my room before the first scheduled meetings. There were only two tracks of meetings (plus the video room, and the yet-undiscovered huckster's hall and art show), and I was agonizing over which meetings to go to. Everything sounded good. Even meetings with topics I didn't understand sounded good.

But before I went to my first meeting, I had to do something about my clothes. I'd brought a black leotard and black sweatpants for exercising in the evening. I switched to them, being as close as I had to what everyone else seemed to be wearing, and I scooted back downstairs.

The con seemed to have grown geometrically, yet again. The meeting rooms were supposed to be on a sort of second floor mezzanine, which could only be reached by taking the elevator to the lobby and then running up a curved flight of "floating stairs". I learned to hate those stairs in the next two and a half days. They were wooden slabs in a tight spiral, made to look as if they were floating in mid-air. Stairs and I don't get along---I broke bones in my right foot, trying (unsuccessfully) to fall down a flight of stairs. Going -up- flights I'm usually fine but, when you went up this flight, the steps at eye-level appeared insubstantial & floating as if they were in zero G. To complicate matters, people kept coming down the stairs when I was going up, and every damned one of them seemed to be wearing a long gown or a cape or both. I was convinced I was going to die on those stairs. On the other hand, those clothes were really cool. And my arms and shoulders were cold from just wearing the short-sleeved leotard. What I wouldn't give for a cape....

**III.**

I went to meetings, and talked to people, all in a wonderful trance of delight and awe. The thing that kept hitting home was how much everyone knew, and how interesting everyone was to talk to. Everyone was enthusiastic. I just couldn't get over that.

I also couldn't get over the concert by Clam Chowder. I didn't know it at the time, but they were not only singing folk music but some filk. I retrieved my tiny tape recorder from my handbag and taped some of the songs. Little did I know that would be the first of what are now several hundred tapes of filk.

At some point in the course of the evening, there was a glitch in the schedule. Someone hadn't arrived from the airport...whatever. I had time to kill. I wandered around the hallways, and discovered the Huckster's Hall. I was in heaven. Books, jewelry, clothes, some tapes (we hadn't really become a video culture yet, but there were audio tapes of something called 'filk'), books, tarot cards, armor and weapons. I wanted all of it. Oh, and did I say books?

But I -needed- exactly one thing, and I needed it right now. The hall was about to close and I had to find me a cape, or I'd freeze. I bought a rust-colored plush-velvet one with a hood, and put it on with great relief and delight. Warmth, and I "fit in" a little better. Well, the hall was closing. Back to the meetings. The rest of the merchandise would have to wait until morning.


**IV**.

With the meetings over for the evening, I decided that I really should try to find the exercise room. After all, I was dressed for it. (Well, the cape would have to come off before I started of course.) I followed the signs, until I could smell pool water, and hear singing. One was on one side of the hall; the other was on the other.

I love music. I investigated the singing first, and found that its source was something called a Bardic Circle. Some kind person on the edge of the little circle explained in a whisper that everyone took turns singing or telling stories. Oops! Not me.

I followed the pool smell, and found my way into the Jacuzzi room. A couple dozen fen were either in the water, or in lawn chairs close to the pool side. The exercise room was beyond them, and it was dark. I didn't care. I plunked myself down in a chair and hung out. Some of the faces I recognized, and others were new, but everyone seemed to have the same characteristics. They were really friendly and really knowledgeable. I just sat and listened, and said a little when I didn't feel like I was making too much of a fool of myself. Honestly, it seemed like even the teenagers knew more than I did. That was really just too much. I went and got me a drink to fortify myself from the shock, bringing it back with me, lest I miss anything. Later on, I found out there was beer in the room.

A little while later, the members of Clam Chowder came in & joined us. People got set up to "sing madrigals". As it turned out, this was shape-note singing, or four-square harmony. I can't read music. I went over to the soprano section, and pretended I could read music. We sang for a while.

Someone suggested that we sing The Hallelujah Chorus. We didn't have the music to the Hallelujah Chorus. Undaunted, we started singing it from memory and got ourselves trapped inside. I'll bet you didn't know that could happen. Neither did we. But there we were, exhausted from a more than full day and still ~~awake~~ up in the middle of the night, and trying our best to sing our respective parts from memory---with a lot of us having no memory left at all. After a few thousand "hallelujahs" in a row, someone shouted over the din that we were lost. Maybe if we tried again from the beginning we could do it! No, we couldn't.

That broke the spell. We stopped singing, and went back to talking. Some of the Clam Chowder members packed up for the night, but I seem to remember a couple of the other ones getting into the pool.

I don't remember going to bed. I may have sleepwalked back to my room but hopefully not by way of the floaty steps.

("Madrigal singing" was always a part of the late-night fannish activity at DarkoverCon. It wasn't filking. That was in a separate room. I've never seen this phenomenon at any other convention I've attended. Interesting thing is that, for all its name, I don't think we ever actually sang a madrigal. For the most part, we sang "Sacred Harp" or shape note singing.)

**V.**

Saturday morning, more than a little comatose, I went off in search of large amounts of caffeine. I found it at the restaurant's breakfast buffet. It was crowded with people, still trying to wake up---at 10:30 or 11, I think. I sat with a bunch of other people, and we yawned our way through breakfast.

Some of the more enterprising amongst the group shanghaied the rest of us into agreeing to meet in the lobby at dinner time and driving to the Royal Exchange to eat.

I went to meetings all day long, ducking into the huckster's hall when there was a lull, and discovering the art show. I decided that next year, I'd have my own pictures in the art show (and I did too.) In the huckster's hall, I got myself into ten kinds of financial trouble, with books. I also fell in love with a dagger, decorated to look like an antique Egyptian weapon. I bought it and the sheath, and then realized I needed a belt on which to attach the sheath. I bought a tooled leather belt with a dragon design on it. That meant I needed a belt buckle. I bought one with an engraved gryphon on it. While I was at it, I bought a holographic pin, with a design that was reminiscent of the swirl of matter around a black hole. I had officially become one of the SF conference serial boughter fen. The fact that I was now in what I would have considered a Halloween costume only 24 hours earlier didn't even register. I was finally dressed properly. Back to the meetings.

That afternoon, I met Marion Zimmer Bradley. She walked. She talked. She was a real live breathing person. She signed a couple of my books. She was the GOH, and she talked to us all, and answered questions after her speech and I was utterly charmed with the whole idea. Later in the day, I went to a panel at which she was a member, and watched several other authors discuss wonderful and exciting things with her. I don't remember what. It didn't matter. This was so -different- from the library association meetings!

I hooked up with the breakfast group, and we drove to the Royal Exchange, a very nice Branmar restaurant which, alas, is no more. One of the coolest things about it was that all the walls were covered with books. It was like eating in a library. We ate, drank, generally stuffed ourselves, laughed ourselves silly, and poked sly fun at all the stuffed shirts around us at the other tables. Then we raced back to the car and back to the con, in time to attend the small "Costume Call". I vowed that I'd be in it the following year---and I was.

## VI.

I was going to go back to the Jacuzzi and hook up with the people from the previous night, but someone told me that the writers and artists were going to be up in something called the Con Suite. So I went there instead. It wasn't the "reception" I was half-expecting to find, but it -was- an excellent choice for a night of relaxed socializing.

Two images remain indelibly impressed on my mind. The first was listening to MZB and a couple of other people discuss the relative merits and strategies of their favorite pro-wrestlers. Marion was incensed about the way one man had treated another in the ring. I sat with mouth a-gape. This intelligent woman---mother of a son, writer of many books, editor and co-founder of a writers' commune of some sort--- believed in pro-wrestling. Alternatively, I was so drunk that I was hallucinating. The second alternative seemed the most comfortable.

Second image: I remember sitting on a sofa with someone named Paige Lewis (Say what! I remember a fan's name, after all!) We had been sitting talking for an hour or two, while various parts of the gathering kind of swirled around us, and different people joined our discussion or brought over discussions of their own. Suddenly, a young man dressed in medieval attire knelt in front of me, in the attitude of a suppliant. He whispered, "My lady..."

Paige and I exchanged glances of bemusement. The gentleman bowed his head, and remained in his position. Paige whispered to me, "I think he's proposing." Charmed at the mere thought (he was reasonably cute), I leaned down to offer some encouragement...and discovered that my courtier was asleep. Or unconscious. We let him sit like that for a little while, then gently tipped him toward the front edge of the sofa, lest he fall over suddenly and do himself an injury.

## VII.

The next morning was also the last morning. I was one of the walking dead from the first meeting through the dead dog concert. I found Paige again in the huckster's hall, where she was working a table which sold what I took to be "fanzines' for the next decade.

They were actually fanfic, collections of stories and songbooks written by fans, inspired by the prominent SF and fantasy in the field. Most of the table's contents were Darkover or Trek tie-ins, including something called "slash." I didn't find out the identity of "slash" until years later.

Eventually Paige became part of my D&D group, but I never made any permanent connections with anyone else at that con. More's the pity! It all boiled down to a lack of money and a lack of transportation. Still does, sad to say. If I could meet with fans every week, I'd be delighted. I used to see Paige at Philcons on occasion, even after she dropped from my group but I don't think she attends cons anymore due to her health.

### VIII.

The following day was a Monday and a work day. So why is there a part VIII, you're asking? Read and see.

I went into work, completely exhausted and completely jazzed by my experience. I didn't want it to end. I didn't want it to ever end. I walked into my office, and decided that the room was really cold, so I might as well leave my cape on.

Two days later, Jon Penn (my supervisor at that time) asked me gently when I was going to stop "going native" and go back to wearing blazers and cardigans to work, instead of capes.

Oh. Damn. I took it off sheepishly, and put it into the out-of-season closet at home. Ready for next convention season. What a shame that, when you have no money and no wheels, convention season comes so rarely.

And I began planning for my next con. I'd do artwork, and have it on display. I'd plan a proper costume and enter the contest. I'd save money for more books. I'd read lots and lots more books and SF magazines, so that next time I wouldn't feel like the stupidest person at the con.

And, maybe, I'd be brave enough to join that Bardic Circle filking thingy. Nah. That was going too far.

Written in 2000 for the single issue of my fanzine, "Stuph".

## How I Learned to Hate Telephones

When I was in junior high, the only person who every called me was Diane Fields—one of my two best friends. I enjoyed her calls—the last ones I would ever enjoy.

In high school Richard Wilson would call me but we rarely had a normal conversation. Richard preferred to recount the plot of whatever science fiction book he was reading. My family only had a wall phone so I stood in the kitchen holding the phone in silence while he recounted the plots chapter by chapter. I had a crush on Richard but this was not fun.

My early education about telephones wasn't so much hands on experience—more thanks to a chapter in Clarence Day's charming, Life With Father. Clarence Day's essay, "*Father Lets in the Telephone*" may have set the tone for my attitude about the pesky gadgets.

Here's what Mr. Day Jr had to say about the early phones and Father,

"When the telephone was invented and was ready to use, hardly anybody cared to install one. ...a telephone might ring every week."

"After ten or fifteen years ... [Father] got one [for the house]. ...Everybody could hear its loud bell. ... It seemed to us rude and intrusive, and from the first it made trouble. It rang seldom but it always chose a bad moment. ...Father .. met these invasions with ferocious resentment. ...There was nothing he could shake his fist at but a little black receiver..."

My dad wasn't the fist-shaking type. However when the phone rang, I think he said words under his breath he had learned while in the Navy in WW2.

That was the first seed.

My mother dealt with the phone when at all possible. Mom was fine with phones and took to both tape recorders and microwaves immediately. VCRs were another matter. I explained that VCRs were really just fancy tape recorders but she wanted no parts of them.

Mom's adamant refusal to upgrade tech planted the second seed.


But back to my dad. I never realized how much he loathed telephones until the day the family went to see the 1967 satire, "The President's Analyst". James Coburn plays Dr. Sidney Schaefer, the personal psychoanalyst of the President of the United States. After a while, Sidney quits because the gig is making him too anxious.

Everyone--especially everyone in the espionage game— wonders what top secrets Sidney might have learned during his chats with the president. Now that he's no longer under the indirect protection of the president's secret service, they all go after him. He isn't paranoid. Everyone really is out to get him.

All through the rest of the film—between being chased, cornered, escaping & having bizarre conversations with various agents both foreign and domestic—Sidney tries repeatedly to call for help. Always without success. He's cornered once more near the end of the film. Defeated but curious, Sidney asks his captors which country or government agency they represent. Answer: they're the phone company's secret agents.

Sidney isn't surprised. "You know, one thing I learned from my patients... they all hate the phone company. It's interesting; even the stock holders of the phone company hate the phone company!"

My father grumbled, "I knew it! Of course it was the phone company."

Vindicated at last.

I'm my dad's daughter when it comes to phones and their parent companies. And my mother's when it comes to ~~over-complicating tech for no good reason~~ upgrading cell phones.

Exhibit One: My long feud with Verizon re billing for services not rendered. When I could get nowhere over several months and dozens of telephone calls—like that's a surprise—a friend kindly accompanied me to a Verizon store.

Twice.

We really thought we had the billing all straightened out that first time. And the second time.

Conceded, the second visit proved successful with the billing problem. But when I got home, Verizon had closed my email account. Hundreds of saved messages were gone forever. Incompetence? Revenge? I'm betting on the latter. Somewhere a memory cell was giggling.


Exhibit Two: I bought my first cell phone via Verizon in 2008 not long before smart phones took off. It was the dumbest of dumb phones but it was smarter than me. Sometimes it deigned to give the signal for an incoming call & sometimes not. Nor did I have any guarantee of success with an outgoing call.

The critter did know how to yell loudly to be recharged, especially in quiet places with no outlet handy. Most frequently it chose to announce its hunger on days when I was serving as a docent for 1$^{st}$ & Central Presbyterian Church's meditation labyrinth. I've never understood how phones can yell that loud when they're out of power.

My next cell—a true smart phone and not from Verizon—had some of the same foibles as the original. I was ~~almost~~ afraid to use it.

Once when I was trying to make a call, a message came up on its screen, "Are you sure you want to change your Operating System?"

Ack! No! No! I panicked. Now what? What dare I touch to tell the phone, "No! Please don't do that!"

I look back on that terrifying moment and wonder. Maybe I should have said, Do that! Change your OS for all I care!

Yeah, I missed my chance. That's probably how you exorcize cell phones.

178

"Lania's Tree"
Lania is a Young One character in "Narenta #2: Earthbow"

## "A Fannish Internet Sub—Creation of a Hyper dimensional Pocket Universe"

To Speculative Fiction Fen & All of the Fannish Persuasion:
The time has come to pass on the secret of

## The B5 Cygnets' Couch and Weekend Retreat

Joe started it when he created Babylon 5 because creating the show created B5 fandom. God had a little something to do with the next part because He once created a round planet with time zones and people living such distances apart that they were in different countries.

Then the Brits or maybe it was the Americans got stubborn about having -their- kind of series TV, beginning and ending according to -their- schedule. Between a whole bunch of time zones and discrepancies in the beginning dates for seasons for the same show--depending on pond-sidedness--SPOILERS were born.

Some of the Brits weren't very hospitable toward some of the Americans because we got to see episodes first. They said we would tattle secret stuph at them and that we should leave until -they- were the ones getting newer episodes than we had seen. That made the Americans all droopy and sad until PAT SWANN came along and rescued us and said she would be our Swan Mommy. (Get it? Swann--swan?) So we became B5 Cygnets (Get it?) and hung out on Jay's server "deepthot" which wasn't Babylon Five's Great Machine tended by the ten Zathri twins—but which, you'll have to concede, was pretty close.

The Cygnets' only official rule was "Be Nice." Everyone knew though that it really meant, "Be nicer than those Brits were to us."

or maybe it meant, "Be nice and don't write down Spoilers in your email unless you put a warning at the top, and then put a whole bunch of Spoiler Space after it because, if you forget to do this List-Momma will send the Narn Bat Squad after you."

And things went tickety-boo or maybe bubble-and-squeak (but probably not) for a long time. Until one day or night--depending on your time zonedness--someone who may or may not have been W/e/s did a not-nice thing. Oddly enough no one's feathers were much ruffled. Not even the Narns in the squad but that may have been because they have scales. Every Cygnet in the group sent shruggy emails to dismiss the whole s/h/a/m/e/f/u/l harmless email--except for W/e/s who simply couldn't get over his embarrassment.

Our very contrite W/e/s reported that he could henceforth be found under the couch since he could no longer face any of us. We humored him for a while, and then a few of us became concerned for his welfare. Others (perhaps) became remorseful for gloating when the Narn Bat Squad tramped past.

Someone--no one remembers who now--someone knelt down at the edge of the couch and suggested that if W/e/s looked around surely he would find something soft to sit on. W/e/s thanked them and reported that he had indeed found a very comfortable overstuffed chair covered in leather of the kind once popular in only the finest men's clubs.

Another Cygnet asked if W/e/s were thirsty or hungry. W/e/s reported that the waiter had long since arrived asking his choice amongst champagne, hot chocolate, iced tea, espresso, a hot toddy, or chicken soup--and that he was at that moment looking at the menu.

Waiter? Menu?

Suffice it to say that those were the last solitary moments W/e/s enjoyed Under the Couch.

We found him seated by a fireplace in one snug corner of a beautifully-appointed chamber. Zathras... No, not that Zathras! Zathras! Zathras were just walking in with one of his brothers. They seemed to have anticipated our arrival because both of them were carrying trays of beverages while simultaneously pushing carts laden with covered dishes of food.

We were still trying to get over our shock when several more of the Zathri struggled toward us pushing handcarts laden with a wide variety of comfy chairs. Another fireplace sprang up in the wall twenty yards away from the first one, and carpeting seemed to grow out of the marble floor like mauve grass.

(It was really weird carpeting! We had Zathras. You know, not that Zathras, the other one? ...we had him send it back to The Great Machine for reprocessing.)

Well, I could go through of the stages of discovery that we went through but I don't want to take away from your pleasure. We had so much fun; we created a separate list just for events, architectural modifications and guests Under the Couch. With a couple of dozen of us keeping all the Zathri and much of the resources of the Great Machine at work, there were a -lot- of modifications!

And of course, the Zathri often anticipated us. We would find new and marvelous or even bewildering surprises on each return visit. A few went back to the Great Machine for reprocessing, plus once in a while we had to explain human aesthetic tastes one more time to a Zathras but, all-in-all, it was grand waiting to see what they would come up with next.

After a while, someone--alas, I can't take the credit--someone hit upon the idea of adding a private wing to Under the Couch so that he/she could entertain visitors of the literary or media variety. WE had already been throwing parties for various groups virtually from the first day we trooped into Under the Couch--hence the need for 6 saunas, only two filled with actual warm water, etc.

This person had other plans.

The Zathri assured us that Under the Couch was hyper-dimensional so, even though we numbered over 20 fen, The Great Machine would have no difficulty adding that many wings to the structure. Even better--we discovered quite by accident--it was possible for more than one Cygnet to plan a quiet evening with exactly the same character as someone else.

No, it is not at all the way it sounds --unless you want it to be.

I could add numerous descriptions but they are from the Cygnets' Under the Couch. To tell you about them would only limit your own discoveries. Besides I doubt very much that the Zathri really want to work on exactly the same projects all over again. I think I hear ten echoes of a groan. Yeah. I thought so. They -love- making up little surprises.

Oh, one thing in case you don't think of it? That hyper-dimensional quality means that Under the Couch is simultaneously near the ocean and the mountains and the desert and Ursa Major and... Well, you get the idea. Do try to group similar wings together. Because it's easier on the human psyche? Maybe. Mostly, it's more energy-efficient.

Enjoy!

**SherryT, a Founding Member of Under the Couch (and of UtC-Anonymous)**

### Comments from the original Live Journal entry—June 13th, 2008

"Hugs to all for being here, lo, these many years!"

Hear! Hear!
We do keep going.

(Sh. I think one of the Zathri may actually be the Energizer Bunny. Or vice versa)
SherryT

(Anonymous)
11 years and counting :)
The most lasting, friendly, accepting and sane group I've ever had the pleasure to associate with. I've got Zathras whipping up a special batch of Heart's Desire* for a celebratory toast.    (* Whatever drink you most want it to be, from moment to moment)

tree_lady
Re: 11 years and counting :)

Hear, Hear! Again.   -Up to the word "sane" anyway.
Sigh. How soon they forget.

I've got Zathras whipping up a special batch of Heart's Desire*...

Ooh! My favorite flavor--variety!   SherryT

# Sherry's Cake is Major Hit at Coffee Hour!  Film at 11!

I finally made the blueberry cake I've been planning for church coffee hour. I do not do homemade. With rare exceptions, I find the results of mixes every bit as good as most people's from-scratch recipes. What do I do instead?

### The secret of my blueberry cake in just 26 easy steps

**1**. Become enamored of a tiny container of dried blueberries. Buy & take home.
**2.** Become filled with anticipatory guilt at the thought of eating said container in the course of one evening, especially given the price. **3.** Resolve to save the container for something special.
**4.** When nothing special comes to mind, go to the store and buy one Quick Bread mix of the blueberry persuasion (I wonder what persuaded it to do that?) and one tub of whoever's frosting as long as it says something like creamy.
**5.** Start with a lasagne pan that will manifestly be too big, but switch in time to the smaller sized pan. Mix the mix with ingredients as listed for the alternative recipe (muffins?) which calls for oil. Add a tiny bit extra oil (scavenged from the bottom of the too-large lasagna pan). **6.** Refrain from mixing until every last lump has been obliterated. **7.** Pour stuff into small lasagna pan. Time travel back to beginning to preheat oven to 375. Put pan in oven. Close door.  **8.** Open dried blueberry container for the first time and panic at how hard those little bug... blueberry knots are.

**9.** Open frosting container and mound dried blueberries precariously on top of frosting. **10.** Confronted by the disaster just begging to happen, find old and bent tomato-slicer (very narrow & long blade). Circumspectly and slowly, fold most of the dried blueberries into the top half of the frosting, in the hopes of moistening them up some.

**11.** Eat any dried blueberries that resist the operation, except for the ones that fall on the floor and commit suicide under your bedroom slippers. **12.** Remove cake after a half hour, and marvel that it didn't burn. **13.** Wash greasy large lasagne pan.

**14.** When the cake is finished cooling (or shortly before that) carefully tip the small lasagne pan over and allow the cake to drop gently unto the middle of the larger pan. **15.** Fuss, fume & otherwise express yourself as you assemble your 3-dimensional cake jigsaw puzzle into something roughly cake-shaped.

**16.** Forgetting where you left off, dump all of the frosting unto the top of the cake. **17.** Go, "Ack!" and desperately try to blend blueberried half of frosting with blueberry-free half of frosting. **18.** Glop frosting around until little glubbies have started over the edges of the cake. **19.** Look at watch. Scream in panic. **20.** Grab plastic wrap in one hand and aluminum foil in the other and try to wrap cake and pan with both simultaneously.

**21.** Get the darn thing safely to the church kitchen. Cut it. Resist much advice involving shifting it all to a tray, and all but smack the hands of people who try to do so. **22.** Listen to people bemoan the lack of paper plates, **23.** Go to church service, and forget all about cake.

**24.** Join with others in fellowship hall, taking care to get a piece of best friend's coffee cake (excellent!) **25.** Be surprised when a couple of people come past and praise the cake.

**26.** Get embarrassed when two people ask for the recipe.

## EgoBoogling, or The Funnest Way For An Author to Ditch Writing

I was EgoBoogling this past Thursday when...

You don't know what EgoBoogling is? You should. Not only authors, artists, actors but internet users in general are susceptible to the disease.

When hungry for fame currently not generated by my books, I seek "ego boost" elsewhere. And in the 21st century, that ego boost comes from searches for my name or my book titles on Google. (Also Wikipedia, Amazon book reviews, Goodreads, The Library Thing, and various social nmedia.)

### Ego boost + Google = Egoboogle.

Tell me you haven't done this. Not briefly in passing, before or after a legitimate Google search? Not at least been tempted?

Thought so.

Last Wednesday a writer friend—who has never mentioned succumbing to the temptation of indulging her innocent curiosity—was having trouble EgoBoogling. She asked for ideas.

Her search rate efficiency was in the cellar because her last name tends to bring up false positives regarding a popular TV show. I gave her a few pointers in the efficient use of Google's Advanced Search parameters and sent her off as happy as a clam.

Wait. Are clams...

Never mind. I refuse to Advance Search "clam" plus "happy".

As misplaced karmic reward for my kind deed, I was immediately bitten by the faunching for fresh EgoBoogle. I gave in the following day.

When you EgoBoogle--unless you were blessed with a distinctive moniker like "Demaris Q. Khalumphek", author of "Zotz"—your search will bring up lots of false positives just as it did for my friend.

Having to wade through ten screens for just one mention of your name or the title of your latest work can be seriously EgoFlating—the opposite of EgoBoogling. We don't need this. Bad reviews, no one showing up at our bookstore signings, or a form rejection to a query email popping into the Inbox an hour after we hit Send all produce more than sufficient EgoFlating.

A carefully refined Google Advanced Search can eliminate at least some of these irrelevant search responses.

But sometimes it's more fun—and more of a time well taking you away from actual writing—if you just put in your name and see what turns up. Since I wasn't doing anything important anyway—just revising this manuscript—I opened up two screens at Google Advanced Search and went at it.

Why two screens? Well, with one I set up my usual EgoBoogle --my name plus detailed parameters for Google's software to focus on or to ignore. Since I didn't have a good idea for today's blog entry, I opened the second screen and input a simple search for my name.

A name as semi-common as Sherry Thompson brings up all sorts of alternative people—just ripe for becoming fictional characters. See? I was working!

I found many familiar alter-egos searching on Google using just "Sherry Thompson"

For instance, I've long been a:

Librarian at Flower Mound High School. (I was a librarian, but not there) Who calls a school "Flower Mound"? I pity their football team...

Staff of the FBC Student Ministry...

Communications and Program Manager in Omaha. I had a great-uncle who lived there...

Yawn.

Owner of the website "Hooked on Stamping". (I must be very conflicted. I never have seen the point of buying an expensive stamp and a stamp pad, so I can make the same design hundreds of times.)

Wow! Here's a new one. "Bill R. Thompson (born 2 April 1949) is a former Australian rules footballer who played in the Victorian Football League (VFL) during the late 1960s. Nicknamed 'Sherry', Thompson spent three seasons playing with Essendon..."

I frequently run across two alternate world Sherry Thompsons, one of who are a deputy sheriff in the Midwest often giving statements to the press and a lesser-known prosecutor. These ladies should get to know each other. Maybe they are each other.

I once was an executive for a cosmetic company but she disappeared. Hopefully not literally!

I'm also a champion female body-builder. Looking in the mirror does not confirm this. Looking at her photos makes me kind of glad.

I used to be a professional clothing designer and made the costumes for "Blossom". Based on her numerous entries, I'm still memorable. Just not to me. How many years ago was that show on?

Speaking of blossoms, I'm involved with the White Charity Blossom of Nebraska which supports nonprofits.

Is there a secret connection between the TV show, the charity and that high school? You're right. We're better off not knowing.

When it comes to artsy Sherry Thompsons, I drew the illustrations for "Our Parade", "What is Love?" and "Spring". To this day and in spite of protests, Amazon conflates my books with hers. Goodreads is only fooled by the book titled, "Spring".

I'm a realtor and a mother with a crazy YouTube video that you can screen. See, I can prove it!

Try Google Images, and you'll find I'm a master of disguise. Now try to find a picture of the real me.

I've died at least once and have mourned the death of someone in the family several times—usually with my husband who keeps changing his first name. What's –that- about anyway? On a happier note I've been married several times. Wait! That can't be right! I don't remember any Google references to divorces. Oh, no! I'm a polygamist! Why did I never notice?

Not to worry! I probably have this multi-marital oversight well in hand since I'm a California divorce lawyer.

As both an animal health technologist and a family practitioner, I save on rent by having both practices in the same office suite. Not to worry—we have two waiting rooms. Yes, we're the ones who gave a toddler a shampoo and put a blue kerchief around his neck. The parents were quite put out. I'm not sure why--their little boy had a blast. Maybe it was the kibble lollipop?

Appraiser, freelance designer, Texas yoga instructor... I work for Kahlo Chrysler, Jeep, Dodge. I'm also part of the Firefighter Nation.

I'm a member of Bayou City Women Bikers. What kind of bikers are we?  Yeah, about that. Is there any connection between my biker street-creds and the time I was booked into the Okaloosa county jail?

I resigned from the District Office Staff somewhere in Australia—probably because the commute to all my other jobs was just killing me. Which explains the obituary notice.

BTW, my targeted EgoBoogle search last Thursday turned up not one new mention of the real me. Whoever she is.

~~~~~

p.s. I come to you ~~hat~~ mouse in ~~hat~~ hand asking for assistance with my EgoBoogle. If you like at least 51% of this book, please consider writing a review or a blog entry about it.     Thanx!

## *Catzis #1*

Cat holidays are coming! Soon we will be celebrating the day that Khiva the Siamese came to live here (two years ago) and the day that Vartha the Maine Coon was born (just one year ago).

Khiva and I agree that Vartha is still such the kitten. Ah, older and wiser furry heads would know. Not.

I've seen this before, but I didn't mention it because I thought I was reading human motivation into cat behavior. But now...

Khiva likes sitting in my lap for long periods of time, and she frequently take naps while she's there. Here.

Vartha will pop up to say hi and get a nice head rub but she's just not into lap-sitting as a pastime. Like I said, she's still very much the kitten. Often Vartha seems to be trying to dislodge Khiva when she's sitting on me.

I always figured she's tempting Khiva to come down and play with her. When this happens, if Khiva looks content, I try to persuade Vartha to lay off by waving something to distract her, preferably something that crinkles or rustles. Normally, rustling things work like magic on Vartha but not when Khiva's on my lap.

I've always interpreted the whole scenario as childlike kitten disturbing the contented adult cat when she's all comfortable.

The other day I paid attention.

Vartha kept reaching up and trying to snag Khiva's tail under her paw. I warned her gently that that wasn't nice and I tried to cup my palm around Khiva's tail lest she wake her up.

Khiva appeared more than half asleep. She was sitting very still but she had her head tilted so she could look down at Vartha.

Any time, Vartha looked about to wander away, Khiva would flick her tail. Vartha would zero in on it, of course, and try to pin it under a paw. As soon as Khiva saw her start to make the attempt, she whisked her tail up and out of the way.

Then she lowered it very slowly, and waved it lazily about-- practically in Vartha's face. As soon as Vartha's attention was focused, Khiva flicked her tail more quickly, all the while looking over her shoulder to be sure of her aim. Then, snatch away, before Vartha could get a firm grip.

I thought I heard purr-chuckling.

Lapsang Souchong, aka "Squeaky"
asleep on the arm of my lounge chair.
(circa 1998)

## *Catzis #2*

Mee-ow! ("My turn to post!")

Vartha:  Our human keeps macking scribbles on here.
Sometimes she mackes scribbles on papper about how shees going to write about us but then she doesn"t, so Im going to right and tell you while she isn't hear...

Khiva: WE are going to write.

Vartha:  I was saying...

Khiva:  Kitten! You didn't even say who our human is.

V:  Don't call me "kitten". And they no already our human. I'm a year old now. I'm as big as yu.

K:  Are not! And you mispelled "you"!

V:  Oh, yeah! Look at what you just did!

K:  What! What did I do?

V: Hah! Fooled her gen. (whisper-scribbles: She frade all the time, even frade do something

K: I not afraid of laps! I sit on laps! Be warm. Sit on hard flat place is not being a cat. No anyone sit on hard cold TV trays? I do.

V: (whisper-scribbles: Honestly, big hssters are bossy and ... spearior.

K: Oh, go play in a box! (whisper-scribbles: She such the kitten. Always getting into boxes and bags. She thinks our humans favorite carry bag is cat bed our human gave her. Dim...

V: Hay! Don't you call me dim-blub, wise-tail! Two ears old, still done understand how to get behind curtins and up on window sill.

K: I prefer the window in the bedroom. YOU still don't know how to ask for special food! Every day, I have to ask for both of us.

V: It's compilcated.

K: (Sigh.) Left front paw on knee. Serious stare. How hard is that?

V: (Pouty) I've been trying.

K: You been using our human like scratch post, moron. It's not the same thing!

V: Hah! I no what I'm doing. I do the pritend scratch post, and the human yells pritend. Then she pets me. Just like uh kitchen.

K: We're not allowed in the kitchen!

V: That's all you know. "Not loud in the kitchen." You get caught and all yu no to do is RUN. Your twice my age and stil dont no how to work that?
Go in the kitchen. Human yels. Run into dinning room and jump on he file box! I do that. She pets evry time! Yu think I always want to snif around the kitchen? Sometimes I want a nice fur rubb.

K: I no... I mean I -know-. Look what you've got me doing! I know how to get patted! I even know how to get my jaw rubbed or my tummy rubbed. Whichever I want...

194

V: Dont want my jaw rubbed! So how wet is water, huh? Wanna tel them how wet is water? Is water two wet for Siammeze's delicate fur?

K: Cats don't like to get wet. I don't know what YOU are.

V: A Maine Coon cat, for the fiftith time! We lov water. Where not es-scared of it cause we got long thick fur.

K: Like duck feathers. (chuckle-purr)
And fur on bottoms of paws, too. Human sings bout your paws. Yu so pat-happy, don't notice rude song! "You gots fur on bottom of paws. Ona bottoms of your paws! Uh bottoms of your paws!"
Why yu skid around corners. Mean INTO corners.

V: I'm all SOFT. That other human said so the other day. Sais she liked patting me. You hid. Again. But I'm soft with all the fur and everyone wants to pat me.

K: Not for long.

V: Whatz that meen?

K: I heard what other human said. Smuch fur make you too warm in summer. You should be clipped...

V: No-oo!

K: Yee-ees! She's going to make you all thin here and thick there, like a poode puppy.

V: (dances sideways) That's a lie! Take that back!

K: (tip of tail twitching) I know what I know.

~ ~ ~ furry-blur ~ ~ ~

Pounce!

Hey!

Stop that!

Oh, want to play rough?

Got your tail!

Don't care! I stand on your tummy!

Not if I pounce your head first!

Wait! Wait!! Your ear's dirty!

What? When? How?

Sh. Calm. I fix it. (licking) Better?

Uu-um. Purr. Thanks. Ooh, that was close! I hate dirty fur emergencies!

Here. Let me freshen up that left shoulder. Half the fur is askew!

Purr. Thanks, sis!

What I'm here fur.

A Collage Made From The Leaves I Collected in 2005.

### Rainstorm Coming

I love that unmistakable change in the air
Little puffs of cool sneaking here and there
Into the dank hanging air.

Big rains are best during the day when I can see
The clouds on the horizon darken to a slightly
Yellowish-gray that's like a surreal sunset.

Watching them roll in.
Hearing the rumbles in the distance.
Was that one a distant plane or the real deal?

Then the glimmer in a far off cloud, the long wait,
The first long rumble. When we were little,
Parents said the giants were bowling.

The first big flash and boom breaks open a seal
In the heavens.

A sudden gust. My hair lifts.
Hot just now, my neck is chilled.

Big drops of rain---
Always biggest right at the beginning of a storm—
Strike cold on my skin.

In the city, on a highway, I smell hot pavement
Scored by a sheet of rain sweeping over it,
Washing it like sheets spurting in a car wash.

The click-clack of windshield wipers,
The hiss of tires.

The opening of umbrellas.
Like parachutes bound to the ground
Waiting for the rare gust to lift them free.

New scents now, rain-released ones,
From this plant,
From its neighbor the tree.

I share a brief hint of what animals sense
Before I flee.

"Long Acres", near Shallotte, North Carolina  (circa 1958)

# Hurricane Hazel

From "Scribblings", September 7, 2008:

"Hazel" is not a typo. Yesterday, I said I would write down my reminiscences of Hurricane Hazel from my childhood, once Hanna had passed through. At the end of this, you'll find an extract from Wikipedia's entry for Hazel.

I'm writing this as I remember it from my perspective as an eight year old--with parenthetical insertions added to explain what was probably going on at the time.

We had been visiting my paternal grandparents at "Long Acres" for the previous week before the hurricane struck and I think we were originally intending to stay longer.

Long Acres was a piece of property belonging to my grandparents—right on the shore of the sound between the barrier islands and the mainland—just outside of Shallotte, NC. That's actually Shallotte, not a mis-spelling of Charlotte NC.

http://www.city-data.com/city/Shallotte-North-Carolina.html

My grandparents had begun improving the wooded property first sleeping in a tent while they added a one-room cabin on their own. They stayed at Long Acres during the summers when my grandfather wasn't teaching at the University of Maryland.

Next step up was a two-floor "house" where neither floor was ever divided into rooms, so far as I can remember. Several beds and at least one bookcase filled the upper floor.

I have a photograph of the outside of the house but not the interior.

Years later--when I was maybe 14--my grandparents had an actual brick house built next to the original house and connected to it via a breezeway. But, that was way in the future at the time of Hazel.

My cousin Stephy, short for Stephanie, was also visiting. She was approximately my age. I don't know where her older brother Lance was at the time. Stephanie was related to my step-grandmother, not to my grandfather. My parents had agreed to take Stephy to Myrtle Beach, South Carolina on our way home.

I have snatches of memory from the early part of the trip. I remember Stephy and I playing games--possibly pinball in those days-- in some kind of open-walled amusement building. Which I assume was in Myrtle Beach.. I remember having dinner in a restaurant and ordering swordfish and being disappointed. Maybe I expected a sword on the side?

The next thing I remember is staying overnight in a hotel when we didn't want to because my mother had a bad headache. My mom was prone to severe migraines. My dad hadn't driven since a bad accident when I was a toddler. If my mom were out of commission as driver, that was that.

We started north late the next morning. It was raining hard and my parents were very anxious about Hazel. We got as far as the ferry--somewhere in the general vicinity of Newport News--and sat forever in the car waiting for the queue to start moving.

Before they built a combination span of bridges between the "mainland" of Virginia and the other bit of Virginia at the southern tip of the Delmarva Peninsula, the chief route between the coastal Carolinas and Delaware was via the link with the ferries. These were huge and held tons of cars as well as their passengers.

But back to me in the car...I was bored and it was pouring rain and windy but I don't think I was scared. Eventually, "the powers that be" began to allow the people at the front of the queue of cars board the ferry.

I remember tense moments as we moved up in the line. My parents wondered if we were going to get on board in the first load. I liked the ferry ride, so I was definitely on their side when it came to getting on the ferry rather than having to wait for the next one.

Well, we made it. Just one problem--they had no business letting that ferry launch. We had been driving north just one step ahead of the hurricane proper. During the stay at that hotel and then our wait in the queue, Hazel had gained ground on us.

I don't remember this from back then, but my parents used to talk about someone screwing up and letting the ferry load and then clearing it to launch when they had no business doing so.

We were literally just past the point of no return when Hazel's strongest winds struck us. The crew warned the passengers to grab on to something--which everyone did. I had my arms wrapped around a painted metal post. I think my mom was grabbing it up above me. My dad was nearby but not holding on to the same post.

The ferry kept tipping sideways and then up and down. I was terrified. I suspect everyone on board was terrified. We could hear big crashing sounds from below deck. As always, all the vehicles had been chained as much as was possible. But in the midst of a hurricane that didn't make every one of them secure.

Eventually, we made shore on the peninsula. I don't remember positively now but I think we might have been in the eye of Hazel at this point, because the slow slow offloading of the ferry comes back to me without the mental image of frantic tossing and turning. Or maybe we were just really secured to the dock.

Anyway we sat in the car in the dark and waited until the cars ahead of us cleared out and my mom could drive off of the boat and unto the road. Water was everywhere. Branches. All sorts of debris.

A bit after this the second half of Hazel swooped down on us. We were on the road, my mom's headache had returned and water began pouring into the car from tiny openings around the doors. It was virtually impossible to see out of the windows, but we could make out blurred shadows of cars that had stalled in the flood and had been abandoned. Some of these were right in the lanes of traffic of course.

I wasn't much caring about stalled cars. I was standing on the back seat (no, seatbelt restrictions in those days) I was standing and looking down at the water covering the floor, and screaming.

I may have kept shrieking from the southern tip of the peninsula the whole way north.

My mom didn't slow down much less stop the car—just kept dodging around stalled cars and debris—for that whole section of the drive. She used to say that that was what kept us from stalling out.

The next thing I remember is driving up to our house and my -maternal- grandparents racing out the door to greet us.

Later on we learned that my paternal grandparents were safe. The shops and so on, built on the closest barrier island (possibly Ocean Isle?) had been swept away as if they had never existed.

I may have added "point of no return" to my vocabulary earlier than just about any child my age—except for the other kids who rode the ferry that day.

*"Hurricane Hazel was the worst hurricane of the 1954 Atlantic hurricane season and one of the worst hurricanes of the 20th century. Hazel killed as many as 1,000 people in Haiti before striking the United States just north of Myrtle Beach, South Carolina and south of Wilmington, North Carolina as a Category 4 hurricane. Nineteen people were killed in North Carolina, and 81 people were killed when it subsequently hit Toronto, Ontario. It is the strongest hurricane ever recorded to strike so far inland."*

You may want to read the whole Wiki entry some time.
http://en.wikipedia.org/wiki/Hurricane_Hazel

## BETWEEN WORLDS

### Interwoven Memories of Ocean City, New Jersey

Night, night, night.
Walking the boards
Close to the cool iron rails.
Caught between slow hissing
sea pulse,
And passing patches of chatter-
laughs
Swimming in a river double-
flowing.

Dark, dark, dark.
Yet lively. Living.
Countless life bursts
Life drawn from smiles and jests
Given back in joy and good will.

Defined by sparkling lights
beyond, above.
Heads bob and float over
massed bodies,
So close-knit by shadows,
Which is which?

Slow. Slow. Slow.
So slow the flows,
Walkers wheel and spin
For space between the gawkers.

They look before.
They look behind.
None see the bright orb,
The sparkling net.

Time is nothing.
Waiting
Here at the cusp, the border,
Is everything.

Wild-scented air.
Moist on arms, legs, face calls.
Fluttered tugging of cloth,
Hair tickling cheeks calls.
I turn and look up.

Floating, floating, floating
A scarred pearl drifts
Through gossamer night.
Always moving.
Always in place.
My delight. My calm.
She who brightens my window
And bids me lift my head.

A few inches are not the whole,
Says the pearl.
With smile as to a friend,
Large orb to small,
Remember, remember,
remember.

She drifts past still clouds.
Into a distance I cannot see,
Can just remember
In this place between worlds.

Thrash. Whoosh. Thrash.
Distant thunder-rumbles.
The sound. The scent. The
chilled skin.

The beloved heartbeat.
I gaze down at the slow throbs,
Mistily visible in their turn

On an always shifting stage.

Humble, each flees before the
next
Wishing to take its rest.
Life in black silk rises,
Is lace-crowned, and falls,
Stitching crest to crest.

Shhh… shhh… shhh…
Froth voicing its last note
In the moonlit dance.
A pause longer than a breath
drawn in,
The shallow builds its height.
The moon tugs. It tumbles,
Hissing a warning, shhh to
younger siblings.

The shy foam dithers,
Caught between demanding
swells,
Makes itself small.
Makes itself gone.

A longer crest creeps closer.
Still bright in scar-mooned lace,
Giving shapely life to the
turbulence beneath.

Ceaseless motion alive.
Faithful, patient, unending,
Dark water gives freely
Wave on wave.

Bright and dark together
Shifting beneath the orb glow.
Foam-garbed this way.
Dark-mantled that.

Shifting, shifting, shifting.
Hair tugs sideways,
Coolness on my neck and back.
The water bows to west wind's
wishes.

Lesser the light now.
The moon pulls its grey mantle
close.

Voices of Sirens call me
landward
With fractures of broken chants.
Notes windswept to me
From a hundred open mouths.

Called by bright songs,
Sweet cacophony,
I turn. I gaze.
I shake my head at no one.
Too soon to join the two-way
flow.

Down a secret path I go,
Eager for unbound toes
To touch the sand.
To touch the sea.

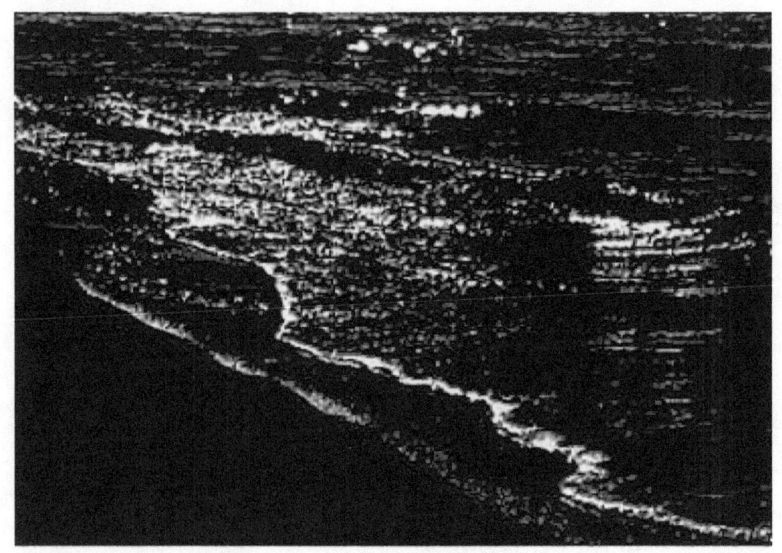

Night Surf
Ocean City, New Jersey

## End of "Reality, Whatever That Is"

(Well, that's a relief)

# *Extracts From My Five Narenta Novels*

## "Narenta #1" Seabird

### "Teaser" from inside the front cover of the first edition

He was racing almost directly toward her, skirting the very top of the embankment as he glanced over his shoulder. Cara caught the dim gleam of a blade, then something worse--the stench of rot borne on the wings of frantic hisses. Cara crouched to avoid being seen, but the werewright changed direction and began scrambling down the slope. Crouching wouldn't help now. Staying as low as she could, Cara propelled herself forward, her arms crossed and braced to strike the werewright's shins.

He saw her a moment before stumbling into her. She heard the swish of his blade. Powerful shins struck her forearms with the unyielding force of logs.

Cara tumbled over backwards, flailing wildly in an effort to slow her fall.

One hand closed on rough cloth. A glancing contact with something metallic stung the fingertips of her other hand. Then blows rained on her from every direction--the muddy slope, the arms and legs of the werewright--which blow came from which was impossible to tell in the seconds that lasted an hour.

… She wasn't moving. Her head was underwater. She got her bruised arms under her body and lifted her upper torso until her nose and mouth rose into the air. Shrieking bored into her ears like twin knives. The sword lay only a foot away from her, half in the water and half out. She stared in horror at the toothed edges and scrambled away from it, still on hands and knees.

The scream had altered to frustrated grunts and labored breathing.

Cara staggered to her feet and turned toward the noise. Just a few feet away, the werewright was fighting its way toward the shore. Cara looked down at the sword, swallowing down the sudden horror of what she needed to do.

She grabbed up the blade and spun toward her approaching foe, lashing out and missing.

Metal flashed as the werewright unsheathed two daggers.

Cara wrapped her left hand about her right and, taking a great breath, struck out again.

## *Narenta #1: Seabird Part 1, Chapter 4*
## *The Shrine*

Someone had placed a seabird-shaped plaque at the very top of the wall. Its black surface had tiny glittery bits scattered on it, possibly to represent stars in a night sky. Cara blinked. The raised panel receded, becoming a bit of night sky glimpsed through a window cut into the wall.

Whoa! Has to be an optical illusion! It didn't get dark in the last few minutes! She blinked, then tilted her head and blinked again but she couldn't trick her eyes into seeing a raised panel.

Patches and slender bars of sunlight brightened the dim interior, their sources the five windows in the remaining walls. Fragments of distant foliage and patches of daytime sky peeked through.

She turned back to the crystal and ebony silk of the seabird window, and trembled in wonder. A dozen half-formed questions welled up. The solemn serenity of that night view quelled them all.

## Narenta #1 Seabird Part 2, Chapter 5
## Cara's Dream in Fiori, from "Many Meetings"

"Reflected light from the column of flame gleamed like copper on the polished-stone walls about her. Golden flashes sparkled on the pebbled floor like trapped seeds of lightning. Tongues of flame licked across the ceiling, searching for cracks in the hewn stone and obscuring it from view.

She drew a step nearer and the column seemed to turn, as though aware of her approach. Threads of golden fire forked from the center of the shimmering inferno and approached her. She lifted her hands, holding them out as if to clasp the exploring tendrils…

Cara awoke with a gasp, and sat up. She stared frantically at her hands, and was amazed to find they were not ash and scorched bone, but her own flesh.

A presence within her seemed to flee, as though shy of her conscious thoughts. She felt its retreat and then its absence with regret and a piercing longing.

It was cool in the room, peacefully quiet. Empty. Drawing the coverlet about her, Cara lay back down."

Illustrated Unicorn, or "Phidias" the unicorn in "Earthbow"

I found the outline of this unicorn in a book filled with very old drawings, printers' marks, etc. and photocopied it because I liked the intricate curls in the unicorn's mane and tail. At some point, the unicorn told me he should be far more intricate. Always happy to oblige a unicorn!

## Narenta #2 Earthbow (1ˢᵗ edition)

Coris' search proved easier than he had expected. Close by one of the candles, a handful of werebane leaves sat half-hidden in a silken cloth by the bedside

Coris knotted the top of the cloth together and stuffed it away.

Back to the outside wall and the climb down to the ground. He shuddered at the prospect.

Then the great hall. Should he slip in through a window or inside and through the guarded corridors? Neither option appealed at the moment. He had best wait and make his decision when his feet were firmly back on the ground.

Multiple footsteps from beyond the bedroom door. Too much clatter for just Lord Cenoc and Sevris. Guards.

Options flashed before Coris, mixed with images of his imminent death. He stood across the room from the window, too far away to reach it without a risk of being seen, and that possibility he couldn't afford. Even a quick run toward it might be for nothing if he became entangled in the decorative sill a second time.

If either of the two lords or a guard saw someone slip from the keep-master's room, a thorough search of the keep would begin at once. The only alternative was to hide in the room and hope he could sneak out later.

Senses heightened by an influx of adrenaline, Coris scanned the room. Cushions and table. The bed. The hearth. Tapestries. Screens.

He settled on the set of woven standing screens. Behind them, was a littered alcove of cubbyhole-like shelves made for the storage of scrolls. He slid the left screen out a few inches, slipped behind it, and then dragged its inner edge a bit closer to its mate.

Coris peeked through the tiny openings afforded by the close-woven vines. He held his breath and waited to see who would enter.

Sevris came in first, walking slowly as though in pain. His discomfort would largely be due to the wereblood not the superficial cut, even though the keep-master had been treated almost as soon as infected. Sevris did not look at all up to this interview with Cenoc.

Cenoc followed Sevris through the door without a word. He paused to glance about the room, disdain etching the curves of his nose and mouth.

For a precarious moment, Coris wanted to burst from behind the screen and destroy the monster that stood before him. Only the guards in the next room, and his urgent errand held him in place.

Sevris led the way to a table near Coris' hiding place.

Coris swore silently to himself.

The keep-master gestured for Cenoc to be seated. His guest lingered near the door a moment longer, possibly looking back toward the guards.

Evidently satisfied, he closed the door, walked over and sank unto the proffered cushions.

Sevris followed him slowly and with difficulty.

Cenoc asked, "How do you feel?" There was less concern than curiosity in his question.

The keep-master shrugged and said nothing, instead unrolling a cracked parchment map that already lay on the table...

Cenoc grumbled, "So this is where you say they are, but what proof do you have?"

Sevris paled at the words. "I have no doubts. As soon as Alarz mentioned Ortaz-Des, I knew he spoke the truth. That's an old Shadow name – sorcerer talk - for Lumnas Pool, not far from here."

Sevris paused and pointed to the map. "Here."

"Yes? So?" Cenoc's probing eyes slid from Sevris' face to his finger on the map. "Oh! A 'protected' valley?"

Sevris nodded.

"Humph. Well, well." Cenoc looked beyond Sevris, wholly involved in his own thoughts. At last he turned back to the keepmaster, his tone businesslike again, "Protected valleys are ignorant piffle! This isn't the extent of your proof, is it?"

"No, my lord. There's an ancient scroll, in the alcove beside you." Sevris leaned forward as if to rise from his cushions, only to grimace and grunt. "If you would be so good..."

Cenoc answered. "Certainly. The wound still pains you?"

He looked at Sevris intently.

The keep-master grunted. "The third row. Its handles are of ebony."

Cenoc rose and turned to the screens.

Pressing his back against the cabinet behind him, Coris grasped his sword hilt and braced himself to attack.

# Narenta #3: The Gryphon and the Basilisk
## (work—in—progress trilogy

### Prologue

Hextor Nigragr, shadow lord, sorcerer and once viceroy of Narenta, waited for his dread master to leave the room before arising. When the door was closed, he stood slowly and gathered his black cape about him with silent hands. He was not yet used to wielding his body again and the movements were slightly awkward.

Venomous hatred in his hood-shadowed eyes, Hextor raged silently at Mexat the traitor--the one the enchanter had turned— longing to destroy him, too. But Wenos Zex had bidden otherwise.

Medea, Hathel, the others on the list were their foes for the moment. The winning of the third Tumult their task. He moved from the fire and drew forth his werestone. There was nothing to do for the moment but wait. Soon it would be time for him to attempt the great theft. In the meantime, Zex had commanded him to watch as Tethra's enchanters chose one of their number as their new commander and then report the information to Wenos Zex.

Hextor stared into his stone and gestured. He could do as bidden—and something else as well. He groped swiftly for the path leading up to the Scroll Chamber where Tethra's enchanters met.

The narthrous from which the ancient doors were crafted burnt his eyes like unshielded sunlight. He blinked.

Stifling a groan of agony, the sorcerer clutched at his forehead, the werestone tumbling from his grasp. The room seemed to tilt first one way and then the other, as if the building were gripped in the maw of an earthquake.

Then all was quiet---except the soft tap of approaching feet from outside the door. He grabbed up his stone in a panic and managed to rise. The footsteps stopped directly outside the door.

Silence. A terrible silence.

Hextor kept his hand clutched about the stone—hiding it. He stared back down at the waning fire with half-closed eyes. Waited. Waited.

No footsteps sounded in retreat.

Hextor forced his thoughts away from the last few minutes. Fingers of his free hand flexing like a vartha longing for the kill, he began silently reciting the information on the burnt scroll. He was halfway through the list a second time before the footsteps retreated.

Teeth clenched tight on a howl of rage, nostrils flaring in fury, Hextor allowed his hatred to boil over him like a shroud. He would NOT be so ordered about! Now—for a little while—yes. But not forever!

He opened his hand from about the werestone, and turned to studying the walls of Eyrie Keep. Then, leaping over them in thought, he studied the vast courtyard in turn and found the door leading to his goal. A few hours still to go. He drew a breath, anticipating the great challenge, longing for it and for the notoriety soon to be his.

~~~~~

NOTE: I'm looking for beta readers for The Gryphon and the Basilisk, specifically someone(s) willing to focus on plot details and who is willing to commit for as much as a year.

Knowledge of the characters and events in previous Narenta series novels is not required. I hope that G&B will be a standalone.

Beta readers don't need a background in proofreading—it isn't their responsibility.

If you would like to know more, follow the link below.

http://scrollchamber.blogspot.com/2014/10/tree-house-tales-collection-due-out.html

Leave your name along with either an email address or your FB/LI URL in the Comments.

Thanks!

# Narenta #1.5 MAROONED
## (Set in the time of the First Tumult)

### Selections from Chapters One & Two

### Chapter One

She felt like she was awakening from a nightmare to find herself in a dream. Chaotic memories of fire, howling or screaming, and fierce wind were replaced in a breath by cool dim blue and a gentle tug she couldn't identify.

She was kneeling. As she worked to stand up, new sensations merged with the flow of cool water on her chilled skin. Her left hand wouldn't move and there was something wrong with her right shin and the toes of her right foot.

The world tilted upright. The shin of her right leg was level with the water-logged surface. Her left leg was drawn up under her, the knee only inches from her chin.

What was wrong with her left hand? She concentrated on making it move, and succeeded in producing only a light stir of fingers. The toes and instep of her right foot were immobile as well.

Water rushed away from her face and she gulped a new breath of air. She couldn't keep doing this. She had to stand up.

### *Narenta #1.5: Marooned*
### *Chapter Two*

"…carefully," warned a hushed male voice. "Don't wake…"

Memory was still reminding her that her sword was gone but instinct had already won that race by several seconds. She sprang up, dagger in hand, before the man could finish his instructions.

Two shadowy shapes leaped back. Steel rang on either side. Striking right, toward the closest target, she felt the tip of her dagger catch slightly on a rib then slide cleanly past the obstacle. Rough cloth and blood touched her hand, as the hilt pressed against the man's body.

The ensuing scream was still building when she pulled the dagger free and spun toward her other attacker.

Metal flashed in the golden moonlight.

She tilted away from the deadly arc, kicked out sideways and felt the sting of her foot striking mail.

The sword was in motion again, its sullen glimmer echoed by the brighter flash of sharp teeth.

(snip)

("Marooned" will be published Spring 2015)

## Narenta # 0.5: "Da Boid, da Tree—Rat 'n da Loser"

### Chapter One
#### Opening Scene: Katan practices hovering.

Katan recited to himself "Upsweep! Downsweep! Bit to the left! Good! I'm hungry. No, no! I'm drifting forward. Less with the chest muscles. Come on, Kat! Focus!"

He found the oddly-shaped clump of mint-green fruits on the cimris tree branch in front of him and refocused his attention on it, adjusting his wing stroke speed so that he was back to hovering approximately three ells in front of the branch and 7 ells from the violet-grassed ground cover splotched between the mud puddles. Typically when he did his daily hovering practice, the only sound he would hear was that of air through his feathers.

Someone passed near his left wing and below him from the sound of their boot treads. He heard a burst of laughter that overlapped with words from a second person passing directly underneath. "Look! He's at it again."

"What is that about anyway?"

"Trying not to hit the tree maybe."

"Sure he's not trying to land on the tree? Maybe a magic spell is holding him off it?"

"Magic spell? Do you –see- an enchanter round about? Ah, he's moon-brained. I hear he bumped into that tree in a drunken stupor and that's how he landed here to begin with."

"Landed? Landed with a ker-thump, say?" One snickering laugh was joined by another.

Once the footsteps faded toward the center of the village, the seabird relaxed.

Katan muttered to himself, "Stupid elders! What do they know? They can't even fly. Do they have any idea... No, no! Focus! You're half an ell closer to the ground."

Hoof beats sounded, approaching from directly behind him. Did this bit of lawn next to the cimris look like a path? Katan decided to pivot in place, both to see who it was and for the practice. Before he made a quarter turn, he had to scoot sideways to avoid the head of yet another human. As fast as his reflexes were, the man's knitted cap brushed against his clenched claws, rucking it sideways to reveal sweat-drenched hair that might normally have been light brown.

"Watch it!" The same words echoed between them.

Katan flew off to one side while the man began dragging his headgear back into place, then yanked it off instead.

"You nearly rode right into me! I had my back turned!"

The man drew his horse to stop and reined it around, so that he was facing Katan,

"Blame my horse if you like! He was facing you and walked me right into you!"

Katan blinked at him, then flew over to his target branch and settled on it. "That is patent nonsense. Were you riding with your eyes closed?"

"I, uh, I drifted off for a..." Leather creaked. The man's head jerked sideways as he stared toward a cart rumbling through the village's palisade gate, one of its wheels letting out a mournful wail with each revolution. He glanced back and his left hand dropped back to his side, revealing the grip of a sword. His right hand loosed its hold on the sheath but retained its hold on the horse's reins.

"What is it to you?"

"You were sleeping? You were riding a horse and sleeping? You might have been..." *knocked off by a low branch* finished only in his thoughts. Obviously the man knew that. He frowned to himself as he studied the man's eyes and the way he used his left hand to sweep down the length of his face. So far as he understood human behavior, that darkness around the eyes and that gesture often meant fatigue.

"So..." Katan tried to think of something neutral or pleasant to say. Are you new here?--I am, sprang to his thoughts and was dismissed. He had only been staying in this village for a few weeks himself but he already knew the residents by sight. Not difficult when you have better vision than anyone within miles. So why ask the question? And why volunteer that he normally didn't live here? The world was a dangerous place--as his parents had warned him before he left. He suppressed a twinge of guilt at that stray thought. He really needed to be moving on.

Launching gently from the branch, he resumed hovering.

The man glanced back from staring over his shoulder – evidently back down the deserted path leading out of town,

It was empty, hardly a surprise so close to gate-closing.

"Forgive me! I, uh,…" He stared really hard back the way he came from and then seemed to relax, judging from the drop of his shoulders and the slight slump of his whole body in the saddle. He turned back to the seabird and asked, "Excuse me, forgive me! Is there a healer –or an herbalist in this village?"

"Little more and her shop would reach out and bite you." Katan grumbled more to himself than the visitor. He tipped his head toward the closest building (description?), taking great care to counterbalance his wing strokes so as not to shift his position.

"There's a human, one of you Latimin(?) Elders who does a few things but for quite a high price. _More than I could afford when I arrived, anyway_

"Also a stohan herbalist. Elpha. Right there. She went off to gather planets a few hours ago. I don't know if she's come back. I've been busy."

Reget tapped his forehead in thank you, took one last glance back up the trail and urged his horse toward the shop.

Pooped and curious, Katan resumed his perch on the branch in front of which he has been practicing.

The man dismounted and tapped on the door.

Katan bill-clacked a laugh.

*Well, if he thinks Elpha is going to answer that, he has a long wait ahead of him.*

Note: The passage—the whole manuscript—is still a bit rough. This is is the first time I've looked at any part of Da Boid in over a year.

# How I Write, or A Smidge of Plot, A Glob of Character*

I began telling myself stories when I was in elementary school, because I often couldn't get to sleep at night. Each night, I would run through the story up to where I left off and then add to it.

Occasionally, I'd get tired of my POV character—who was often myself—and try out my current story from inside someone else's thoughts. When I did this, sometimes I found myself backtracking in my "plot" because this other character was more interested in something else that was going on, or because he or she had "arrived late" in the story and I was just plain nosy to see what she or he had been up to before walking on stage.

Decades later, writing "Seabird" set the formal pattern for my characterization—and my plotting. I work out a skeleton plot and always—nearly always—make sure I have an end to the story. Then, I set the storyline aside. I begin with two or three characters and get to know them—beginning with the protagonist. I "learn" far more about them than can possibly fit into the story.

I don't use physical character sheets—I have the equivalent inside my head possibly leftover from my days as a D&D game-master.

When I can think of nothing new about a particular character, I switch to another one; usually beginning with how they react to the character(s) I've already developed.

In the process of developing these interrelationships and everyone's individual motives, juicy little nuggets pop into my head. Look at that! This guy plays a flute! That one's a poet and a bad one, and his mother abandoned him under tragic circumstances when he was very young.

I know the name of that person's horse, and I know why his girlfriend gave it that name. And so on.

Eventually, I reach critical mass when it comes to my characters, and I go back to writing the story. Actually, by now, I already have some scenes scribbled down. Decades ago on index cards; now keyed in as Notepad files.

My skeleton outline has put on a lot of weight, but still has room to grow. Developments in characterization don't cease until I type "The End".

\* No, writing is not like baking blueberry cake.

~~~~

*Below are a couple of my favorite and more bizarre characters—and how they developed.*

## *Khiva the stoah*
### ("Earthbow" and "The Gryphon and the Basilisk")

Khiva is a sentient arboreal animal. She was supposed to be in just two scenes. In the first, she surprises someone who is secretly crawling into a window and in the other she fortuitously gets a different character out of a fix.

Khiva is based on my experiences living with cats and watching squirrels. I gifted her with the prehensile tail of a monkey because she needed it for the plot. And she's a chatterbox-mostly for the fun of it.

That was it for her—at first.

As I wrote more and more of Earthbow, it kept getting darker and darker. Not what I had planned at all. Earthbow badly needed comic relief. I thought about bringing in another human character or making one of my protagonists more self-deprecating, but neither solution seemed to fit.

Then I remembered Khiva. I went back and thought through her character in depth, realizing in the process that she really had more going on in her furry little brain than I had given her credit for. She hates her job as a plant-gatherer for a human herbalist. She, like most stoahs as it turns out, is very into equal rights for stoahs, believing that the stoahn people deserve to be called the "fourth people" alongside the traditional "three peoples" of Narenta.

She seems self-centered if you just listen to her chatter, but she actually has a soft heart for anyone in trouble or in pain. She's a bit vain—not that I blame her with such great fur. And she's addicted to rosehips. Before I knew it, she was threaded throughout "Earthbow", essential to its plot, and had claimed a role in its sequel.

**Note**: Khiva is also the name of one of my cats. She (the cat) was named after the character.

~~~~~

## <u>Bert–and–Marsha–from–Hoboken</u>
### *"Marooned"*

Or, how not to do characterization except in an emergency. Now I ask you, do Bert & Marsha—much less Hoboken—sound like names from a fantasy novel?

I wrote most of Marooned during National Novel Writing Month, a few Novembers ago. For those of you who know nothing about NaNoWriMo, participants attempt to write 50,000+ words of one novel during the month of November.

NaNoWriMo founder Chris Baty wrote a short NaNo guideline or handbook titled "No Plot? No Problem". His core piece of advice is to ignore your internal editor and just get the words down. December January, etc can be used for your National Novel Editing Month if you choose. Any month can be used for revising and editing except November.

I had done some (legal) prepping for the latest challenge before November 1st of that year, via my usual method of nailing down the characteristics and motives of my two principle characters.

I was busily writing away one day (1667 words per day, minimum) when I realized that the protagonist needed to hear news from a neighboring village and--without cell phones, Palantiri or the internet—that meant I needed eyewitnesses to show up in the village where my protagonist was staying.

I was so rushed with the daily need to reach my NaNo quota, I couldn't take time to figure out eyewitnesses' names according to my Narenta naming conventions. I hadn't a clue what their village was called. (I still don't.)

So, Bert & Marsha strolled into the village where the main characters were and announced they had fled Hoboken. I have never characterized on the fly so much in my life. Suddenly they had three children. Or was it two? Marsha started acting like a real dim supermom.

Bert refused to fit the role of dad. Argh! I backtracked and stuffed Bert in jail. Why? A nameless character had attacked my protagonist the previous day, and I still didn't know anything about that person except that they were now in jail. "Jailbird" became Bert. Combining characters solved that problem!

Ah! Marsha had arrived from Hoboken with their three, no, seriously two children were enough... M arrived with their little boy and girl in tow, only to discover that dad was in jail! The children needed their dad! Marsha set about breaking Bert out of jail. Outstanding!

Next thing you know, I realized* that Bert was not who he professed to be. Poor Marsha! And like that.

Whoosh! Rush characterization for a NaNoWriMo novel is so much fun.

Bert, Marsha, and Hoboken are still awaiting their real names but I do know a lot about them. I had better! "Marooned" should be completely finished by now. And proofread. And yet another December has started without me.

*Literally realized. That's what happens when I'm writing.

www.ingramcontent.com/pod-product-compliance
Lightning Source LLC
Chambersburg PA
CBHW021137130626
46554CB00005B/1540